MVFOL

*Crazy Hot*

Also by Melissa de la Cruz

*Beach Lane*

*Beach Lane: Skinny-dipping*

*Beach Lane: Sun-kissed*

*Angels on Sunset Boulevard*

*Girl Stays in the Picture*

*The Ashleys*

*The Ashleys: Jealous?*

*The Ashleys: Birthday Vicious*

*The Ashleys: Lip Gloss Jungle*

# Crazy Hot

## A Beach Lane Novel

## Melissa de la Cruz

SIMON & SCHUSTER BFYR

New York   London   Toronto   Sydney   New Delhi

SIMON & SCHUSTER BFYR

An imprint of Simon & Schuster Children's Publishing Division

1230 Avenue of the Americas, New York, New York 10020

SIMON & SCHUSTER BFYR is a trademark of Simon & Schuster, Inc.

For information about special discounts for bulk purchases, please contact Simon & Schuster Special Sales at 1-866-506-1949 or business@simonandschuster.com.

The Simon & Schuster Speakers Bureau can bring authors to your live event.

For more information or to book an event, contact the Simon & Schuster Speakers Bureau at 1-866-248-3049

or visit our website at www.simonspeakers.com.

Also available in a SIMON & SCHUSTER BFYR hardcover edition

Book design by Christopher Grassi

The text for this book is set in Adobe Garamond.

Manufactured in the United States of America

This SIMON & SCHUSTER BFYR paperback edition June 2013

2 4 6 8 10 9 7 5 3 1

The Library of Congress has cataloged the hardcover edition as follows:

Crazy hot / by Melissa de la Cruz

p. cm.

Summary: Eliza, Jaqui, and Mara are just beginning their careers, but find themselves all together in the Hamptons once again since Eliza's new stepmother needs a nanny.

ISBN 978-1-4169-3961-0 (hc)

[1. Au pairs—Fiction. 2. Wealth—Fiction. 3. Friendship—Fiction. 4. Dating (Social customs)—Fiction. 5. Hamptons (N.Y.)—Fiction. 6. New York (State)—Fiction.] I. Title.

Fic—dc22 2007   2007278261

ISBN 978-1-4424-7412-3 (pbk)

ISBN 978-1-4424-7417-8 (eBook)

*For Mike and Mattie*

*Live your life with arms wide open,*
*Today is when your book begins,*
*The rest is still unwritten.*
                    —Natasha Bedingfield, "Unwritten"

*Don't waste your youth growing up.*
                    —Anonymous

# eliza is *not* the new au pair

ELIZA THOMPSON TAPPED LIGHTLY ON THE GAS PEDAL of her candy-apple red CLK convertible, zipping around the clunky gray station wagon that had been blocking her way. Didn't they know better than to putter down the Montauk Highway at five miles *below* the speed limit? She sighed happily as she cruised along, flashes of bright blue ocean in the distance peeking out through the trees, her rumbling engine the only noise disturbing the crisp June air.

Once she was safely past the offending family-mobile, Eliza patted the steering wheel and tightened the silk Hermès scarf holding back her long, platinum blond hair. With her Chloé sunglasses and her white halter dress, Eliza felt like she'd come straight out of the movie *Casablanca*. The dress was one of her own designs, inspired by the scene in which Ingrid Bergman and Humphrey Bogart explore the Parisian countryside in a convertible not so terribly unlike Eliza's own.

Eliza loved her new car, but it was also a reminder of how much things had changed—the car was a guilt present from her parents, who had separated earlier this year. Eliza was in the middle of a studio critique as a first-year student at Parsons when she got the news. She'd been so excited to present her vision for her fall collection: an elaborate fantasy of black satin baby-doll dresses and velvet capes, perfectly in step with the current gothic mood in fashion—but then her cell phone rang just as she was about to go up.

Eliza had flipped open her cell to the deafening roar of hair dryers—her mother was always at the salon—and then proceeded to listen as she rather candidly told Eliza that she was leaving Eliza's father for a much younger man. Her new trainer at the Reebok gym, to be precise. Eliza had stared at the sewing machines lining the Parsons workroom in a state of total shock. Throughout her dad's business scandal, his bankruptcy, and then his consequent comeback, her mother had stood by his side, just as stoic as Sienna Miller taking back Jude Law during Nannygate. Eliza had always had her suspicions that as soon as her parents got comfortable again, old (bad) habits would resurface, and here they were. Why did money always have to change everything?

Eliza's cell phone rang, playing Justin Timberlake's "SexyBack," and after giving her hips a little jiggle she picked it up. "Hello?"

"Hey, gorgeous. What's shaking?" Her boyfriend Jeremy Stone's deep, sexy voice reached her ear.

"Hey, yourself." Eliza smiled. "And I'm what's shaking,

actually—I just got a new ringtone and I can't stop dancing every time someone calls."

Jeremy laughed into the phone. "Oh yeah? I wish I were there to see it."

"I wish you were too. But I'll see you soon enough—I'm on the Montauk Highway right now, less than half an hour from my dad's house." She had to mentally remind herself not to say *parents'* house—her mom was with her boy toy, sunbathing in Saint-Tropez and Capri for the summer, and she'd left the house in Amagansett entirely to Eliza's father.

"Really? Think he'll be there with her?"

Eliza's father had responded to the news that he was being left by his wife by immediately finding himself a new girlfriend—who just happened to be more than twenty years his junior. Suzy Finnemore was a divorcée who ran an enormously profitable hedge fund and was notorious for her affairs with even more powerful men. While Eliza didn't relish the idea of spending the next three months with a quasi-stepmother, it would be better than hanging out in the city all by herself. It was already the second week of June and New York was like a ghost town, all the "right people" having absconded to their summer houses around Memorial Day.

"Oh God, don't remind me." She rolled her eyes. "I really don't feel like having to play daughter to some woman who's not that much older than I am."

"Hey, don't worry about it—I'm sure you guys will get along fine." Jeremy's voice was consoling. "And besides, you'll be so busy with the new store you'll hardly even be around, you hotshot designer, you."

"Thanks, J." Eliza couldn't suppress her grin. Jeremy always knew the right thing to say. Back at Parsons, she'd recovered from the shock of her parents' separation, presented her collection, and ended up receiving the highest grade in her design class. She'd been chosen as one of five students to show during Fashion Week in February at the big Bryant Park tents. Buyers from Barneys, Bergdorf's, and Kirna Zabête had clamored for her childlike yet edgy collection—the *Times* had described it as Courtney Love meets Wednesday Addams.

Bolstered by their enthusiasm, Eliza had decided it was high time she opened her own store. And since her clothes had been such a huge hit last summer in the Hamptons, what better place to do it? She'd found a tiny little space in an alley just off Main Street across from Scoop and Calypso and had the entire place painted a pale pink—the exact color of the inside of a seashell. Her name would appear in lowercase Arial letters— eliza thompson—on the pink-and-white awning. Just thinking about her little boutique made her heart leap.

She held the phone close to her ear, wishing Jeremy were here so she could kiss him. It was hard to believe they'd already been dating for three years—Eliza skipped over the part when they had taken a break after the first summer due to the long-distance thing. Jeremy, with his warm brown eyes and delicious head of curls, was the sweetest guy she'd ever met. She couldn't imagine being with anyone else.

"But I really should go—I'm almost here. And I got so distracted talking to you that I think I may have just run over a pigeon."

Jeremy laughed. "Okay, call me later. Love you, babe."

Hearing those three sweet words, Eliza sighed. No matter how many times Jeremy said them, it still made her skin tingle.

It was going to be another perfect summer in the Hamptons. Except, of course, for one thing: for the first time since they'd met, Mara wasn't going to be there. She'd landed some kind of job backpacking through Europe, writing about off-the-beaten-path locales—as in stinky hostels and cheapo pubs. Charming. Eliza thought travel should involve five-star resorts, hot stone massages, piña coladas by the pool, and the occasional hot pool boy—and nothing less. But she knew Mara would love it. And at least Jacqui would be nearby with the Perrys.

Eliza sped along the last stretch of the highway and found herself pulling up to the Thompson estate in Amagansett less than fifteen minutes later. Her parents always called it their "shack" or "the cottage," even though the house was the size of a fortress. It was a beautiful old place—solid, weathered, sprawling, and distinguished, with none of the grotesque McMansion details or gargantuan proportions that were popping up all over the Hamptons. A stately colonial with a two-story portico, a row of impressive columns, and an antique bronze oil-rubbed lantern over the doorway, the house had been in her mother's family for years. There was even an authentic Indian tepee in the back, where Eliza had played house as a kid and had first smoked pot as a teen. It was home.

"Dad!" she called, pushing her sunglasses up on her head and scrambling out of the car. "I'm here!"

She was about to unlock the front door when it opened. "Dad?" Eliza stopped short. A man in his late thirties stood there, wearing a white Lacoste shirt, faded Edun jeans, and moccasins—no socks.

"You're not my dad," Eliza said stupidly.

"No. But you are definitely a babe." He extended a hand. "Rupert Thorne. Pleasure's all mine."

Eliza kept her hands by her side. "I think there's been some kind of mistake," she said hesitantly. "I'm Eliza Thompson."

"Honey, is it the au pair?" a female voice called from inside.

Rupert's smarmy leer only deepened. "I certainly hope so." He winked.

"I'm not the au pair. I live here. Or at least, my family does. During the summer. This is our house." She ignored the sleazy up-and-down look he gave her and dug her phone out of her purse, speed-dialing her father.

He picked up after about ten rings. "Sweetie! Are you stuck in traffic?"

Eliza could hear the clinking of ice cubes in a glass. It occurred to her that she could always tell which parent was on the line by the background noise—with her mom it was hair dryers, with her dad it was the chink-chink of ice in a glass. "Dad, there are people in our house. What's going on?"

"Oh, sweetheart, I forgot to tell you. Your mother rented out the house without telling me." The sound of ice was now drowned out by a loud clamor and the sound of shrieking. Where *was* he? "I think it's payback for selling the yacht in Portofino without telling her. But don't worry, there's lots of room at Suzy's. There are a few extra rooms in the east wing, near the kids."

Suzy's? Kids? Eliza frowned. Did that mean those insane whoops in the background were her *children*? There had been no mention of children before this. Eliza cast a grumpy look at Rupert Thorne, who was still staring at her, practically salivating. She'd so been looking forward to staying in her own room, with her own things, in her own house. This did not sound promising.

"It's right off Dune Drive," her father said. "You can't miss it. It's the largest one on the block, with all the Greek and Roman statuary out front. Turn left at the Pietà."

Eliza sighed. She didn't have much of a choice. She walked back down the steps and toward her car, ignoring Rupert Thorne as he called after her, asking if the au pair wanted to come play house.

Eliza's dad was right: she definitely wasn't in any danger of missing Suzy's house. If the Thompsons' "cottage" was the epitome of a Gatsby-like Hamptons past, Suzy's home was decidedly the Hamptons future. It positively screamed new money, with its elaborate mailbox—an exact replica of the house itself—and a massive roof that made it look like the house was sinking into the ground under its own weight. Until now, the Reynolds Castle had been the largest and most ostentatious house in the Hamptons, but the Finnemore mega-mansion certainly gave it a run for its money. And Eliza was going to have to call this monstrosity home for the whole summer?

A white-jacketed butler took her bags, and another servant led her to the terrace. Her father was splayed out in a lawn chair, a pitcher of margaritas by his side, and Suzy sat next to him, holding a BlackBerry and jiggling a six-month-old baby in a Björn carrier. A portable Sony plasma television was set up in front of her, and on the screen was a view of the stock exchange. The shrieking sounds Eliza had heard on the phone were of traders screeching orders to their runners.

"Hey." Eliza nodded at both of them and then bent to give her father a kiss on the cheek. She'd met Suzy a couple of times before and didn't think of her as a woman so much as a blur— she was always on the move, with her three constantly ringing cell phones, two hovering assistants, and her trademark mane of frizzy red hair. For the life of her, Eliza couldn't figure out why Suzy didn't just have it straightened. She could certainly afford it.

"This is Cassidy." Suzy smiled, motioning to the baby as she texted furiously with one hand. "I know it's an unusual name for a boy, but I've always loved the name and was worried this might be my last shot to use it!" She turned her attention away from the BlackBerry for a moment to beam down at the baby boy in her arms. "And sorry for the chaos—the au pair is supposed to arrive today and *of course* she's already late."

Eliza took a glance around. What chaos? There were three kids sitting quietly on lounge chairs by the pool, two of them playing chess and one reading. It was downright peaceful—so different from what she'd encountered that first day at the Perrys' when she was their au pair for the summer. She shuddered just thinking about it. Thank God she'd never have to do *that* again.

Suzy followed Eliza's eyes. She gestured to the two boys hunched over the chess table. "Logan is the regional champ in the under-ten category. We're traveling to D.C. this fall for nationals," she said proudly. The somber-looking seven-year-old wore a pair of round glasses that gave him an owl-like demeanor. "Logan is teaching Wyatt how to play chess," Suzy added. Eliza looked across from Logan to the chubby little five-year-old who sat across from him, his forehead wrinkled in intense concentration. She'd never seen children who sat so perfectly *still*.

"And that's Jackson with the book. He and Logan are twins, obviously." Jackson was a carbon copy of his brother, down to the owl glasses.

"Obviously," Eliza agreed, trying to keep the shock and awe out of her voice. Jackson was reading *The Greatest Story Ever Sold: The Decline and Fall of Truth from 9/11 to Katrina*. She raised an eyebrow. Whatever happened to comic books?

"The author was on CNN the other day and Jackson insisted on getting his book." Suzy sighed with a wry smile. "It's like that with everybody who comes on that channel! I can never get him to watch anything else."

"Oh," Eliza said simply. She didn't even watch CNN now.

"And that's Violet, behind me," Suzy tilted her head backward and Eliza looked past her to see a thin, pale girl seated at a patio table, hunched over her computer. She'd been so quiet, Eliza hadn't even noticed she was there. "She's first in her class at Horace Mann," Suzy whispered, leaning toward Eliza. "But she gets embarrassed when I tell people that." She turned toward her daughter and called out to her. "Violet, honey! Say hi to Eliza!"

Violet peeked over the screen of her laptop. "Oh, hi," she said shyly, not coming out from behind her computer.

"Nice to meet you, Violet," Eliza called out. She couldn't help but mentally compare Suzy's passel of wunderkids to the Perry kids and their many developmental problems.

"Are you the au pair?" Violet looked at Eliza quizzically.

"No." Eliza shook her head. "No, I'm not." And then she smiled. Even if the Finnemores did seem like perfect children, she knew all too well that looks can be awfully deceiving.

# jacqui discovers that even the best-laid plans often go awry

**JACQUI VELASCO WOKE UP TO THE BRIGHT JUNE SUN** shining through the window of her Upper East Side studio. She took one glance at the purple NYU sticker on the glass and smiled. It was going to be a great day. Every day was a great day ever since she'd gotten accepted into NYU. Finally. Her fifth year at St. Grace had been absolute torture—she'd had to take precalculus to finish the math requirements and qualify for admission—but it had all been worth it when she received the fat envelope she'd been waiting for since last April. Jacqui threw her arms above her head with a big yawn, gave the sticker a little kiss, and started to get ready.

She was officially in, officially accepted, and ready to begin her freshman year in September. Tuition was expensive, and as a foreign student Jacqui hadn't gotten much financial aid, but thankfully one more summer with the Perrys would take care of her contribution for her first year. She pulled on one of her usual kid-friendly-but-still-New-York-savvy outfits—comfortable but

11

skintight J Brand skinny jeans with a long cotton tunic (machine washable for spit-up stains), and a pair of French Sole ballet flats—and tied her long, ebony locks back into a practical ponytail.

Jacqui headed out the door and toward the Perrys' town house, just a short walk away. The family was leaving for the Hamptons the next day, and Jacqui had to make sure all the kids were packed and ready to go. There were only three of them this time—the girls, thirteen-year-old Madison and nine-year-old Zoë, were spending the summer at an Australian tennis camp, which left only William, Cody, and new baby Eloise.

"Hey, everybody! I'm here!" she called as she closed the Perrys' town house door behind her. But when she made her way into the living room, she was met with not the usual "everybody" but instead a very odd assortment of people.

Ten fat, matronly women, to be exact. All of them with ruddy, chubby cheeks and sweet cherubic smiles. Add flat hats, carpetbags, and black umbrellas, and you would have ten Mary Poppinses.

Jacqui's skin prickled in warning. What was going on here?

"Uh, hi," she addressed the group, closing the door behind her and shoving the front door key back into her purse.

"Hello, dear, are you here about the position?" one of the women asked in a cheerful British accent. She looked Jacqui up and down. "What part of London are you from? You don't look like a local."

"London?" Jacqui echoed, a foreboding feeling rising in her chest. "No, I—where's Anna?" She didn't wait for an answer and instead strode purposefully through the room and toward the heart of the house. William, twelve and already almost as tall as she was, rolled down the marble hallway on his skateboard. He looked more like his big brother, Ryan, every day. "Hey, Bill—where's Anna?"

William gestured toward the kitchen as he kept rolling by.

Jacqui quickened her steps, practically running into Madison as she turned the corner. Madison looked trim in her tennis whites, swinging a Dunlop racket. Her face lit up when she saw Jacqui. "Hey! I'm leaving for Sydney tonight, but I hope you come visit!"

"To Sydney?" Jacqui winked. "How about I see you when you get back."

"When I get back?" Madison's brow furrowed. She strummed a finger along the taut strings of her tennis racket. "Anna hasn't told you?"

"Told me what?" The anxious feeling in Jacqui's chest began to expand.

"That's just like her and Dad. Ugh!" Madison leaned in and gave Jacqui a quick, close hug. "But anyway, don't forget—e-mail me!" With that she trotted off, swinging her racket lightly as she went.

Jacqui shook her shoulders and continued to the kitchen, where she found Anna looking flustered, holding her phone close to her ear and scribbling notes on a yellow legal pad. Baby Eloise sat in her high chair, cheerfully throwing rice cereal everywhere, but Anna didn't seem to notice.

Anna held up a manicured fingernail when she saw Jacqui, mouthing, "One second." Jacqui immediately went to work, wiping Eloise's mouth and tray and scooping the baby up as she began to cry. She was bouncing her on her hip when Anna finally snapped her phone shut.

"Jacqui, you're here. Thank God. It's been such a horrid morning. Of course everything has to happen at the last minute." Anna rubbed her temples and took a gulp of coffee from the mug in front of her.

"What's going on? Who are all those people in the foyer?" Jacqui was both dying to know and totally afraid to hear the answer.

"Oh, right—they're candidates. Of course I have to find a baby nurse and a nanny in less than twenty-four hours!" Anna sighed in her usual melodramatic fashion.

"Excuse me?" Jacqui started. A nanny? Wasn't that pretty much *her* job?

"Didn't we tell you—oh, of course not. You weren't here last week," Anna said a bit peevishly.

Last week Jacqui had gone to Brazil to visit her family, a belated graduation gift from the Perrys. She'd spent the week bonding with her grandmother in São Paulo and her family in Campinas, getting reacquainted with her younger brothers—

whom, she thought sadly, she knew less about than Cody and William. It was great of the Perrys to pay for her ticket, but why was it that every time they did something nice for her, there was a catch?

Anna took out her bottle of Vicodin and popped two pills. She'd scheduled a C-section to deliver Eloise and then had liposuction and a tummy tuck (apparently standard procedure with Upper East Side deliveries), but that had been nine months ago and she was still hoovering painkillers. "The fact is, we're moving to London," Anna said crisply, taking a sip of water. "Kevin's opening up a branch of the law firm there, and we've got to move immediately. Some big trial or something to do with the royal family and Diana's butler." Anna closed the Vicodin container and rolled her eyes, although Jacqui knew there was nothing her employer liked better than to drop (clang!) such big names. "And we've been invited to Highgrove for some big dinner—you know, with the Prince of Wales." This time there was giggling to accompany the name-dropping. "It's tomorrow night. I wonder if Camilla is as much of a bow-wow as she is in pictures?"

"Oh." Jacqui was startled. "London? Tomorrow?"

"I know, it's a shock to me too, but Kevin's already found us the most darling little pad near Hyde Park." Anna finally noticed the rice cereal Eloise had been throwing and moved the bowl out of her reach. "It's next to Madonna and Guy!" (Clang! Clang!) She turned to face Jacqui again. "Be a dear and help me with the interviews—you know the kids so well, you can pick a good replacement, can't you?"

For a moment, Jacqui was too stunned to say anything. She froze, trying to process everything Anna had just said.

"I really am sorry, but it looks like we won't be needing you this summer after all, especially since we need someone who can stick out the whole year, and with you off to college and all . . ." Anna's shoulders rose in an exaggerated shrug, and she knit her eyebrows in concern. "But I hope this will cover it. . . ." She fished out an envelope from her red patent leather Jimmy Choo Ramona handbag and extended it toward Jacqui. "It's not for the whole three months—more like a severance."

Jacqui automatically stuck out her hand and took the envelope, mumbling, "Thank you." She stood there numbly, her arm still extended, unable to move.

Anna waved a hand. "And of course we'll need the keys back to the studio. But take your time. Kevin's decided to sublet it for the summer, but you can take two weeks to find a new place." She squeezed Jacqui's shoulder. "Don't worry, I'll give you a great reference, and you shouldn't have a problem finding another family in the city to work for."

Anna's cell phone rang, and she smiled at Jacqui and nodded definitively, as if to say, "We're done here." She picked up her cell phone and resumed her busy travel arrangements.

Jacqui nodded, her throat dry. Just like that, in one fell swoop, she was unemployed and homeless. What now?

# mara finds it's a lonesome planet indeed

**MARA WATERS HUSTLED THROUGH JFK WITH A BRISK,** confident step. She'd just finished her first year at Columbia, acing all her finals and scoring an almost perfect GPA. She smiled just thinking about it. Mara had quickly discovered she was one of those girls who were made for college. In high school she'd been "just Mara"—pretty smart, pretty nice, pretty average all around. But with the polish and poise she'd gained from summers in the Hamptons—not to mention discovering the wonders of butterscotch highlights and professional eyebrow tweezing—she had turned into "that Mara."

As in, that Mara who had thrown the biggest bash the dorm had ever seen (what better training than those numerous Hamptons soirees?). That Mara who had the best clothes of any freshman—hello, her best friend was Eliza Thompson, up-and-coming designer. And that Mara who'd snagged the best internship in the city freshman year. Her old boss from *Hamptons* magazine had been true to her word and had put her on staff at *Metropolitan Circus*.

"You got everything?" David's voice broke into her thoughts. She adjusted the handle on her bag, hoping that it wouldn't burst open to reveal all of her underwear to the entire airport. "With a bag that overstuffed, I certainly hope so," he teased, and kept on walking.

That Mara was also dating "the David." As in, the David who was editor in chief of the *Spectator*, the college newspaper, as well as the David who lived off campus in his own sweet bachelor pad in Trump Place, with a view of the Hudson River from his bedroom window. The David who was president of St. Anthony's Hall—better known as St. A.'s—the snobbiest and most elite fraternity on campus, with its sprawling mansion on Riverside Drive.

And that Mara and the David made the perfect couple, particularly because they had all of the same interests. David was an aspiring writer as well, and Mara thought that if they ended up together, they could have one of those Joan Didion–John Dunne relationships—editing and critiquing each other's work while vacationing at the Four Seasons in Maui.

"Wait up! It's no fair—you've got longer legs!" She giggled as she quickened her pace and tried to catch up with him, her rolling suitcase jostling around behind her as she went.

They were off to Brussels, the first stop on their Lonesome Planet agenda. The two of them had been picked to write the latest European edition of the student-friendly travel guidebook, and Mara was looking forward to spending the whole summer in the most romantic places on earth with David—discovering the hidden treasures of Florence, Venice, Paris, London, Prague, and a host of other fabulous cities. She couldn't wipe the smile from her face when she thought of it: the two of them comparing notes, writing pieces, and sharing everything from croissants to gondola rides. Okay, so maybe the gondolas were a bit of a fantasy—the Lonesome Planet guides were specifically about the cheapest and most out-of-the-way locations, which meant they wouldn't exactly be splurging on tourist attractions or staying in five-star hotels. But still . . .

"Mar, we have to hurry!" David called back to her as they raced up to the check-in counter. Mara bounded up beside him and he placed their bags on the scale.

"We're on the ten thirty to Brussels," Mara said breathlessly. "We have e-tickets."

The airline employee gave them a brisk nod. "May I see your passports, please?"

David slid his forward while Mara fished in her purse, finally pulling hers out and placing it on the counter with a loud *thwack*. While the agent looked over their passports David leaned in and gave her a quick peck on the cheek, stroking her sleeve.

"This one is fine," the agent said, handing David's passport back to him along with a boarding pass. "But this one is expired." She pointed to Mara's beaten-up passport, which she'd gotten ages ago but had barely used until the past few years. "Do you have your new one?"

"Oh no!" Mara exclaimed.

"You didn't!" David's face fell. "I told you."

He had. He had left sticky notes all over her dorm room reminding her to make sure her passport was current—with exclamation points and the occasional smiley face. She had used it last during her trip to Cabo with the girls and she'd been sure it was still good and had meant to check, but with finals, and finals parties, and, well . . .

The people in line behind them shuffled their bags forward, antsy to get their boarding passes. "Hey, what's the holdup?" an angry-looking woman with a mop of frizzy dark hair asked crabbily.

"Oh my God. I'm so sorry." Mara felt herself flush red as she grabbed her bag again and they stepped away from the counter.

"We're going to miss our flight." David's forehead wrinkled in concern.

"Hey." Mara cupped his face in her hands. "I know it sucks, but it'll be fine. I'll get a new one tomorrow, and we'll only be delayed a day."

David smiled and seemed to relax. "You're right," he said, pulling out his phone. "I'll call the Lonesome Planet office and let them know what happened." He dialed and placed the phone to his ear. "It's ringing," he whispered, cupping a hand over the speaker. "Hi, can I have the assignment office, please? It's David Preston. Listen, there's been a little problem. . . ."

He walked away as he talked to their editor, pacing back and forth. Mara thought she heard him raising his voice, but she bit her lip and focused on the departures board, patiently waiting until he came back.

She watched as David snapped the phone shut and walked back to her, his brow wrinkled again. "What did they say?"

"Well, it's sort of complicated." David looked down and started to play with the tag on Mara's luggage. "It's Saturday, and the post office is closed. So the earliest you can get it renewed is Monday, which means the earliest we can leave is Tuesday. We're supposed to have covered Brussels and be in Madrid by then."

"So . . . what does that mean exactly?" Mara wasn't sure she wanted to know the answer.

"The three days throw off their schedule completely. Everything's already pre-booked. And they've got someone who can cover for you. She's already in Brussels." David put a hand on her arm. "Mara, I'm sorry, but . . . they fired you."

Mara felt the tears start to bubble up in her eyes. He brought her in for a hug, wrapping his arms tightly around her waist.

"How could they?" she whispered, nuzzling David's shoulder. She stepped back and shook her shoulders, trying to regroup. They could still have a great summer. They were together, and that was all that mattered. "Well, it's not the end of the world. . . . We can still travel Europe together . . . and now we don't have to stay in all those dumpy hostels!" She looked up at David, hoping to find him smiling.

Instead, he looked worried. He glanced down at his watch.

"You can't be serious," she said flatly, realizing there was only one reason he'd be checking the time.

"Mar—"

"I mean, you're still thinking of going? After they fired me for a tiny little mistake?" She felt herself go pale with shock.

"I mean . . . it's sort of a big mistake, Mar. And I did remind you to get your passport renewed," he pointed out. "About a hundred times."

"You know how busy I was!" Mara heard herself start to whine. "I had that story due for the magazine and my dinosaurs final!" Like many English majors, Mara was fulfilling Columbia's two-semester science requirement by taking a class on prehistoric reptiles. So far she'd only used the course information to compare her college acquaintances to the various species of dinosaurs. Her professor was a total stegosaurus—hunchbacked and scaly.

"Mar, I'm really sorry. But you know this is a huge opportunity for me. . . . If I want to get a job at the *Times* after graduation, they're really going to look at what I did with my summers. I'd be writing a whole book!"

"It's a guidebook," Mara corrected, feeling herself start to pout.

"It's a start." He checked his watch again. "Look, if I don't go now, I'll miss my flight."

"It was *our* flight just a few seconds ago," Mara said, unable to keep the bitterness out of her voice.

"I know this totally blows, but I swear, if you were in the same position, I would understand. I wouldn't want you to miss out on this chance." He grabbed her hand, his eyes pleading. "Please, Mara. It's something I really feel I need to do."

"If it were me, you'd just let me go?" Mara asked skeptically.

David shrugged. "I would never get in the way of your dreams." He looked down at the floor again. "You know, maybe part of you just didn't want this that much. I mean, if you had, you would have remembered to renew your passport, right?" He looked up and into her eyes, and she watched him transform from loving boyfriend to ambitious young writer. "This is a job, Mara, not a vacation. Maybe you're just . . . not cut out to be a journalist."

Mara was speechless. Didn't want this that much? She was the one who had found the listing on the college job board! The one who had hounded the two of them to apply! She was the one who'd never been to Europe before!

David rocked back and forth on his New Balance sneakers, waiting for her to say something.

She sighed. "Go," she said finally.

"Yeah?" He tilted his head and looked into her eyes. "You're okay, right?"

"Just go, David." She nodded, a defeated half smile curving her lips. He was right. She didn't want to stand in the way of his dreams, and it was her fault for not being more responsible. It was totally unfair that one little mistake would cost her an entire

summer, but Mara had lived long enough to realize that sometimes, the Rolling Stones were right on the money—you can't
always get what you want.

He gave her a kiss on the forehead. "You're the best. I'll call
you from the hostel. Love you." With that, he turned and raced
off to the gate.

Mara stared at his retreating back, still clutching her expired
passport. A few minutes ago, she'd been ready to board a plane to
Europe, but now her perfect summer—not to mention her perfect boyfriend—was vanishing right before her eyes.

# au pair means "extra set of hands" in french. so why not have two?

"AND THIS"—ELIZA POSED DRAMATICALLY IN THE SHOP window—"is where the cotton candy machine is going."

"The cotton candy machine?" Jeremy chuckled, shaking his head.

"It's edible pink!" Eliza squealed. She ducked her head so she wouldn't hit the ceiling and climbed off the ledge in front of the shop window, making sure not to topple over on her four-inch Yves Saint Laurent platforms. "Isn't that such a great idea? It's going to be like a carnival of pink in here!"

Jeremy smiled. "Except for the clothes, of course." He turned to marvel at the racks of clothing neatly lined up by the wall, still wrapped in dry-cleaning plastic.

"Of course." Eliza flicked her wrist in mock-diva fashion. "I mean, please, no one actually wears pink. It's cute, but strictly for babies." Eliza's summer collection was completely mono-chromatic—just as everything in her fall collection had been black, for summer everything in the store would be white: white bikinis, white sundresses, white capri pants, white jeans, white caftans, the perfect white button-down shirts. It was a perfectly Hamptons-pleasing collection. Eliza knew lots of girls who never wore any other hue for all three months—in fact, she was one of them. With the all-pink walls, the handful of pink Pucci chairs, the aquarium filled with pink tropical fish, and the pink cotton candy machine, the white clothes would stand out all the more, practically screaming for attention.

"And we'll put the mannequin here—the one based on Marilyn Monroe in *The Seven Year Itch*." Eliza giggled, standing in front of the fan and trying to keep her skirt down, just like her idol once had on top of a subway grate. "I mean, that is the most iconic white dress in history."

"You're nuts," Jeremy said fondly, coming up to stroke her hair. "But you're my nut."

"Can you believe I have this store? I had to raid my trust fund to do it, but whatever." Eliza whooped. "This is huge, J. I mean, this is, like, so scary, but so exciting."

"Speaking of exciting," he said, sweeping her into his arms. "I wanted to tell you about what happened to me today. . . ."

Before he could finish his sentence, the front door whipped open with a clang, and a harassed-looking Swedish girl tumbled in.

"Is this Eliza Thompson shop?" the girl asked.

"Yes, it is," Eliza said, untangling herself from Jeremy's embrace. "But I'm afraid we're not open for business yet."

From behind the girl, Suzy's wunderkids from earlier that morning appeared, fanning out inside the store. Violet started gently fingering the clothing, as if afraid it might jump up and bite her, while the little boys dispersed in every direction.

"Are those fighting fish?" Logan asked, coming up to the aquarium and pressing his nose against the glass. The startled fish fled from his magnified face, scattering throughout the tank.

"This is crooked." Jackson straightened a framed photograph of Marlene Dietrich in a white tuxedo that was hung low by the sweater table, getting fingerprints all over the carefully buffed frame.

Wyatt came up to Eliza and tapped her on her shin. "I have to pee," he whispered, cupping a hand over his mouth as if he were sharing a big secret.

"Yes, they're fighting fish," Eliza told Logan as she began to steer Wyatt toward the bathroom. They were perfectly sweet kids, but really, what were they doing in her store?

"This is silk? Where is it made?" Violet held up a white pareo, reading the tag as if it were an information plaque at a museum.

"Actually, the silk comes from a farm in Thailand where the silkworms only eat organic leaves." Eliza smiled, feeling a small surge of pride. She turned to the Swedish girl. "What's going on?"

"I leaving. I get modeling contract. Miss Suzy said Mr. Thompson say you will deal with children—you were also au pair."

"My father said *what*?" Eliza felt herself turning red. Of *course* her father would assume she had nothing better to do than babysit his girlfriend's children—he'd never really taken her fashion design career seriously. He'd been totally miffed when she postponed Princeton for Parsons.

"I leaving," the girl said again, removing the Björn carrier from her chest and handing the baby to Eliza.

Eliza looked down, completely perplexed. How had she wound up with a six-month-old in her arms? Cassidy cooed and gurgled, and she felt her heart melting at the sight of him. But really—she had no time for child care this summer. She had a business to run. "Hey, you can't just—wait!" she called after the Swedish au pair, but the girl was already out the door.

Eliza turned to find Jeremy giving Wyatt a piggyback ride from the bathroom, while Logan and Jackson each clung to one of his knees, mirror images of each other. He approached Violet, who was standing by one of the racks of clothing, looking like she didn't know what to do with herself. "You want to try on some clothes later? When everything's all set up?" he asked.

"Okay," she said with a shy smile, nodding.

"Sounds good. But how about we all clear out of here for now and let Eliza finish her work. There's an outdoor circus down the block." He gently set Wyatt down and then took the baby from Eliza's arms. "I'll take them for a while, don't worry," he told her, giving her a quick kiss on the cheek.

"Thanks." She nodded gratefully. Her eyes misted. She'd forgotten how good Jeremy was with children. He was going to be an awesome father someday—some far, far distant day in the future.

When Jeremy had every last kid out the door, Eliza stopped to think. So Suzy needed an au pair, did she? Maybe even two au pairs? There were four kids and a baby, after all. Quite a handful.

Eliza knew just who to call—if it wasn't too late.

# jacqui finds comfort
# in a stranger

**JACQUI WALKED OUT OF THE PERRYS' TOWN HOUSE** feeling like she'd just been sucker punched. All of her plans—her well-laid plans—had disappeared in a puff of smoke. Or, more precisely, in an invitation from Buckingham Palace. Jacqui took the envelope Anna had given her out of her bag and peeked at the check. Looking at all the zeros, she instantly felt a little better. Still, it wasn't nearly enough to cover the entire first year's tuition, especially if she was going to have to find a new place to live for three months on top of that. What good was getting accepted into NYU if she couldn't actually afford to go?

Jacqui made peanuts at Daslu, the designer store in Brazil she'd be forced to work at if she went home—the job was all about the free clothes, which weren't going to pay for college. She pictured the NYU admissions office opening the envelope with her contribution in it and finding a Versace gown instead of a check. She tried to laugh at the image but instead found herself blinking back tears. It felt just like last year when she'd been told she was a perfect candidate except for the whole math requirement—close, but no cigar. She wiped her eyes. There would be no NYU in the fall.

Jacqui walked blindly through the streets of New York, not knowing or caring where she was going. She went up Fifth Avenue, past a construction site—they were no doubt building another set of ten-million-dollar luxury apartments, as if the city needed more— and tried not to notice the construction workers leering at her.

"Baby, don't look so glum—I'll cheer you up!" one of them shouted at her as she walked past, but she just threw him a dirty look and kept walking.

Jacqui used to be flattered when men ogled her, but now she was just disgusted.

Someone had once told her that even in a city full of beautiful women, she stood out like an orchid among roses. But what had being pretty really gotten her in the long run? She looked at herself in a shined-to-perfection shop window, taking in her razor-sharp cheekbones and lustrous dark eyes. Her whole life, Jacqui had wanted to prove that she was more than just an amazing body and a beautiful face. It had been so difficult for her to take the embarrassing fifth year of high school, getting left behind as her friends went to college and regaled her with their success stories. She didn't resent Eliza and Mara's accomplishments, but she did wish she had a few of her own under her belt. Being beautiful didn't seem like an achievement—she'd done nothing to deserve her good looks, other than winning the genetic lottery.

Without realizing where her feet were taking her, Jacqui found herself in the middle of Central Park. She spotted a park bench and sat down, watching a family of mallard ducks float on the pond. She wondered if they were hungry and wished she had something to feed them. Whenever Jacqui took the Perry kids here, she thought of Holden Caulfield in *The Catcher in the Rye* and his fascination with the ducks—he always wondered where the ducks went in the winter and why, despite the inhospitable cold of New York City, they always came back. Why did they try to live in Manhattan when it obviously wasn't a place for a duck? It clearly wasn't a place for a poor girl from Brazil, either. Jacqui felt the tears coming again and blinked furiously.

She'd been kidding herself, thinking that she fit in here. The Perrys had been her substitute family, so much so that she didn't even know her real family anymore. But when it came down to it, she was still considered the help. Help that could so easily be dismissed. It was a painful wake-up call.

*I'm not going to cry, I'm not going to cry,* she thought fiercely, even as two fat tears slid down her cheeks and plopped onto her lap, staining her whiskered jeans.

She blinked to find a white cotton handkerchief being held under her nose.

"Oh. Thank you," she said gratefully, keeping her eyes to the ground. She blew her nose on the handkerchief, taking in the sweet smell of freshly ironed lavender. It was as large as a formal dinner napkin and softer than Kleenex. Who even carried handkerchiefs anymore?

"I'm sorry. I think I've soiled this," she apologized, balling it up in her hand. She looked up to see who'd given it to her, expecting a white-haired old lady with a plaid hat, but instead found herself looking at a tall, towheaded boy built like a football player, with broad shoulders and a rugged bearing. He was about her age, Jacqui guessed. He had quintessential all-American good looks, from his thick blond hair and clear, cornflower blue eyes to his straight, roman nose.

"I'm Pete Rockwood," he said, holding out his hand.

She shook it. "Jacqui Velasco." She held out his handkerchief. "Thanks again."

"Not at all. Keep it. You need it more than I do." He smiled gently.

Jacqui nodded and looked up at him again. He had a camera around his neck—a small digital Canon Elph, but still. He was clearly a tourist. Somehow she didn't feel the usual disdain she felt for the provincial hordes that swarmed upon Manhattan in the summer months. He was too . . . cute for disdain.

"You take care now." Pete gave her another kind smile and turned to walk away. Jacqui was shocked. He wasn't even going to stay and make small talk? In her whole life, she'd never met a single guy who'd given up the chance to flirt with her. She couldn't decide if she was impressed or insulted.

"Hey!" she called out after him.

He turned around.

"Where are you going?" she asked.

"To St. Patrick's. My family's waiting there."

"Oh . . ." Jacqui said. She didn't want to keep him, but she didn't much feel like being alone right now either. "Well, what are you doing here, then?"

Pete smiled and gestured to the scene before them. "I just wanted to see the pond, you know. Have a little J. D. Salinger moment. I'd always wanted to see the ducks. We have ducks in Indianapolis too, but it's not the same."

Jacqui felt like she'd just been knocked in the chest. He'd been thinking of *The Catcher in the Rye* too? "Do you have to meet them right now?"

Pete walked back and sat down next to her on the bench. "I guess not." He removed a plastic bag full of bread crumbs from his back pocket and handed her some. Together they started tossing the crumbs to the ducks on the water.

"Sorry to keep you; it's just . . . it's been a crappy day." She tossed a crumb to one of the hungrier-looking ducks.

"Yeah? What happened?" Pete turned and looked at her, really looked at her, waiting patiently for her to tell him.

Jacqui didn't know why, but she felt like she could trust this Pete Rockwood. Maybe it was something about taking comfort in a stranger, someone who didn't know anything about her, but before she knew it, she was unburdening herself to him, everything coming out in a torrent—her hopes for NYU, the Perrys' shocking abandonment, her doomed future.

Pete listened quietly, asking the right questions, never interrupting her or making snap judgments. Throughout all of her experiences in America—with the super-rich Hamptonites, the spoiled and self-involved New Yorkers—no one had ever treated her so . . . nicely. He was so gentle and sweet, strong and solid at the same time. What was this Indianapolis place, and were all the guys there like Pete?

His voice broke into her thoughts. "You know, you've been dealt a bad hand—but as my granny says, when life hands you lemons, make lemonade." Pete grinned, and his teeth were so white he looked like he should be in a Crest commercial.

"Lemonade?"

"You know, figure out a way to make things work for you." He shrugged. "It's not an exact science. But something will come up. It always does." He smiled shyly and his hair fell into his eyes.

"Are you always this optimistic?" Jacqui asked.

Pete nodded. "Yeah, actually. I mean, that lady—Anna, right?—she said she'd give you a great reference. And that there's a family that's going to need you." He picked up the camera and held it up to one eye, squinting. "Well, you'll probably have a job by tonight." He snapped a few photos of the ducks and the surroundings but never once asked to take her photo. Another first.

"You think?" Jacqui wrinkled her brow doubtfully, although Pete's positive outlook was starting to rub off on her. Anna had said someone would need her. After all, this was Manhattan. A family with young children must be in search of a good nanny right now, right?

"Of course. If NYU is what you want, it won't just . . . happen." He shrugged again. "You'll make it happen. All you have to do is follow your heart, and your dreams will come true." Pete snapped another photo, then put down his camera and turned to face her. "I know it's totally corny, but I've always believed it." He stood up, brushing the crumbs from his jeans, which weren't dark-rinsed or low-rise or even remotely trendy—nothing like the jeans worn by guys who chased Jacqui around nightclubs. They were just plain, straight-leg Levi's 501s.

"You're going?" Jacqui suddenly felt disappointed, though she wasn't sure why.

"I have to go meet my family—our flight leaves tonight. Going back home to Indy." He sighed and crumpled up the now-empty plastic bag, putting it in his pocket—most likely to find a recycling bin for it somewhere.

She nodded and briefly considered asking him for his e-mail address or phone number. But what was the point? He lived in Indiana. She'd likely be on her way back to Brazil soon. Or, if Pete was right, starting classes at NYU.

"Well, it was nice meeting you, Miss Jacqui Velasco." Pete offered her his hand.

She shook it warmly. "You too, Pete Rockwood." She grinned at his formality. It was sweet and unexpected.

On a whim, Jacqui took Pete's camera from his hand and

stood next to him, holding the camera away from their faces and snapping a picture of the two of them. "I want you to remember me." Jacqui smiled.

"Aw." Pete broke into a wide grin. "I don't need a picture for that. But thanks."

Jacqui watched him walk in the direction of St. Patrick's, and she felt content. Even though she knew she'd never see Pete again, she was happy to have met him.

And just then, as Pete disappeared behind a giant leafy oak tree, Jacqui's cell phone began to sing the tune to Led Zeppelin's "The Lemon Song."

Jacqui glanced down at the screen and saw Eliza's name.

Had the lemonade arrived?

# good friends have great ideas

MARA SAT UNDERNEATH THE FLUORESCENT LIGHTS OF the airport Pizza Hut, chewing her slice of pepperoni but barely tasting it. She was still slightly shell-shocked. How could David do that to her? She'd always appreciated how much David shared her passion for writing. Well, he shared her passion, all right—so much so that he was on a plane to Brussels while she was stuck at the baggage terminal. Even though she'd told him to go, she'd really wanted to scream, *Stay! What do you mean you're going to Europe without me?*

She couldn't decide if she was angry or proud. *You would do the same thing,* he'd said. But would she? Would she have been driven enough to follow her dreams, even if it meant walking away from him? *This isn't a vacation, Mara.*

Well, maybe that was fair—wasn't that what she'd been secretly fantasizing it would be? A romantic, all-expenses-paid vacation through Europe's most glamorous capitals with her wonderful and worldly boyfriend? Had she not been taking the trip seriously enough? Was she really not cut out for journalism?

The sound of her phone playing Fergie's "London Bridge" startled her. She picked it up immediately. "Liza! Hey!" Mara smiled. She could really use a friend right now.

"Hey, yourself!" Eliza's cheerful greeting lifted Mara's spirits immediately.

"I'm so glad you called! Oh my God, you'll never believe what just happened. . . ." Before Eliza could say another word, Mara poured out the whole sob story, taking care to recount every horrid detail—except for her doubts that maybe David was the teensiest bit right about her not taking their job seriously enough. "So what do you think?" Mara asked as she finished up her story. "Do I win the award for worst start of the summer ever or what?" She tried to laugh at herself but couldn't muster more than a half smile.

"Actually, I think it's fantastic!" Eliza chirped.

"Um, excuse me? Did you hear what I just told you? I pretty much got dumped and fired at the same time!" Saying the word *dumped* made Mara feel less sad—and more angry. She took a bite of the crust of her pizza, tearing it with her teeth.

"David didn't dump you. He said he loved you, didn't he? I bet he's going to bring you back like ten thousand pounds of Perigord truffles from Paris." Eliza's voice was soothing. "And so what if you got fired? I have a job for you!"

"A job?" Mara asked, the slightest bit of hope seeping into her voice. Eliza was really well connected—maybe she knew of an opening at a fashion magazine or something?

"My dad's girlfriend has these kids. . . . They're practically angels. Nothing like the Perrys. At all. I mean, the seven-year-olds basically read at college level," Eliza said enthusiastically.

"And?" Mara switched her phone from one ear to the other and squinted, wondering where this was going.

"Well, the thing is, the au pair they'd hired just quit—nothing to do with the kids, of course; she just landed a modeling job—so they're hiring!" Eliza sounded so gleeful, as if she had no doubt Mara would take the job in a snap.

"Au pair?" Mara asked doubtfully. It had been two years since she'd played babysitter. Last summer she'd had a kick-ass internship at *Hamptons* magazine. Chasing after a pack of kids, changing diapers, and wiping drool sounded like a big step backward. "I don't know, E." Mara's eyes wandered around the Pizza Hut, finally settling on two eight-year-old boys who were taking the toppings off their pizza and throwing them at each other across the table. Little monsters.

"She's paying a lot," Eliza wheedled.

Mara's curiosity got the better of her. "How much?"

"How's fifteen grand a month sound?" Eliza asked.

"That's a lot of money," she conceded. Even though she'd been lucky enough to win grants and scholarship money to fund her college tuition, with the cost of living in Manhattan, college was very expensive indeed. Her internship at the *Circus* wasn't putting anything in her pocket, either—it paid in freebies and premiere tickets.

Mara didn't want to be a sellout, but beggars couldn't be choosers, and at the moment, she certainly felt like a beggar.

"And there's more: Jacqui's in too. Plus I'll be here and we can all spend the summer together! It'll be a blast!"

"Oh my God, Jacqui too?" Of course. Jacqui would be with the Perrys in the Hamptons. The money was tempting, and so was the promise of friends, but not the job itself. "I mean, I would love to be with you guys, but I kind of feel like I need to do some writing—you know, show David I'm cut out for it." She looked over at the eight-year-olds again, who were now sword-fighting with their crusts. "He said my heart wasn't in journalism. Taking a job as an au pair sort of feels like giving up, like . . . proving him right."

"Well," Eliza said thoughtfully, "maybe David is right."

Mara practically dropped her slice of pizza. "Excuse me?"

"No, no—hear me out. Maybe your heart isn't in journalism. Because you're so much more creative than that. You're too romantic, too much of a . . . free spirit. Maybe you'd be better at writing a novel. Why don't you come out this summer and try writing a book? You know, like one of those funny Candace Bushnell–type things. About the beautiful people and the glamorous life and how it's not so beautiful and glam after all."

Mara sighed. Eliza always had outrageous, over-the-top ideas for everything. She couldn't write a novel. What did she know about it?

"All those nanny books are hot right now," Eliza went on. "You could write a funny one about your experiences with the Hamptons set. The kids and their demands. The parents and their crazy expectations. I predict best seller!"

Against her better judgment, Mara was starting to grin. "That's ridiculous."

"No, it's not, and you know it. C'mon. You'll make a lot of money, get to hang out with me and Jacqui, get some notes for your blockbuster. That'll show David, won't it?" Eliza wheedled.

Mara picked up her tray and tossed the contents in the garbage. "You're quite the saleswoman, Miss Thompson!"

"Does that mean you'll do it?"

"Yeah." Mara grinned, picking up her bag again. "I'm in."

"Woo-hoo!"

Mara laughed as she strode purposefully out of Pizza Hut and toward the terminal exit. It was great to have a friend like Eliza. Someone who could steer you in the right direction, even when life sent you totally off course.

"So," Eliza's voice came chirping through the phone, "how soon can you be in the Hamptons?"

Mara glanced down at her watch. She grinned. "As soon as they're ready for me."

# is there such a thing as attachment nannying?

**AS SHE STEPPED OUT OF THE TAXICAB ON DUNE DRIVE,** Mara found herself greeted by a twenty-foot-high statue of Michelangelo's *David*. Enormous reproductions of several of the most famous sculptures in Western history stood on the lawn in front of the mega-mansion, casting long shadows that stretched all the way to the road. If she'd renewed her passport, Mara thought glumly, she'd be seeing the real *David* in Florence—with *her* David at her side—instead of its rather tacky facsimile. But then a welcome sight greeted her among the fake Greek kouroi, chasing her negative thoughts away.

Jacqui was sitting on the curb, cigarette in hand. She quickly stood as she saw her friend. "Mara!" she cried, running up and throwing her arms around her. Mara hugged her back fiercely. Jacqui's thick, glossy mane of hair tickled her cheek.

Mara finally managed to stand back and smile. "What are you doing here? Did the Perrys send you over to borrow a cup of sugar?" she joked, straightening the straps of her pale yellow sundress.

At the mention of the Perrys, Jacqui's face fell. "No. I'm not working for them anymore. They moved to London."

"To London?" Mara asked, totally taken aback. It was her turn to look distressed. "All of them?"

Jacqui nodded, putting out her cigarette with the heel of her wedge sandal. "C'mon, let's go in." She linked her arm in Mara's and the two of them walked up to the front door together.

Mara took Jacqui's arm and followed her blindly, lost in thought. London. If the whole family had moved, that meant Ryan was in London too. Which meant he wasn't going to be in the Hamptons this summer. A small part of her—one she didn't even know existed anymore—suddenly . . . deflated.

When Ryan and Mara broke up last summer, they'd promised each other that they would be friends and that they'd keep in touch. They'd tried, but without much success. Ryan had e-mailed several times, and Mara had called him a bunch too, but the e-mails had been short and the phone calls stilted. In the end, Mara couldn't remember who was supposed to get back to whom, and the correspondence dwindled, until she had to rely on third-party information from Jacqui, who worked for his family, or Eliza, who was one of Ryan's oldest childhood friends and traveled in the same social circles.

Mara took one last look at the *David*, that enduring portrait of male perfection, as they climbed the steps and thought with a sigh about the two guys in her life who she'd once thought were perfect—Ryan and David—but whose relationships with her had either *not* endured or had turned out to be less than perfect.

The door opened moments after they rang the bell, revealing a glowing Eliza, her skin tan against a chic white halter dress. *"Hola, chiquitas!"* She threw out her arms and enveloped them in a three-way hug. She finally pulled back and led them into the house. "Welcome to our humble abode," Eliza said slyly, gesturing grandly with one arm.

*"Meu Deus!"* Jacqui exclaimed as they took in the size of the foyer, the gold-gilt furniture, and the breathtaking view of the ocean through floor-to-ceiling windows. The five-thousand-square-foot room had a sunken conversation pit with buttery leather couches and crystal coffee tables, and twin six-by-ten-foot Jackson Pollock canvases flanked the fireplace, almost identical to the ones that hung on the entrance to the third floor of MoMA.

Eliza ushered them into a messy office on the ground floor. "This is Suzy," she said, gesturing to the area behind the paper-covered desk. They turned to see a frizzy-haired woman talking into her headset while miming instructions to a few staff members who stood patiently, somehow understanding her nonverbal cues and scribbling down notes.

Suzy took off her headset and smiled at the girls. "Hi! You must be Eliza's friends. Come, sit!" She motioned for them to take a seat around the conference table, and her staff members slunk quietly out of the room.

Eliza followed them to the door. "I'll see you guys later; I have to jet to the store. Jeremy's putting the downlighting in the dressing rooms and I have to make sure he got the pink bulbs—super-flattering!" She waved her hands and blew them kisses as she shut the door.

Mara turned to look at Suzy again. She wondered if she was going to be as difficult as Anna Perry had been. She'd certainly heard of Suzy Finnemore, hedge fund queen, and had been expecting a hard-as-nails dragon lady. Someone blown out and Botoxed to within an inch of her life. But the woman who sat at the head of table had a blowsy, harried manner—not to mention a rumpled wardrobe. Quite a departure from the perfectly polished Hamptons housewife—which, Mara realized, was exactly what the difference was. Unlike those women, Suzy actually *worked* for a living—in fact, she ran a very successful business. She didn't have time to sit around and have manicures all day. "So let me begin by saying, I usually don't work with a nanny." Suzy moved one of the piles of paper over so they could see each other more clearly. "I raised all the kids myself."

Jacqui raised an eyebrow. Now, this was interesting.

"My ex-husband and I were total attached parents. We took Violet everywhere and when the twins came, we did the same thing. With Wyatt, we had just started the fund, so it was a little more difficult, but we managed. But then my ex left for Australia to go on a 'walkabout.'" She made quotations with her fingers and, seeing the girls' confused looks, explained. "It's one of those things the aborigines do, to find out who they are. It's been a year and a half and he's still looking." She threw up her hands, as if shrugging it off. "In the middle of our divorce, I found out I was pregnant with Cassidy. Since he was born, the fund's taken off, and I've found that I barely have time to see to my own needs, much less theirs. And the last thing I want to be is a slacker mom. So I've decided to reevaluate my nurturing methods." She leaned forward, her intelligent brown eyes flashing. "Here's the deal. I just want you guys to think of me as your manager."

Mara wrinkled her brow in worry and turned to Jacqui, whose lips were curling in amusement.

"By that I mean, since I can't be a full-time parent anymore, on the floor and in the thick of things, I need you girls to be me—to think of my children as your children. To do everything that I would do if I had the time." Suzy grabbed a stack of child-care books that were sitting behind her and pushed them down the table. *Your Baby and Child. Dr. Spock. What to Expect the First Year. The No-Cry Sleep Solution. The Happiest Baby on the Block. The Contented Little Baby. How to Talk to a Teenager. Encouraging Your Gifted Child.*

"And then—this is the manager part—I need you to report back to me. I want you guys to keep logs on the kids. Write down everything they do and how they're reacting to the world. Are the activities worth their time? Are they developing at the normal rate? They're all gifted, so I want to make sure they're all being challenged enough. Bored people are boring."

Jacqui cleared her throat. "I think Mara should keep the log. She's a great writer, so maybe it should be her responsibility."

Suzy shrugged. "Sure. I don't care, as long as it gets done."

Mara sighed inwardly but tried to keep a polite smile on her face. She couldn't help but be reminded of their first summer as au pairs, when Eliza and Jacqui routinely blew off their responsibilities to party, leaving Mara holding the diaper bag.

But as she glanced at the stack of books in front of her, a light flipped on in her head. A log would be a great way to keep notes as material for her book. Maybe she could even do it online, as a blog. . . . Everyone had one now, so that could be a great place to start. It would be good practice for writing every day, and maybe she could turn those notes into her book.

"Thanks again for taking the position on such short notice." Suzy stood and smoothed out some of the wrinkles in her suit, even though it looked like it had never seen an iron in its life and might never be able to recover. "Eliza has sung your praises to the heavens, so I'm sure I won't be disappointed." She held out her hand and shook both of their hands again, as if she'd just concluded a successful business deal. "I'll be reviewing the log every week and tailoring their activities and development according to what I find in it. I want a high yield on my investments, so to speak." Suzy winked to let them know she was kidding. "So just make sure they don't crash and burn."

Mara nodded. Even if all didn't go according to plan, she was used to putting out fires. She'd already been burned once today.

# these girls can't keep their clothes on for long

"AAAAND HE'S OUT," MARA SAID, SLIPPING OFF HER shoes and plopping down on her new bed's cushy duvet comforter. After parting ways just ten minutes ago to put the kids to sleep, she was already back to her new bedroom, and Jacqui was sprawled out on the leather sofa.

They'd spent the better part of the day being "debriefed" on each of the Finnemore children, learning all about their likes and dislikes, their goals, their academic achievements, even their medical history. Suzy was unbelievably thorough and wanted to make sure her au pairs were well versed in all possible information related to their charges. It was like cramming for finals at Columbia all over again. But the kids themselves were remarkably easygoing and good-natured.

"I didn't think a kid could go to bed that quickly. I just put him down in his crib, like Suzy told me, and left him there. Five minutes later, he's snoring." Mara hadn't believed it at first, having expected six-month-old Cassidy to fuss and holler, but the baby actually adhered to the rigid sleep schedule that was posted by his crib, as if he were well aware of the task at hand and wanted to stay on target. "Suzy said he'll sleep through the night, so we're off duty. Amazing." Mara shook her head and reached behind her for a pillow, wedging it under her head.

Jacqui laughed from the sofa, her glossy black hair spread out across the armrest like a fan. "Tell me about it! Can we clone those *meninos*? I read them a story, tucked them in, and that was it." Jacqui sighed happily, splaying her arms out on either side of her and letting her body sink into the soft cushions. "They almost don't need us," she added wistfully. Her success with the Perry children had led Jacqui to earnestly think about majoring in child development. The Finnemores were a cakewalk compared to her former charges, but part of her missed the challenge.

"We've got it made," Mara agreed, glancing around the enormous room she'd been given in the children's wing. It had a flatscreen television, a renovated bathroom with a Jacuzzi, a cushy double bed, and an Eames sofa. The whole room was furnished in a very modern style, in black and white with red accents—white walls, a jet-black duvet on the bed, a black leather couch with red cushions. Jacqui's room was identical and right next door. Compared to the Perrys' tiny, ramshackle servants' cottage, this was heaven.

"*Fala sério!*" Jacqui cried, sitting up. She picked up the remote from the floor and tried to figure out which of its hundreds of buttons would turn it on.

There was a rap on the door and Eliza walked in, looking a bit grimy from her day at the store—meaning, her hair was the slightest bit out of place and her pants were wrinkled. "Hey, ladies." She smiled.

Mara opened one eye. "Why, hello, m'dear."

"Nice digs, huh?" Eliza sat down beside Jacqui on the leather sofa and Jacqui scooted over. "I told Suzy there was no way she was going to stick you in the service wing. My room is just down the hall." There was a twinkle in her eye as she bounded from the couch and looked from one girl to the other. "You all aren't too tired, are you?"

"Why, what do you have in mind?" Jacqui sat up. She was always up for a little fun.

"I found some champagne in the fridge." Eliza removed a magnum of Cristal from her enormous Chanel bucket bag. "I think we should celebrate!"

Mara groaned.

Jacqui grinned.

"C'mon, Mar," Eliza pleaded. "What are you, a Sturbridge Puritan again? Or maybe you're a stiff Ivy Leaguer now," she teased. "Don't tell me you've forgotten how to have fun!"

"All right, all right." Mara sighed, slipping her shoes on. "But we better be back at a decent hour—according to Suzy, the baby wakes up at six!"

Eliza led them through the house to the patio, past the pool, and down to the trail that led to the beach. It was a gorgeous night. They kicked off their shoes and walked for a while in silence, taking in the moonlight and the calm sea. They eventually came to the secluded spot near the old Perry homestead, Creek Head Manor. "Weird." Mara broke the silence. "I had no idea we were so close."

"Yeah," Eliza replied. "Pretty much all the houses in this part of the Hamptons are connected to the same beach—you just have to know where to walk." She dug a toe into the sand. "Anyway, I thought this would be an appropriate spot to bring you girls on our first night."

The three girls grinned mischievously, thinking of their skinny-dipping excursion of two years ago. They turned to look at the Perry house, memories of their first summer together rushing back. Mara put an arm around her friends' shoulders. Eliza and Jacqui didn't know that this spot held extra significance for her—it was where she'd first spent a night with Ryan, sleeping side by side in sleeping bags on the beach but not so much as kissing. She shook off the thought. This night was about her and her girlfriends, not her history with Ryan.

Eliza pulled the bottle out of her purse and handed it to Jacqui, who did the honors, popping the cork and sending a spray of bubbles onto the sand. The three girls giggled. Eliza reached into her purse again and produced three plastic cups. "I propose a toast—to the start of the summer." She raised her red Solo cup, careful not to spill its contents on her white dress.

Mara's eyes glinted in the moonlight. "I propose revising your toast—to the *new* start to the summer!" she said with a laugh.

"Yes," Jacqui agreed, raising her glass. "Here's to getting a—what is the phrase?—a much needed do-over!"

"Hear, hear!" they all cheered, sipping down the cold bubbles.

The surf was rolling in gently, and the sand was refreshingly cold and wet on their feet. A soft ocean breeze blew, and the sky was blanketed with stars. All three girls couldn't help but feel lucky to have yet another summer to spend in such a magical place.

Mara looked back at the Perrys' house again. "Just imagine, if those first au pairs had worked out, we never would have met," she said softly, referring to the fact that the three of them had been hired as the "B team" after the first group of au pairs had been unceremoniously fired by Anna before the Fourth of July. During the past year, the three of them had been in New York at the same time, but they hadn't been able to see each other nearly as much as they'd have liked. Eliza had been busy with her new arsty friends, hanging out at the basement of La Esquina with the fashion crowd, while Jacqui had no spare time between juggling the kids' schedules and her studies. Not that Mara could talk about being busy—she'd been so wrapped up in David and Columbia that more often than not, it was she who canceled on dinner dates and brunch plans.

She looked over at Jacqui and Eliza, who were leaning on each other and happily sipping their champagne. Mara felt a shiver of delight. With the whole summer stretching ahead of them, it was time to reconnect and reacquaint with her old friends. She couldn't wait. She'd made some good friends at college—her roommates, a debutante from Georgia and a Nantucket preppie, were both really sweet—but they were no Jacqui and Eliza. Somehow, the experience of surviving the Perrys' dysfunctional family dynamic and the rigors of the Hamptons social scene had bonded the three of them for life.

Mara threw pebbles into the water, making them skip. "This champagne is making me hot," she said, feeling a warm rush to her cheeks from the alcohol.

"Well," Eliza said in a practical tone. "There's only one cure for that."

"Are you thinking what I'm thinking?" Mara grinned.

In answer, Eliza kicked off her clogs and took off her sweater. Jacqui watched with an amused expression. "Are we really going to do this?" she asked.

"Hey, it's practically tradition!" Eliza replied.

Jacqui slid out of her skinny jeans and Mara shrugged off her sundress, following Eliza to the water. The cold waves lapped at their ankles and the breeze tickled their skin.

"This is *it*!" Eliza laughed, expressing what all three of them felt. That they were wild and free, at one with nature and the world, their best friends at their side. This was what life was all about—the ocean, the stars, and friendship. This was what they'd waited all year for.

"Let's never grow up!" Mara cheered.

"Never!" Jacqui agreed. *"Jovens para sempre!"* Forever young.

And with that promise, the three of them bounded into the surf.

# mara finds a new way to warm up

*BRRRRR.* **MARA STARTED SHAKING FROM THE COLD, TINY** goose bumps forming all over her wet arms. Whose idea had it been to go skinny-dipping in the Atlantic Ocean anyway? Maybe she hadn't drunk enough champagne—Eliza and Jacqui didn't seem to feel adverse to the chill. Jacqui was doing a handstand in the waves, while Eliza floated lazily on her back.

It was with relief that Mara heard her cell phone ringing. Any excuse to get out of the ice bucket. She splashed over to the beach, jumping up and down to warm herself up. Three sets of clothes lay strewn about the sand: Eliza's in a messy pile by a log, Jacqui's all in a row—she apparently liked to strip as she made her way to the water—and Mara's folded neatly by the side of the dune. Her phone kept jingling from her left jacket pocket, breaking the perfect silence of the night.

Mara crouched down and picked up her jacket. Who could be calling so late? Maybe it was David, calling from Brussels to apologize and tell her how much he missed her already? She pulled out the phone. It stopped ringing the second she picked it up. Of course.

"Mara?" A voice behind her startled her. A very, *very* familiar voice.

Mara almost jumped out of her birthday suit—not that that was possible. She turned around. "Oh my God!" Her hands flew to cover herself though she realized there was no need—he'd seen it all before. Because Ryan Perry was standing in front of her, an amused half smile on his face.

Mara's dark chestnut hair was plastered to her cheek, half her body covered with sand. She was so shocked to see him that the only words that came out of her mouth were, "Why aren't you in London?"

"Well, hello to you too," Ryan said amiably. His honey blond hair shone under the moonlight, and his two dimples winked in his smooth, tanned cheeks. He looked just as handsome as ever, if not more so. But his face was totally unreadable. He was acting so blasé, as if he ran into naked ex-girlfriends all the time. Mara willed herself to act as nonchalantly as he was—even if he had the advantage of being fully clothed.

"Oh, sorry—it's just that you caught me by surprise."

"I can see that." He grinned. "You make a habit of walking around naked these days, Waters?"

Talk about new habits. Calling her by her last name was a new habit *he'd* developed since they'd broken up. That and calling her "dude." *Dude?* Mara was no dude. She was "babe," "good-looking," "sweetheart." Not "dude."

"Learned it from you," she shot back flirtatiously. Ryan was a free-spirit bohemian, and during the summer they'd spent on his family's yacht, just the two of them, there had been a lot of naked sailing, naked deep-sea fishing, even naked breakfast-eating.

"Touché, my friend." Ryan laughed, and Mara decided to ignore the "friend" comment. "You know my habits all too well—I'm always one step away from joining a nudist colony." He smiled wickedly.

Mara laughed. "It's good to see you," she said, trying to keep her voice level. How did you have a normal conversation with a guy you used to love? Especially when one of you was naked? Not wanting to bend over for her clothes, Mara took some of her long hair and tried to reposition it so that it was covering her chest. There. That was better. She crossed her arms for further coverage.

"You too." Ryan nodded and looked down, digging a toe in the sand.

"But seriously, why *are* you here?" Mara tried to suppress the waves of excitement flowing through her. Not that it meant anything, especially since she had a new boyfriend now. A very cute boyfriend. Although said cute boyfriend had left her stranded at the airport that morning. Definitely not a cute move.

"You heard about London, huh?" Ryan said. "Yeah, the family moved overseas, but I'm staying at the house here until they find someone to rent it. But what about you—aren't you supposed to be bumming around Prague or something? A friend of mine is doing Lonesome Planet, and I saw your name on the list. What are you doing here?"

"Taking a swim!" Mara yelled, and with that she ran toward the jet-black ocean and dove into the waves. She'd had enough of the conversation—it was just too weird and surreal to stand there in front of Ryan without any clothes on and make small talk. Cordial and civilized had never been their style.

Mara put her head down in the water, her heart racing. Ryan Perry. And he'd been keeping tabs on her, too. Seeing him was like hearing an old song come on the radio—bringing up so many old feelings and memories that you can't tune them out. Mara swam to where her friends were still bobbing happily.

"Hey, is that Ryan?" Eliza asked, squinting and craning her neck to get a better look at the figure on the beach.

"Ryan! Come join us!" Jacqui yelled mischievously, kicking up one bare foot.

Ryan just waved at them from the shoreline. Mara was relieved to see him finally turn on his heels and walk back to the house. Because even though the water was totally freezing, she felt warm and tingly all over.

# jeremy shows eliza her future, eliza doesn't know if she wants to look

**"WHERE ARE WE GOING?" ELIZA STRETCHED HER FEET** out in front of her on the dashboard of Jeremy's truck, admiring her new pedicure—shell pink, to match the decor of her boutique, of course. The past several days had been a mad rush to get everything ready for the store launch that weekend, and she'd hardly even seen the girls since they'd gone skinny-dipping their first night. She was glad to even have snuck in some time with Jeremy.

"You'll see." He smiled, putting a hand on Eliza's slim ankle. "It's a surprise."

"You know I hate surprises." Eliza mock-pouted.

"You'll like this one," he said mysteriously.

"Fine, be that way," she retorted, pretending to be miffed. She sighed, inhaling the woody, loamy scent of Jeremy's truck. Despite running his own successful landscaping business, Jeremy had yet to trade in his decades-old pickup for something more expensive. When he'd pulled into the driveway to pick her up earlier, his car had looked hilariously mismatched sitting next to Eliza's CLK convertible. But Eliza didn't mind. Maybe the old Eliza would have badgered her boyfriend to trade up as soon as he made more money, but this Eliza didn't care about image the way she'd used to. She liked Jeremy's truck. It was sensible and sturdy—just like him.

Jeremy drove into one of the quiet, secluded older neighborhoods in Sagaponack, filled with white clapboard houses and picket fences. The streets were lined with enormous maple trees bowed low, their green leaves blowing gently in the breeze. The sun was just beginning to set, giving the whole scene a warm, pinkish tint. "Close your eyes," he instructed.

"Do I have to?" she whined, crossing her arms over her chest defiantly.

"Yes, and not one more peep from you, young lady." Jeremy put on a mock-serious, teacher-y voice, taking one hand off the wheel to wag a finger at her.

Eliza closed her eyes obediently. She hadn't been lying—she hated surprises. Eliza was the type of girl who made lists of presents for other people to get her every time Christmas or her birthday rolled around. If she received a gift that deviated from the list, she promptly returned it for store credit. She could never even read a mystery novel without reading the last page first to see whodunit. She hated suspense. But she wanted to please her boyfriend.

She wondered what trick Jeremy had up his sleeve. He'd been

acting anxious all evening, alternately jittery and excited. They were so comfortable with each other, so familiar with every crevice of each other's body, every variation on each other's moods, that she could tell instantly when something was going on. Sometimes she felt like they were turning into an old married couple.

The car came to an abrupt stop and Eliza heard Jeremy get out of the cab, walk around, and open her door.

"Can I open them now?" she asked.

"Not yet!" He took her elbow and helped her to the ground, steadying her as she wobbled a bit on her chunky white Calypso espadrilles. They walked forward a few feet.

"Okay, now," Jeremy said.

Eliza opened her eyes. She was standing in front of an old, regal mansion—one that needed a lot of work. The paint was peeling, the cornice crumbling. Still, it was beautiful. It reminded her a little bit of the dollhouse she'd played with as a kid, which had looked a bit like an old British manor—her own personal version of a Barbie dream house. "What's this?"

"Remember I told you about old lady Greyson? One of my oldest clients?"

"Yeah." Eliza nodded slowly. She vaguely remembered him talking about one of the old ladies whose gardens he tended, charging much less than he should have. Recently, he'd been acting as her pseudo-caretaker, making sure she'd taken her medicine and that she had enough groceries to see her through the week, feeding her cat, various little things. Jeremy was a sweetheart like that. But was this really her surprise? He'd taken her to meet some cranky, possibly senile old lady? Were they going to have to read her bedtime stories and give her an oatmeal sponge bath?

"Well, she passed away this week." Jeremy looked down at the ground, kicking at a pebble with his shoe.

"Oh—I'm so sorry." She touched his arm. Whoops. She felt like a jerk now. "I . . . didn't know you guys were so close."

"Neither did I," Jeremy said. He looked back up at her, his eyes shining. "She was a really sweet old lady." He paused. "Anyway, she didn't have any family. She used to say I was the only one who cared about her in the end, but I didn't realize it was true."

"That's so sad." Eliza wrinkled her brow. "It must be terrible to die alone."

Jeremy didn't seem to hear her. He was gazing at the house, as if in a trance. "She left me everything," he said softly. "Her entire estate, stocks, bonds, everything. Including the house." He continued to stare at it, as if he were hearing the news for the first time and not the one delivering it. "I know it looks like it's falling apart, but it's got good bones and it's in a great location. With a little work, a cosmetic touch-up, it could really be something."

Eliza looked at him. He was standing so still in the golden light, looking up at the old house as if it held all the answers in the universe. All at once it sank in for her what this meant. This house was *his*. "Oh my God! Jeremy!" Eliza squealed.

"I know." He turned and smiled. "She always said she wanted the house to go to someone who would take care of it. Don't you think it's beautiful?"

"It's fabulous," Eliza agreed. "You'll make a fortune renting it out next summer." She smiled. If anyone deserved a break like this, it was Jeremy. Maybe nice guys really did finish first.

"C'mon." Jeremy took her hand. "Let me give you a tour."

He unlocked the front door and they walked inside. The house still had the stuffy smell of age and neglect, but Eliza could see that it was a grand house indeed. "Look at this kitchen," he said, showing her the front "master" kitchen and then leading her to a second kitchen in the back. "It's called the scullery." He ran a finger over a dusty countertop. "In the early twentieth century, when the house was built, kitchens were only for the help, so they were hidden from the rest of the house." He gestured to the middle of the space. "I'm thinking of opening this up and making a big island so that it feels more modern," he said. "Though I'll of course defer to your taste, since the kitchen is the lady's domain." He turned to her and wrapped her in his arms, a sly grin spreading across his face.

"Like you'll ever get me to cook," Eliza said dryly, leaning her head on his shoulder. Jeremy well knew that when it came to preparing dinner, she was much more likely to shell out for a private chef than to put on an apron.

"There's more I want to show you." He grabbed her hand and took her upstairs. "See, there's a study off the master bedroom that can be turned into a nursery." He gestured to a small room with tall windows that really did look like it would fit a crib nicely.

"But why go to all that trouble before you know who's going to live here?" Eliza asked, puzzled. "I mean, what if the people who move in don't have a baby?" She walked over to the window and looked out at the enormous, beautiful yard below, the white gazebo cloaked in the orange glow of the setting sun.

"Well, what about when *we* have babies?" Jeremy asked innocently, coming up behind her and kissing her neck.

"Babies!" She turned and swatted his arm. "Jer, *we're* babies."

Jeremy just kept nuzzling her ear as if he hadn't heard her. "Eleven bedrooms," he whispered. "We can have a big family. A whole soccer team!"

"Sure, I'll just pop them all out while I'm cooking away in the back kitchen." Eliza laughed. He was joking, right?

He led her back downstairs and out to the garden. They walked through the overgrown yard, past the willow trees, and to the gazebo she'd seen from upstairs. Looking through it, there was a beautiful view of the ocean in the distance. "And I was thinking . . . this is where we'll have our wedding," Jeremy said softly, pointing to the gazebo. Eliza's heart thumped in her chest. Jeremy wasn't just fantasizing about the future. No. He was planning it.

It was so beautiful, and yet . . .

"E., I want you to have this," Jeremy said, slipping a ring on her finger. Her left ring finger.

Eliza looked down in a daze. It was an enormous, glittering rock. A huge, princess-cut diamond. A princess for a princess—just like she'd always said she wanted. Eliza had always been very vocal about her bridal preferences, tossing her opinions out in the air the way she did with everything. She had no idea he'd actually been *listening*.

"Jer . . ." She didn't know what to say. She wasn't even really sure what had just happened. Did this mean . . . ?

"I love you," he said, pulling her to him and kissing her under the setting sun.

Eliza kissed him back, and when she opened one eye to look at her hand, her new ring winked at her, almost as if to say, *Gotcha!*

## www.blogspot/hamptonsaupair1

### about me

Hello. Hello. Is this mike working? Ha. Just kidding. I'm new to this Internet thingy. But allow me to introduce myself. I'm M., a nineteen-year-old au pair in the Hamptons. And no, I don't have a webcam. Besides, contrary to popular belief, I don't just hang out in my bikini and neglect the kids all day. It's a lot of work taking care of five overachieving children under the age of thirteen while their mom yells at you for feeding them non-free-range chicken nuggets. (Not that it's happened yet—it's only been a week—but I'm just saying.)

### my charges

VIOLET is twelve going on thirty-five. She speaks five languages and can probably balance the federal budget. Her advanced-Mandarin tutor arrives every other day. Otherwise, this summer Violet is busy with art, drama, sculpture, Bikram yoga, experimental dance and movement, etiquette, horseback riding, and violin. Her schedule is busier than that of a CEO of a large financial company. I know, because her mom is one, and *she* actually has time off. Violet's goal? Early admission to Harvard (Mom was class of '92), a Rhodes Scholarship, and world domination. Violet displays all twelve signs of extraordinary ability according to *Twelve Signs Your Tween is Gifted.* She is well balanced, well rounded, and incredibly mature for her age. Sadly, I have not yet seen her laugh.

LOGAN and JACKSON are seven-year-old twin child geniuses. Logan has composed a piano solo in the style of Chopin and beat the former Soviet chess champ when he was five years old. Jackson wrote a one-act play that was produced by a New York theater company last year. (Title: *A Car Seat Named Desire.*) They are obsessed with CNN and ending global warming and are full-fledged members of the Libertarian party. Logan asked me with total sincerity what I was doing to lower my carbon monoxide emissions. Told him I myself don't even own a car anymore—I sold my Camry to pay for my first year at Columbia. These days I drive their mom's Lexus hybrid. Does that count?

WYATT is five and has proven the theory of relativity. Joke! Wyatt has eaten a sandwich. As far as I can tell, he is a normal five-year-old with five-year-old likes and dislikes: Tonka trucks, Legos, PlayStation 3, SpongeBob. His mother is convinced there must be something wrong with him.

CASSIDY is six months old, and he's already beginning to crawl. (Yes, Cassidy's a boy—thank God I'm not going to be around during those difficult, name-teasing preteen years.) His toilet trainer comes twice a week. Cassidy is proficient in BSL (baby sign language). I myself cannot speak BSL and therefore did not understand that Cassidy wanted a bottle rather than a cuddle, which resulted in major vomit. *Vomit* is gross in all languages.

Seriously, they're all adorable, and their mom is surprisingly down-to-earth considering she lives in a thirty-thousand-square-foot house. We'll see how long it lasts.

### personal notes

Taking care of kids isn't my *entire* life. I'm also here at the beach with my two best friends in the whole world, and between the three of us, we have a lot of fun and get into a lot of trouble. (Not necessarily in that order.)

E. is a designer diva, probably the best-dressed gal on the Atlantic coast. She's blond, gorgeous, funny, and will lend you the Pucci shift off her back—a girl after my own heart. She's opening her own store in the Hamptons this summer and has asked me to model at the opening! Me? Model? Bet you really wish I had a webcam now, huh?

J. is a South American sexpot, as well as one of the sweetest, nicest girls I've ever met. She's been unlucky in love in the past, and I've noticed she's been a bit subdued since we arrived. Every time I turn around, she's googling "Pete Rockwood, Indianapolis" on the computer. I asked her what the deal was, but she wouldn't tell me. No worries—J. will spill when she's ready. She's not one to keep secrets from friends. Unless, of course, it's about how one's boyfriend fooled around with one's other best friend a couple of years ago. But that's an old story and all is forgiven between the three of us. Seriously. Said ex-boyfriend is old news. Ancient history. Totally. Anyway, moving on . . .

My boyfriend D. and I have been together for almost a year. We were supposed to spend the summer in Europe together, but alas, as they say—"the best-laid plans of mice and men . . ." or "Life happens when you're busy making plans." Anyway, who knew that passports can expire? Last I saw him he was hightailing it to gate 24 in terminal 3 at JFK. He has sent a number of apologetic e-mails and texts but has yet to call. Should I give him the cold shoulder when he does ring? Or fake happiness? Which is more likely to prompt gifts of handmade Belgian chocolates?

**Till next time,**
**HamptonsAuPair1**

# jacqui meets the
# boys from oz

JACQUI GLIDED DOWN MAIN STREET, ENJOYING THE warm sunshine and colorful shop windows and almost forgetting the troop of children trailing her. A sweeping boulevard lined with weeping willow trees, rustic shingled cottages, and hand-painted signs as far as the eye could see, Main Street could have been in any quaint New England town. Filled as it was with dog-walking, child-toting parents, it was impossible to believe that this was one of the most fashionable places on earth. But on closer inspection, those tiny cottages actually housed storefronts for flashy designer labels and expensive apothecary stores, the dogs were hypoallergenic purebreds, and the children's play clothes were made from imported French cotton.

All three Finnemore boys were happily licking generous ice cream cones as they marched behind Jacqui in an orderly fashion. Logan and Jackson were quietly discussing the merits of last night's *Hannity & Colmes* debate, while Wyatt was devouring as much ice cream as possible while making sure not to spill any on his stubby little chin. She smiled, feeling a bit like Julie Andrews's Maria in *The Sound of Music*, the well-loved nanny with her rosy-cheeked, happy troop. Of course, Maria never wore sexy white Stella McCartney jumpers like the one she had on. But then again, Maria was a nun.

Jacqui stopped to look at a Calypso display in one of the cottage windows, admiring a handwoven leather belt. Without her having to tell them to, the boys immediately stopped behind her, waiting patiently.

Just as she had predicted, the kids were an easy bunch to manage. Their first week had been hassle- and trouble-free, with nary a tantrum or a toy thrown. In fact, the little boys were *so* serious Jacqui hoped to shake them up a bit. Violet was so studious she hardly ever went outside. Even the baby never cried. Well behaved was one thing, but these kids were so calm they were practically Stepford. Jacqui, trying to squeeze some fun into the kids' challenging schedule, had brought them to the ice cream counter as a treat, and they'd looked almost bewildered when she told them they could get anything they wanted.

Jacqui leaned in toward the show window, shading her eyes with her hand to block the reflection off the well-polished glass. The store had some beautiful things, and she immediately missed being able to buy what she wanted without worrying how much it cost. Payday was a few weeks off, and Jacqui knew exactly how she wanted to spend it: in their short jaunt, she'd made a mental note of the floaty sundresses at Tracy Feith, the newest thong sandals at Scoop, and a wallet-busting crocodile bag from Georgina.

Jacqui sighed. Those were things she wanted, all right, but she knew she wouldn't buy them. Suzy was paying her handsomely, and Jacqui intended to save every penny of it just to be safe. She'd had the rug pulled out from her once already this summer, and she wanted to have backup plans for her backup plans.

"I'm dripping," Wyatt whined, startling Jacqui from her reverie. "I tried to stop it from melting, but I couldn't."

"Oh no, sweetie." Jacqui bent down to help dab the front of his shirt, which was covered with sticky ice cream residue.

They had run out of napkins a few blocks back, so Jacqui rifled in her handbag for suitable alternatives. She came across the invite to Eliza's store opening that night—Eliza probably wouldn't be too happy to find out her invite was being used to wipe a five-year-old's face, but what she didn't know couldn't hurt her. Jacqui squatted down and began to gently wipe off Wyatt's face with the soft paper, crouching so low that the short-shorts on her jumper rode even farther up her thighs, and bending so far forward that she was dangerously close to revealing to the world that she was not wearing a bra underneath her eyelet top. She was almost done cleaning him when she heard the distinctive click of a camera shutter.

Jacqui jumped at the sound, teetering on her wooden Chloé wedges. *Meu Deus!* Was it the paparazzi again? But what would they want with her? She'd been keeping a low profile ever since Eliza's impromptu beach fashion show last summer. The camera continued to click and Jacqui rolled her eyes. Seriously, what did it take to be left alone these days?

She straightened, whipping her head around, about to unleash a smart retort—until she noticed who was behind the lens.

A lanky guy with shaggy, light brown hair and deep blue eyes stood on the sidewalk, squinting into his camera. He was dressed in a pair of worn cargos and a thin, faded All-Blacks T-shirt. "Hello, love, just hold that, will you? Brilliant! Now if you could just turn this way . . ." He motioned with a hand, still looking through the viewfinder.

Jacqui bristled. Who did he think he was? She was minding her own business, taking care of the kids in broad daylight on Main Street. She could tell from his accent he was Australian— she'd watched enough *Crocodile Hunter* with the Perry kids to be able to differentiate a Brit from an Aussie—and maybe things were done differently Down Under. Still, she certainly didn't need to add *paparazzi* to her list of things to deal with.

"Right there, perfect," the photographer said, just as Logan pulled on the hem of her jumper.

Jacqui looked down at the owlish little boy, trying to keep the annoyance out of her voice. "Yes, sweetie?"

"Why is that man bothering you?" he asked. "Doesn't he know about privacy law?"

Jacqui couldn't stop a grin from spreading across her face. "I don't know. Why don't we ask him?" She finished wiping Wyatt's face and gave him his ice cream cone back.

"Am I bothering you? I'm so sorry." The photographer smiled and his whole face lit up. He held the lens up to his eye again. "Could you hold that pose, please? Perfect, thanks. And maybe turn your chin down just a bit?"

Jacqui found her chin moving down automatically, her eyes locking with the camera's lens. Dozens of photographers in Manhattan had told her she was made for the camera, and the way her body seemed to respond to his directions naturally, almost against her will, she began to wonder if it were true.

"Jacqui . . . ," Jackson whined from behind her, his voice breaking the spell of the camera's flash. "I dropped my ice cream." She turned to face him. The little boy was dangerously close to tears, pointing to where his ice cream cone rested upside down on the sidewalk. "It was my fault—I was trying to count how many diamonds there were in the waffle cone and it fell," he added miserably, staring at the drippy pink mess. Jacqui hurried to his side, bending to give him a big hug.

"No worries, mate, we'll get you another." An even deeper voice startled her.

Jacqui and the kids looked up to see another man, identical to the first photographer except with even shaggier hair, so long that it licked the edge of his shirt collar but artfully tousled. He wore a rare vintage concert tee and his cargos were the seven-hundred-dollar designer kind—as she crouched down, the Maharishi logo was just at Jacqui's eye level. He winked at her and she felt a thrill zigzag up her spine.

"Don't mind my brother," he said, nodding at the first photographer. "Atrocious manners. Thinks he can just start taking photos of any girl off the street without asking permission." He shook his head in mock frustration, his shaggy locks bouncing adorably back and forth. "Let me introduce us. That's Midas there and I'm Marcus." He held out a hand. "We're the Easton boys. At your service, mum."

Midas waved from behind the camera. "Hello there!"

"Jacarei Velasco." She stood, extending a hand. Instead of shaking it, Marcus leaned forward and kissed it. She smiled. "But you can call me Jacqui."

"But why should I when Jacarei is such a pretty name?" Marcus's eyes twinkled. "You're from Brazil then, yes?"

Jacqui nodded, surprised. She straightened the hem of her jumper, hoping it hadn't ridden too high. "You know Brazil?"

"We were just there last month, shooting in Praia da Baía do Sancho." He nodded, naming one of the country's most beautiful and remote beaches. "We had to hike a few miles on foot to get there and helicopter in the models. But it was worth it."

She couldn't help but grin. Whenever she met anyone who had been to her country, it was usually only for Carnaval in Rio. It was refreshing to meet someone who understood that there was more to Brazil than women in feather bikinis dancing the conga.

Midas resumed his monologue as he continued to snap away with his camera. "Yes, those eyes, very good. Very Linda. And my

God, those legs. Haven't seen a pair like that since Karolina. And that hair rivals Gisele's."

"Where were we?" Marcus frowned, ignoring his brother and studying the kids, who were looking up at him openmouthed. They clearly weren't quite sure what to make of the two big boys who had so suddenly and noisily interrupted their quiet walk. "I remember, you, sir, had lost your ice cream and need a replacement, yes?" he asked, bending down to tickle Jackson's chin. "Now, what flavor can we get you?"

"Passion fruit, please," Jackson said politely.

"Good boy." Jacqui smiled. The kids had chosen low-fat fruit-flavored ice cream rather than the chocolate variety all on their own. Suzy had taught them well.

Marcus loped off to fetch the cone from the nearby Scoops storefront and returned momentarily, handing it briskly to Jackson with an elaborate bow. "Your wish is my command."

Jackson reached out for the cone. "You're silly," he observed. Marcus responded by stretching his face into a contorted grimace and sticking out his tongue. Jackson giggled and Logan, after a minute, followed suit. Soon, Wyatt was laughing too. It was the first time Jacqui had seen the kids let loose, and she giggled along with them.

"They're adorable. Yours?" Marcus raised an eyebrow, his sleepy-sexy eyes twinkling.

"*Deus!* Of course not, I'm only nineteen!" Jacqui laughed. If he wasn't so adorable, she would have been extremely offended.

But she'd always had a soft spot for Australian accents, and his was particularly yummy.

Marcus drew a hand across his brow, pretending to look greatly relieved.

Midas, who was still taking photographs, mumbled, "Perfect. And undiscovered, I can bet on it. But how?" He finally put the camera down and addressed Jacqui directly, wiping the sweat off his brow. "You're not with any agency, are you?"

Jacqui shook her head. She had been mistaken for a model so often in Manhattan, it was always tempting to lie and say that she was so people would stop bothering her about it already.

Midas fished in his pants pocket for his card and handed it to her. "I'd love to take more photos of you if you're interested."

She took the card and put in her pocket, crumpling it with her fingers. She wasn't sure if she even believed they were real fashion photographers, and besides, she'd heard that line *many* times before.

"Oh, playing hard to get, are we?" Marcus teased, having noticed the discreet diss. "What my brother is too shy to tell you is that we just arrived here from Sydney to scout locations for a magazine shoot, and you're just the face we're looking for."

Jacqui shook her head again, more firmly this time but with a smile. "You're both very sweet, but it's just not for me." Once upon a time, Jacqui eagerly traded in her looks for anything it could bring—the use of older men's Black AmEx credit cards, free drinks at a bar, a better table in restaurants. But she was tired of being treated like an empty-headed doll. She wanted to prove

to the world that she was a serious girl with serious ambitions—
to be known for the size of her brain rather than that of her bust.

"Don't tell me we've found the only girl in the world who
doesn't want to be a model!" Marcus laughed. "You're going to
put Tyra Banks out of business!"

Midas shrugged. "Just think about it," he said, in a serious,
professional manner. He began putting away his camera and nodded, the conversation already over for him. "Let's go—we told
Tonne we'd check out the pond to see if we can use it for the
shoot."

"Hang on a sec," Marcus said, still eyeing Jacqui. "Sure you're
not interested? We don't bite, you know."

Jacqui returned the smile. "I'm not. But if you guys really are
fashion photographers, you might want to come by my friend's
party tonight. She's opening her store." She dug out the invitation, which was only slightly grimy from having been used as a
napkin. "Eliza Thompson. She's the biggest thing in the
Hamptons right now." Okay, so that might not be true—*yet*—
but it would be soon. She stretched out a hand with the invitation and Marcus took it, his fingers lingering over her own for a
brief moment.

"Good on ya." Marcus nodded as he drew his hand away,
smoothly pocketing the invite. "See you there."

Jacqui watched them saunter down the street until an insistent
tug on her hem reminded her that there were other, smaller boys
who needed her attention as well.

# eliza's ring only promises misunderstandings

**"IT'S SO TIGHT!" MARA EXCLAIMED AS ELIZA TIGHTENED** the straps on the white floor-length mermaid gown she'd asked Mara to model at the store-opening party.

"It's *supposed* to be tight," Eliza replied, cinching it so that the dress showed off Mara's lithe figure to spectacular effect. With its fishtail hem and crisscrossing straps in the back, it was one of her favorite pieces in her collection. "See?" She stepped back and turned Mara toward the mirror.

Mara took in her reflection. She had to admit, the constriction of her breathing might actually be worth it. If there was one thing you could say about Eliza's designs, it was that they flattered a woman's figure. She smiled at herself in the mirror, sneaking a glance at Eliza's beaming face and the messy bedroom behind them.

In typical Eliza fashion, her room at the Finnemore mansion looked like a hurricane had hit it—clothes, papers, and trash were strewn about everywhere. Balled-up designer gowns littered the carpet, along with tangled bikinis, wet beach towels, empty Fiji water bottles, and various fashion magazines. The dresser was covered in cosmetic cases, hairbrushes, and jars of face cream and lotion. Eliza had only lived in the room for a week, and yet it already looked like she'd been there for years. It was a minor miracle that she emerged from her messy room looking immaculately groomed every day.

Mara's phone vibrated with a text message on the dresser beside her, and she grabbed it while Eliza knelt down to pin the hem on her gown. She flipped up the screen.

VU FRM EIFFEL TWR GR8. BUT NOT SAME W/O U.

David again. He'd e-mailed her from Europe a few days after he'd arrived, explaining that it was hard to get an Internet connection and that his cell phone charged astronomical fees for international calls. But he'd quickly discovered he could send text messages for the usual fee and had taken to texting her multiple times a day to let her know exactly where he was—and, inadvertently, what she was missing.

Like Jacqui, Mara had found the kids to be a breeze, but being back to playing nanny was still quite a letdown after her glorious summer plans had gone awry. Mara had spent the afternoon chauffeuring Violet to her various tutors, baby Cassidy strapped in the backseat, while Jacqui took the boys to their lessons. She had given them both their dinner, and Violet had gone to bed early to get ready for her Mandarin exam the next day, and the baby was already asleep. While nannying the Finnemores wasn't all that difficult, it also wasn't the Eiffel Tower.

Mara texted back. PARTY TONIGHT. AM BUSY.

There. That should let him know she was preoccupied with her own glamorous life. Not that it was that much of a stretch—in the long, elegant white gown, she couldn't help but feel glamorous, and she did have a fun night ahead of her with her friends.

"That should do it," Eliza said, knotting up the stitch and cutting the thread with her teeth. She brushed lint off her knees and stood up. "Where's Jacqui?" she asked, glancing at the bedside clock, which was partially obscured by a pair of dangling bra cups. Whoops, maybe when she got a spare moment she should clean up a bit in here. Not that she ever *had* a spare moment. She was already past due at the store. The caterers should have arrived by now, as well as the army of publicists who were working the event. According to Eliza's schedule, her staff would be assembling the gift bags right this moment. She'd only waited because she wanted to see how Jacqui looked in the outfit she'd chosen for her.

"She called—she was running late with the boys. Jackson got sick in the car and they had to stop at a gas station, but she'll be here," Mara answered, examining her profile in the mirror. The dress was a bit *ta-da!* and she had been worried about being able to pull it off, but Eliza was right—it did look better tighter.

"I hope she gets here soon. I want to make sure her dress fits perfectly—I'm worried it's too low in the chest," Eliza fretted.

"When has that ever been a problem with Jac?" Mara laughed. The girl lived in low-cut outfits. "Décolletage is Jacqui's middle name."

"I know." Eliza nodded with a wry smile. "But I want to make sure it looks Mischa Barton sexy, not Jessica Simpson sexy." She ran a hand nervously through her hair.

"Oh my God. What is *that*?" Mara shrieked as an enormous diamond ring on Eliza's hand caught the light.

Eliza wondered what had gotten into Mara until she noticed the rock on her finger. She usually wore it stone-side down to deflect attention since she didn't know what to make of it yet. She felt more comfortable showing the world she was wearing a plain platinum band, but the ring had turned around when she wasn't looking, and the five-carat rock was now front and center.

"Is this what I think it is?" Mara said, sticking her face a centimeter away from Eliza's hand so she could see it better. "When did you get this?" She looked up at Eliza curiously.

"Last Sunday," Eliza admitted, chewing her bottom lip. She'd been uncharacteristically tight-lipped about the news, having not breathed a word to her friends. She pulled away, picking up a powder brush from the vanity and dusting her nose, as if getting a six-figure diamond ring from her boyfriend happened every week. She just didn't feel like getting into it.

She and Jeremy still hadn't had a proper conversation about what had happened that day at old lady Greyson's. Every time she felt like bringing the subject up, she couldn't find the right words. Asking him exactly what he'd meant by giving her the ring seemed so . . . rude. Especially since Jeremy was being so unbelievably sweet and supportive of her store opening. This week he'd sent her flowers out of the blue and offered to help set up at the party, even though he had a big deadline on one of his jobs. He was acting like something very important had now been settled between them. The problem was, Eliza couldn't shake off a feeling that felt anything *but* settled. Did the ring mean what she—and now Mara—thought it meant?

"Why haven't you said anything?" Mara demanded, swiping the brush away from Eliza and putting a hand on her hip like an angry schoolteacher. The three of them had met up every night for dinner or a nightcap that week, and Eliza had kept absolutely mum on her romantic situation.

"Uh . . ." Eliza didn't know what to say. Jeremy hadn't exactly gotten down on his knees, and she hadn't said yes or anything. Eliza had decided it was more of a "promise" ring than anything, like one of those rings the Bachelor gave when he didn't want to commit to marriage but the producers still wanted to finagle a happy ending. Because really, how could you get engaged to someone you'd met on reality television? Or in Eliza's case, how could you get engaged when you were only nineteen years old? She wasn't barefoot, pregnant, or Paris Hilton. Be serious!

Before Eliza could explain, Mara pulled her in for a tight hug, almost tripping over the thick June issue of *Vogue* splayed out on the carpet between them. "Congratulations! This is sooo exciting! You and Jeremy! Hooray!"

"*O que está acontecendo?*" Jacqui called from the doorway. "What's happening?" She made her way to her gleefully hugging friends, who broke apart and smiled when they saw her. "Is it too late for me to shower? I'm all covered in ice cream." She was exhausted from dealing with Jackson's tummy troubles. Passion fruit ice cream might be fat free, but it was too acidic for the little boy's stomach. She'd spent the last hour in a cramped gas station bathroom, dealing with the consequences.

"No, it's not too late, but here, let me show you what you're wear—" Eliza reached for the white dress hanging on the closet door, but Mara cut her off with a whoop.

"Eliza's engaged!" Mara cried, grabbing Eliza's outstretched hand and thrusting it toward Jacqui to show off the ring.

*"Que beleza!"* Jacqui breathed, blinded by the flash of the diamond. "Congratulations! He proposed?"

"We're totally going wedding gown shopping!" Mara cheered before Eliza could answer, hopping up and down—or at least as much as she could in the tight dress.

"Of course!" Jacqui agreed, squeezing Eliza's hand excitedly, still gazing at the ring. "It's huge!"

Eliza shrugged, her mouth slowly turning into a smile. She looked at her two friends' beaming faces. She wished she could explain about the ring's true meaning, but she wanted everyone to be excited for tonight. Compared to an engagement ring, explaining that it was only a *promise* ring just didn't sound as, well, promising. Why ruin the moment?

# it's the same old hamptons, but an all-new mara. . . .

MARA COULDN'T HELP BUT SUPPRESS A SMILE AS SHE circulated about Eliza's boutique, watching the sleek blond socialites wage silent wars against each other in their efforts to secure a bikini or silk pareo. Mara gasped as the handbag tug-of-war unfolding in front of her suddenly escalated into violence. A towering figure in a multicolored Missoni caftan with billowing sleeves wrenched the prized white straw-and-leather tote away from her rival's grasp. The loser of the battle, an overly tanned woman in a transparent Gucci sarong, promptly flew backward onto the shoe display.

Needless to say, Eliza's store opening was a tremendous success.

It was all-bets-off shopping mayhem as the affluent customers—who were used to getting exactly what they wanted—found they had to fight tooth and manicured nail for the precious and dwindling selection of must-have pieces. Salesgirls rushed to keep up with the customers' demands, and the line to the furiously ringing registers snaked through the store, nearly reaching the sidewalk.

Mara's job was to walk slowly around the store—to "swan," as Eliza had instructed—showing off the evening gown and answering questions about it, while Jacqui did the same on the other side. The two of them had completed several laps of the place already, and the party was in full swing. An army of cater-waiters in white pants and white T-shirts emblazoned with the pink eliza thompson logo brought out a tempting array of dishes, bartenders were pouring pink champagne into crystal flutes, and the store was filled with the buzz of partygoers happily drinking, eating, and shopping.

It wasn't as flashy or insane as the Sydney Minx opening last summer, where Eliza herself had arrived in a helicopter and walked the runway. But that was a good thing, since Sydney Minx was kaput and in the boutique's former place was another yoga studio. Hopefully Eliza's label wouldn't suffer a similar fate.

Mara reached for a shrimp puff and chewed on it slowly, surveying the room with an experienced reporter's eye, taking care not to get oil on her white silk dress. She spotted Garrett Reynolds, her former flame, holding a woman's purse under his arm as his girlfriend, a pouty condiment heiress famous for her public tantrums, disappeared into the dressing room underneath a huge pile of clothing.

"Look what the cat dragged in." Garrett smirked when he saw Mara and strolled over toward her.

"Hi, yourself." Mara smiled politely, steeling herself for one of Garrett's digs. "What are you doing here? Don't you summer in South Africa these days?" she asked with a hint of derision, referring to his comment last summer about how the Hamptons scene was as "over and out" as a Clay Aiken record.

"Got shot in the ass while on safari," Garrett growled. "I thought it best to stay in safer waters."

Mara tried not to laugh and failed. "I'm sorry." She chuckled.

"Go ahead, have your fun," Garrett allowed with a debonair wave of the hand. "It's not every day you get mistaken for a white rhino. Thankfully, the settlement was enough to buy me my own place out here," he added, craning his neck and preening at his reflection in the mirror. "It's south of the highway, with a view of the ocean. I'm renovating—you should come visit when it's done."

Building his own place? Was his family's totally ostentatious, five-hundred-million-square-foot castle not enough? "Sure, when it's done." Mara nodded, forcing a smile. She knew the visit would never happen.

It was just like Garrett to suffer a humiliation but come out even richer from it, Mara thought as she walked away. Two women already loaded down with shopping bags stopped and asked where to find the dress she was wearing, and after pointing them in the right direction, Mara decided she had to do a little shopping of her own. She grabbed one of the white string bikinis from the racks before they were all gone and bumped into another familiar face.

"Sexy, aren't they?" Mitzi Goober appeared beside her, her one-year-old daughter strapped to her chest in a Gucci baby carrier. The über-publicist dragged her daughter to every event, no matter how late or how inappropriate. Little Soleil had been to everything, including a party for the launch of a new line of vibrators. Knowing Mitzi, she probably thought it was never too early to get her daughter started socializing with the crème de la crème.

"They're cut Brazilian style," Mara explained, knowing Eliza had patterned the swimsuits after the tiny tangas Jacqui was so fond of.

Mitzi clucked approvingly. "Brazil is hot again. I'll make sure I mention that to *Vogue*."

"You're Eliza's publicist?" Mara asked, momentarily shocked, although she shouldn't have been. Eliza never let anything like notoriety get in the way of hiring "the best," and vituperative personality aside, Mitzi got the job done. The place was teeming with dozens of reporters getting drunk and fat off the free booze and eats.

Mitzi nodded, craning over Mara's shoulder to see if there was anyone more important she should be talking to. Now that Mara was no longer a reporter for *Hamptons* or on staff for *Metropolitan Circus,* the fact that Mitzi had said hello to her at all was a big concession to courtesy.

Thankfully, Mara was rescued from Mitzi's indifference by Lucky Yap, the friendly paparazzo who had been Mara's mentor in the past.

"There's my girl!" Lucky gushed when he saw her. "You look deeevine!" he enthused, taking a few shots of Mara for old times' sake.

Lucky was dressed in the latest Hampton obsession—orange robes and shawls modeled after the ones worn by the Dalai Lama. His Holiness was making a pilgrimage to the Hamptons that summer, and his devoted followers showed their dedication by donning colorful togas similar to those worn by his Tibetan monks over their Lilly Pulitzer capris. Wooden prayer beads had even replaced wooden Marni necklaces as the season's hottest accessory.

"Thanks, Lucky. And you look very . . . orange!" Mara said, once again at a loss for words at the sight of Lucky's outrageous outfit. "Like a sunset!"

"It's tangerine, my dear, tangerine," Lucky corrected. "Feel this," he ordered, taking Mara's hand and placing it on the shawl. "It's made from Mongolian antelope hair. Softer than a baby's butt!"

Mara was just about to ask Lucky if his shawl was an illegal shahtoosh—she suspected that it was—when the portly photographer bolted to the front door. "Oh, oh, oh! Gotta dash—there's Chauncey Raven stepping out of the limo! I hope she's wearing underwear this time; I can't sell hoochie shots to *People* magazine!" And with that he dashed off to snap the pop-star-turned-single-mother, whose every exit from a vehicle was akin to a gynecological exam.

Mara watched him leave with a fond eye. No one ever changed in the Hamptons. It was the same old moneyed crowd, the same old taut and tanned faces—even if some of the face-lifts were new. She yawned, covering her mouth with the back of her hand. The party was fabulous and all, but her feet were starting to swell from the high-heeled sandals Eliza has picked out to match the dress. If only she could sit down. Or better yet, lie down. There was a comfortable bed with her name on it not too far away. Surely Eliza didn't expect her to model the gown all evening? If she bade her goodbyes now, she could still catch a late-night rerun of *Ugly Betty*.

She found Eliza in a brightly lit corner of the store, flushed and happy, surrounded by clients and the fashion press. She wore a slim white satin tuxedo with nothing underneath, showing off her deep Flying Point beach tan. Mara made eye contact and Eliza broke away from the group with an apologetic bow to say hello to her friend.

"What's up? Having fun?" Eliza asked, straightening a stack of T-shirts on a table next to Mara, ever the mindful hostess.

"For sure, but I'm pooped," Mara said. "My feet are killing me. Will you be very angry if I bail?"

"You're leaving?" Eliza hugged the T-shirts to her chest and then laid them down flat. "So early?"

"I'm sorry," Mara said, feeling a little guilty. She wanted to be there for Eliza, but she'd been standing in the same stilettos for almost two hours now, and she was tired. It had been a long day, and she was ready for it to be over. "But see, the dress is already sold out," she said, motioning to the empty rack. "You're a hit! You don't need me."

"Flattery will get you everywhere." Eliza smiled. "But you're really going?"

"Yeah." Mara sighed. "I haven't been to a party like this in ages, and I'd forgotten how *exhausting* they are. If another socialite asks me where I get waxed, I'm going to hurl. You know David's idea of a good time is a *New Yorker* lecture." Mara shook her head in a "what are you gonna do" gesture, shrugging.

Eliza put the shirts back down on the table with a slap. She knew Mara was just trying to be funny, but she felt a twinge of irritation nonetheless. Ever since Mara had started dating The Amazing David (which was what Eliza had begun to call him in her head, since Mara was prone to gush about him), there had been a lot of little comments like that. Mara, who'd once been so intimidated by snooty velvet-rope events when she was a Hamptons newbie, sometimes sounded like she now thought she was "above" the trivial social scene.

"Okay, go home." Eliza nodded briskly, trying not to show how hurt she was. It was the opening of her first boutique, and Eliza had hoped that once the party wound down and all the celebrities and journalists left, she and Jeremy and her two best friends could celebrate privately—she'd even set aside a tray of caviar and a bottle of champagne for just that purpose. But if Mara wanted to leave, who was she to stop her?

Mara gave Eliza a kiss on the cheek. She held up the bikini. "And I'll totally pay you for this when I get paid next week, okay?" She waved goodbye to Jacqui across the room and made her way toward the clipboard squad guarding the entrance. After a night of run-ins with her Hamptons past, she was relieved to be finally leaving. The second she got in the door at the Finnemores', she was going to take off her shoes and massage her aching feet.

There was a huge crowd of people still waiting to get inside the party, but she saw a familiar dark honey blond head walk to the front of the velvet ropes, cutting through the mass of hopeful partygoers like a hot knife through butter.

Because Ryan Perry was *always* on the VIP list.

He caught her eye and her heart stopped at the sight of him. And just like that, Mara completely forgot about her tired, pained feet.

# brangelina's got nothing on jereliza

BEFORE ELIZA COULD FEEL TOO UPSET ABOUT MARA abandoning her, she was pulled away by Mitzi Goober, who was hyperventilating in excitement.

"The 'Tawker' writer's here! And she wants you *now*," Mitzi said, her manicured nails digging into Eliza's arm. "Tawker" was a must-read Manhattan-based gossip column that appeared daily in one of the major papers.

"Wait! Can I go say hi to my boyfriend first?" Eliza asked, seeing Jeremy enter the store, looking handsome as ever in a nice linen suit. He had been at the store earlier to help but had left to change out of his overalls. He waved to Eliza and started to make his way toward her.

"No time for boyfriends!" Mitzi ordered, pushing Eliza toward the "Tawker" gossipeuse.

"All right." Eliza sighed, gesturing apologetically in Jeremy's direction. Given that Mitzi had strapped her baby to her chest, maybe there *was* no time for relationships when you were trying to make a living on the New York social circuit. Was she going to have to strap Jeremy to her chest to get to spend any time with him?

Eliza pasted on her most winning smile as she prepared herself to take on the reporter's questions. She knew she had to ace the interview or else be subjected to enormous ridicule. "Tawker" was merciless in its coverage of Manhattan movers and shakers. It had even instituted a popular section called "Dumbass of the Day," wherein various players on the Manhattan social scene were relentlessly savaged. Never appearing in that column was considered a great achievement among a certain set.

"Hey, nice meeting ya." The gossip writer, a perky, twenty-something brunette quickly shook her hand before diving right in. "So, which stuff did Chauncey Raven buy? The underwear, I hope? God knows the girl needs it, huh?"

Eliza laughed and then provided all the lacy details. She knew that celebrities' shopping habits were standard fodder for the gossip press.

The "Tawker" editor followed with a few softball questions about the launch party and who had been invited, and Eliza carefully answered every query, making sure not to use the word *like* in every sentence or say anything that could be used to humiliate her—with one careless answer, she could be painted as another rich blond socialite trying to buy her way into a career in fashion.

Eliza was proud of her own composure, but she could tell that after only a few minutes, the reporter could barely contain her boredom—she was already checking her watch. *What was up with everyone tonight?* Eliza thought, annoyed. First Mara bailing early, and now it was so obvious the "Tawker" writer was talking to her only because Mitzi had forced her to. Well, screw her. Eliza wasn't going to embarrass herself just to give "Tawker" something to talk about. Though she was dying to get some press—the store wouldn't survive without it.

"Well, thanks for your time," the girl said, giving Eliza a fake smile. "I'll let Mitzi know if we run an item."

"Sure." Eliza nodded, pushing her hair away from her face, knowing full well that a passing mention on Chauncey Raven's lingerie purchase would be the only coverage her store would receive. Still, she'd take any press she could get.

"Hey, is that an engagement ring?" the reporter asked suddenly.

"Oh yeah, I guess," Eliza said, looking at the ring again as if for the first time.

The writer whistled. "What is that, five carats? It's a monster!"

Eliza nodded, blushing a little. It really *was* huge. But then, hadn't she always insisted to whoever listened that she would never settle for anything less? "Five carats—anything less is a speck. An insult. A piece of dust!" "Five carats or don't bother!" But now, it did seem absurdly large. It looked gigantic on her finger.

"So who's the lucky guy?" the writer asked, taking a slug of champagne, her interest in Eliza apparently renewed.

"Jeremy Stone," Eliza said with a warm smile.

"Jeremy Stone," the girl repeated, furrowing her brow. "Why does his name sound so familiar?"

"He's a really great landscape architect," Eliza gushed, beaming. So maybe "landscape architect" was pushing it—Jeremy was just a glorified gardener when you came down to it. But whatever her ambivalence toward the ring, one thing was for sure—she was very proud of Jeremy.

"No, that's not why," the reporter said dismissively, waving her glass of champagne around as she furrowed her brow in thought. "Jeremy Stone. . . . Hey, I remember now. Isn't he the guy who just inherited the Greyson pile?"

What a way to put it. "Um, well, yes . . . ," Eliza said slowly.

"Damn, girl. You made a killing! You're marrying the Greyson heir!" The "Tawker" writer immediately lit up and brought out her iPod recorder. "So when's the wedding?"

*The Greyson heir? Wedding?* "Uh, we're not really sure. . . ." Eliza blanched. *Wedding?* Who said anything about a wedding? She wanted to explain that the ring signified more of a "promise" than an engagement—Jeremy had never even said anything more about it; he just looked happy to see the ring on her hand—but no words came out. The "Tawker" writer seemed really interested in the story, and Eliza felt the hunger for publicity start to gnaw at her.

"Um . . . next . . . next year?" Eliza hedged. Besides, if it *was* an engagement ring, which everyone seemed to think it was—

and what was the harm if they did?—then that would mean there would have to be a wedding at some point. . . .

"You gonna wear white? God knows you have enough white in this store. Design the dress?"

"Um . . ." Eliza began to feel her cheeks become very red. Just as she was trying to back away from the aggressive reporter, she was accosted by several of her old friends from Spence.

"Liza! Oh my God! We just heard! Congratulations! And by the way, that is an ice rink!" Lindsay said, admiring the ring while the other girls oohed and aahed.

There was nothing like a ring viewing to cause a commotion, and soon even more reporters were swarming around. *New York* magazine wanted to know if they were having the reception in the city or on the beach. *WWD* inquired as to the ring's provenance (Neil Lane from *Beverly Hills*). The *Observer* asked if she would do a "bridal blog" on their site. Every question directed toward Eliza had nothing to do with her store launch or the collection but instead focused on her engagement to Jeremy "Five Carat" Stone, as the "Tawker" reported had quickly dubbed him.

It was everything she'd ever dreamed of for herself when she was growing up, and yet—and yet—the ring was starting to feel incredibly heavy on her finger. And she was beginning to become just a teensy bit annoyed that not one of the reporters had asked about her new collection.

Finally, when Eliza could no longer hide the fact that she

didn't have very many details on the impending nuptials, the rest of the reporters ended the bridal inquisition and scattered to attack the goody bags, leaving her alone with the "Tawker" writer once again.

"So, did he have anything to do with the store?" she asked Eliza.

She caught sight of Jeremy across the room. He was politely talking to a few buyers from Japan, who didn't know anyone else at the party and spoke limited English. He really was such a sweetheart. "Oh yes, he built the whole interior," Eliza replied. "According to my design, of course." She smiled fondly, thinking of the two of them throwing paint at each other over the winter and how they had laughed when the ceiling caved in, covering them in plaster, while Jeremy was renovating. She glanced at the corner where he was laughing at something the Japanese buyer was saying.

She caught his eye and he raised his glass to her. She raised hers to him, feeling a pang that she hadn't even had time to say hello. No matter—if the ring promised anything, it was that they had all the time in the world.

# mara doesn't speak ex-boyfriend

**"RYAN," MARA BREATHED. AFTER THAT NIGHT ON THE** beach, she'd chalked up that odd jittery feeling she'd felt on seeing him to the fact that she was naked at the time. But now that she was fully clothed, why were her hands still shaking? And why was her throat suddenly dry? Was it just because David was thousands of miles away? And had left her stranded in an airport? Maybe if David were here, seeing Ryan wouldn't affect her so much. She tried to get ahold of herself and stood up straight, willing her voice to stop trembling. "Good to see you."

"Oh, hey," Ryan said, looking a bit uncomfortable when he spotted Mara at the door, blocking his way. "You're off?" he asked. "I mean, it's obvious you're leaving. But didn't the party just start?"

"No, I mean, yes, I mean, I don't have to," Mara said, kicking herself for sounding so flustered. What was it about Ryan and those beautiful greeny blue eyes of his that turned her into a blithering idiot?

"You don't—I mean, you don't have to stay if you don't want

to. But if you want to, it's, uh, cool." Ryan shrugged, sounding a little nervous himself. "I mean, you can do whatever."

A few people behind him waiting to get inside the party began to harrumph and complain. "Excuse me!" an annoyed forty-something woman cried as she pushed past them, clutching her pink invitation. "Can I get through?"

"Yes, of course," Ryan said, jumping out of her way and into the store. Mara immediately followed him back into the party. They found a quiet corner by the wall of handbags.

"I thought you hated these things," Mara said abruptly as Ryan accepted a caviar-stuffed blini off a white-tuxedoed cater-waiter's tray.

"I thought you lived for these things," Ryan retorted, licking sour cream off his fingers.

Mara frowned. That was a sour statement. She had spent last summer chronicling the social scene for *Hamptons* magazine, which necessitated attendance at dozens of these kinds of events—events at which Ryan had rarely made an effort to join her, choosing to sulk at home at being abandoned by his girlfriend instead. "I'm not writing for *Hamptons* this summer. I'm back on baby duty," Mara explained. "The Finnemores? Eliza's dad is dating the mom. They live a few streets over from you guys."

"The house with all the fake statues?" Ryan asked.

"Bingo."

A smile fleetingly appeared on Ryan's lips, but it disappeared just as quickly.

"Oysters?" A cater-waiter appeared, offering fat bivalves on a tray of ice.

"Sure," Ryan agreed, knocking one back while Mara grimaced. She could never quite stomach raw seafood. They stood in tense silence for a moment. "Anyway, it's Eliza's big day, so I thought I should be here," he said finally, looking down at the pink terrazzo floor. "Is it me, or is everything pink in here?"

"Everything's pink," Mara confirmed. Oh. So he was here for Eliza. He and Eliza went way back, and nothing ever seemed to affect their friendship. She was suddenly a little jealous of that, and took a big gulp of champagne from her glass.

"Dude, that is so Eliza." Ryan laughed.

*Dude.* There it was again. There was just something so *platonic* about that word. Ryan called Eliza "dude" all the time, and Mara had liked that he did, since it meant that he thought of her as a buddy and not as a girl he'd once hooked up with. Then again, what did she care? She had a new boyfriend now—not that she was thrilled with David at this particular moment. He'd just sent her a photo of the Louvre from his camera phone with a note that said I LOUVRE YOU. Great, but how about an I Louvre You call?

It was silly to be so awkward around Ryan. They had a history together, and there was no reason they couldn't be friends. "You know, we should hang out sometime," Mara proposed, adopting a super-casual tone. The fact that her heart was beating quickly was probably just the stuffy air. There were too many people in the boutique and the air-conditioning system couldn't keep up.

"Yeah." Ryan nodded. "I'm sure I'll see you around this summer." He took two chicken skewers from a passing tray. "I missed dinner," he explained, blushing slightly.

"'See me around'? You're not getting away that easily," Mara teased. Did he *really* just give her the "see you around" brush-off? "We should get together. What are you doing for the Fourth?" she pressed, now determined to squeeze a real plan out of him.

"Dunno." He shrugged, looking around for a trash can for the skewers and shoving them into his pockets when he couldn't find one.

"C'mon, you always have big plans." She thought of her first summer at the Hamptons, when Ryan had saved her from a disastrous Fourth of July taking care of the Perry kids by herself. She'd spent the holiday with him these past three years. Why couldn't they just hang out like they used to?

Ryan shrugged. "A couple of the guys might be getting together for a barbecue down by the house. Not a big deal."

"What time?"

"Around noon or so."

"Cool, I'll bring beer."

"Uh, okay." Ryan nodded, taking the empty skewers out of his pockets and placing them on a passing tray.

"See you then," Mara said cheerfully, willfully oblivious to how reluctant Ryan was about extending the invitation. Boys could be so immature! She'd practically had to invite herself to the shindig. If he could be friends with Eliza, why couldn't they be friends too? It couldn't be that hard, could it?

"Ryan! You made it!" Eliza squealed, bursting on the two of them and giving Ryan a friendly hug. She looked puzzled to see Mara. "I thought you'd left!"

"I was just—," Mara said, but Eliza had already pulled Ryan deeper into the party. Mara watched them walk away, arm in arm.

The Fourth of July was next Saturday. A week wasn't a very long time, but for Mara it suddenly felt like an eternity. She hitched the shopping bag that held the minuscule bikini on her shoulder. Maybe she'd wear *that* to the barbecue, just to remind him that she wasn't exactly one of the guys.

"Dude" indeed.

# good-looking guys get away with everything

*WALLFLOWER* **WAS NOT A WORD THAT CAME TO MIND** when describing Jacqui Velasco, but that was exactly what she felt like at the store opening. Modeling had been fun at first. Eliza had picked a daring, thigh-scraping strapless A-line dress for her to wear, and the white fabric stood out against her deep mocha tan. Jacqui had enjoyed vamping it up and helping guests decide which of Eliza's sexy white dresses looked best on their figures.

But a few hours later, almost all the racks were bare, and she had to inch around the room, which was getting more jammed by the second with the late-night crowd, who were more interested in the free cocktails than in the clothing.

Other than Eliza, who was busy being a social butterfly, and Mara, who had just left, Jacqui realized she knew almost no one at the party. That had never fazed her before—in her hard-partying days, she could make a friend in the instant it took to pop a champagne cork—but between trying to get into NYU and working for the Perrys, it had been a while since she'd been the life of the party. She grabbed another glass of champagne, her fifth of the evening. Ooh. She should stop. But she'd felt ridiculous standing all alone, dressed to the nines with heavy makeup on, looking like a dismissed diva while everyone else was gathered in tight-knit cliques. Drinking had given her something to do.

Oh, well. No one would even notice if she tiptoed out the door right now. She could just put down the champagne flute and sneak out the back. Eliza would understand. It wasn't like she needed Jacqui to be there anymore for moral—or model—support. Almost everything in the store had already sold out. And besides, Jacqui had a big day with the kids planned for tomorrow. The twins needed to be at their gifted seminar in Wainscott by eight, and Wyatt had his practice session for his upcoming KRTs (the Kindergarten Readiness Tests, which was to preschoolers what the SATs were to their high school counterparts) shortly afterward. So it would probably be best if she just left now. . . .

"Don't I know you from somewhere?" A voice startled her from behind.

Finally. Someone she knew. Jacqui turned and began to smile until she realized who it was. Some smarmy-looking thirty-year-old-guy trying too hard to look cool with his slicked-back hair and his vintage Rolex, jangling his Bentley car keys. Why did he look so familiar? Then it hit her. The Hollywood hotshot. The chicks-gone-crazy party. That first memorable summer in the Hamptons. Rupert Thorne. Otherwise known as a Thorne in her side. Raising his smug head again.

"I think you're confusing me with someone else," she said, pushing past him and trying to get as far away from him as possible.

"Whoa, don't be that way, beautiful!" he called after her.

As she stormed away, she bumped into Eliza, who had just finished giving another interview. "You all right?" Eliza asked. "You look tense."

Jacqui shrugged. "Listen, *chica*, it's late. . . ."

"Don't say you're leaving too! I can't believe Mara's already gone!" Eliza wailed, running her fingers through her hair in dismay.

Jacqui was about to apologize, but just then there was a communal buzz from the party as two gorgeous guys appeared in the doorway. She and Eliza turned to look. Jacqui smiled. It was the two cute Aussies she'd met that afternoon! She was glad to see some familiar—not to mention handsome—faces. Midas looked a bit scruffy and tired. He was still wearing the same worn T-shirt and pants that he'd had on earlier, but Marcus looked freshly shaven and had changed into a dashing white linen suit.

She began to wave, but Eliza tugged on her arm. "Oh. My. God. Do you know who those guys are?" Eliza whispered fiercely, pulling Jacqui close. "That's Midas and Marcus Easton—they're the hottest photographers in fashion right now!"

"Really?" Jacqui asked. So they hadn't been lying or pretending to be something they weren't. That was good to know. So many guys called themselves "photographers" when really all they did was run up-skirt websites. Not that Jacqui had ever been on one, thank you very much. But she'd seen the Chauncey Raven shots.

"Don't tell me you haven't heard of the 'Saucy Aussies'?" Eliza asked, forever shocked that other people could be so ignorant of the fashion industry.

"The what?" Jacqui raised an eyebrow, amused.

"That's what they're called because they do these really cool, almost risqué fashion shoots. *Vogue* can't get enough of them. Midas is known for his 'touch of gold.' He's really the genius behind it all. A lot of people say Marcus is just along for the ride. That he doesn't do anything but hold up a reflector. But you know, the 'twin' thing works to their advantage. I mean, they're both great-looking, so why not have two beautiful guys on a shoot instead of one? Oh my God. Oh my God. I can't believe they're here!" Eliza squealed, unable to conceal her excitement. She was speaking so loudly that several guests turned to look.

"Why? You've got almost everyone here," Jacqui said, pointing to a famous actress who was leaving the party with four goody bags stuffed under her arm. "It looks pretty A-list to me."

"You don't understand—every year Midas and Marcus pick one model and one designer to follow—they do this thing called 'reality fashion,' where instead of doing formal shoots and stuff, they just follow a model wearing the designer's clothes the way a normal person would—you know, everywhere from the bedroom to grocery shopping—and then they do a big spread in *Vogue* showing all the designs. If they pick my line, it could launch my career!" Eliza explained, anxiously smoothing the lapels on her satin tuxedo and giving her hair a good shake.

"That's so funny, I bumped into them earlier with the—," Jacqui began, but her words died as the two boys walked right up to them.

"There she is," Marcus said, putting a friendly arm around Jacqui. "The girl of the moment."

"Thanks for the invite," Midas added, fiddling with the zoom lens on his camera and pointing it at the Marilyn mannequin. "This is a great store. Love the high-concept thing."

Eliza looked confused and turned to Jacqui. "You *know* these guys?"

"Sure. We're all best pals here. I'm Marcus. That's Midas. Cheers, big ears," Marcus said merrily, taking a champagne flute from a waiter's tray, his hand still draped casually around Jacqui's neck. "Brilliant! Pink and white! Like being in a big cotton candy machine."

"That's the idea," Eliza replied smoothly, not quite sure if she'd just been complimented or insulted.

"Guys, this is my friend Eliza Thompson that I told you about," Jacqui said, making introductions all around.

Midas shook Eliza's hand with a firm grip while Marcus was content to wave lazily, still attached to Jacqui's side.

Jacqui felt his hand trail from her neck to her waist, giving her a light squeeze. Maybe all the bubbles had gone to her head—she usually didn't like a guy to be so forward—but she leaned comfortably into his embrace. After all, who could resist a Saucy Aussie?

# supermodels are discovered, not made

**"THANKS FOR COMING TO MY PARTY," ELIZA SAID SHYLY** to Midas. She felt a little bit like a seventh grader throwing a birthday party, and she hoped he wouldn't be able to detect her nervousness.

"No worries. You're all this?" Midas asked, motioning to the store as a whole and closely inspecting the row of portraits of famous actresses from the thirties and forties that lined the wall leading to the dressing rooms. All of Eliza's fashion icons were up there. Greta Garbo in a feathered nightgown. Bette Davis smoldering in a sequin bolero. Katharine Hepburn in her signature men's-style trousers. Joan Crawford in her wasp-waisted suit—the only woman who could make shoulder pads look good.

Eliza nodded, glancing in Jacqui and Marcus's direction as they drifted off on their own, Marcus's hand brushing Jacqui's hip in a possessive manner. That was fast. She turned back to Midas. He wasn't as flashy or slick as his brother, but he was certainly very cute. His deep blue eyes focused on her with shining intensity.

"And you did that," Midas was saying, gesturing to the hot number that Jacqui was wearing. The dress was covered in white acrylic beading that made it shimmer in the light.

"Uh-huh." She nodded stupidly. The Easton brothers were total career launchers, and first impressions were everything. Her palms were practically sweating. Why was it so warm in here? Who was in charge? Oh, right, she was.

"It's very sixties, isn't it?" Midas asked.

"I was inspired by Twiggy," Eliza admitted. "But I wanted to update the shape and the fabric. Not make it feel so retro. I like to put my own twist on things. The fabric is actually washable, so it's practical too." As the words spilled out of her mouth, Eliza felt herself begin to relax. Talking about her designs had always come naturally.

"This is lovely as well," Midas said, taking a modern-looking kimono jacket from the nearest rack and studying it intently, as if he were going to be tested on its details. "What's the theme of your whole collection?"

Eliza smiled, flattered to be the object of such concentrated scrutiny. Finally—*finally*—someone was asking about the idea behind the line. "Well, as you can see, it's all white because I wanted to keep it really simple and monastic but still sexy." She gestured around the room at the various outfitted mannequins, as most of the other clothing had been snatched off the racks.

"Along with the beachy basics, I also did ten standout pieces that are unique and one-of-a-kind, each with a story behind it. Like this mermaid gown," she added, finding one last copy of the dress Mara had worn earlier. "I call it Venus Rising. Jacqui's dress is Carnaby Street, and the kimono is called Monet, partly because the impressionist painters were obsessed with Japanoiserie and partly because it kind of looks like a painter's smock."

"Nice." Midas put the kimono back on the rack and inspected the one-piece halter jumpsuit next to it. "And this?"

"It's called Angel's Flight. It's very Farrah Fawcett from the seventies." Eliza laughed guiltily. "I was having a little fun."

"You've really thought all this through." Midas raised an eyebrow, his dark blue eyes scrutinizing her as closely as they'd studied the clothes.

Eliza nodded. "Of course. I think it's so boring just to wear clothes. Fashion is all about fantasy. I want women to be able to feel transformed—and transported—by my clothing."

"I get it," Midas proclaimed. "I like it." He put a hand on his stubbly chin and looked at her, deep in thought. Eliza smiled, feeling a bit awkward just standing there in silence. She wondered what he was thinking behind those intense dark eyes. Finally, Midas spoke.

"I think we might have a proposition for you," he said slowly. "Let me just have a quick chat with Marcus." He glanced around for his brother, who was deep in conversation with Jacqui on the white velvet couch in the middle of the store, their two perfect forms posed like living mannequins. "Hey, mate, could you come over here a second?" Midas called.

Marcus shrugged and stood, giving Jacqui a quick goodbye kiss on the hand that made her giggle. It was obvious they'd both drunk a lot of champagne in a very short time.

"What shakes?" Marcus asked as he approached, hands jauntily in his pockets as if he were out for a stroll.

Midas whispered in Marcus's ear, and Marcus began nodding, then started shaking his head. Midas looked stymied, but Marcus only shrugged. Then they stepped away from each other. Eliza expected Midas to say something, but it was Marcus who cleared his throat.

"Congratulations . . . uh . . . Eliza Thompson?" he said, reading her name from the logo on one of the shopping bags. "You've just won Project Runway."

"He's being a goof," Midas said with a fond but dismissive shake of the head. He turned to Eliza with a serious look on his face. "But I'm glad he agrees with me. Listen, we'd like to do a shoot based on your line. It's just what we're looking for. I like the stories behind the clothes, I like your ideas, and I think we'll have fun working together."

Eliza was flabbergasted. "Are you serious?"

"Serious as a lawsuit," Marcus interjected cheekily.

"You're going to do a shoot—on my line—wow," Eliza breathed. She was so excited she almost tottered on her high heels. Sure, she'd had orders from Barneys and Bergdorf's, but the Easton brothers choosing her clothes to photograph brought her to a different level entirely. They only shot the *best*. It was like being picked for the major leagues.

"And we want your friend Jacqui to be the model for the shoot."

"Jacqui? Fabulous!" Eliza trilled. "I think that's a great idea!" She looked over to where Jacqui was artfully draped on the couch. The girl looked poised even when she was sitting down.

"I know. She's a natural." Midas nodded. "She's exactly what editors are looking for right now. You know the super-skinny skeletal look is out. Models dying from starvation and all that. Out, out, out. They want healthy. They want exotic. They want a girl with curves. She can be the new Gisele. You said your clothes are about telling a story, about transforming a woman. I think she can convey that—with her looks, she can read as Caucasian, Hispanic, even part African or Asian, like Jessica Alba. She's unique and universal at the same time."

Eliza nodded, her enthusiasm building.

"There's just one catch," Midas added, a preemptive note in his voice.

"What's that?" Eliza's brow furrowed. There was *always* a catch.

"Marcus already asked her to do it, and she turned him down flat."

Eliza frowned. How could she have forgotten about Jacqui's distaste for modeling? Whenever Eliza invited her out with her and her fashion buddies in the city, she always declined, saying she knew how models partied. Not that Eliza could really blame her—Jacqui's sole venture into professional modeling had resulted in a disastrous fauxhawk haircut. "Jacqui doesn't want to be a model, and I don't think we can change her mind." Eliza sighed. "But surely we can find someone else?"

"Oh." Midas looked troubled. "I'm afraid it doesn't work that way. We always look for the right combination—model and designer—and if one doesn't work out, we'll have to find another label. I'm sorry. So unless you can convince her otherwise . . ." He shrugged, his voice trailing off.

"I'll talk to her," Eliza said, trying to make her voice more optimistic than she felt. There would be no convincing Jacqui. Talking to her, you'd think modeling was akin to clubbing baby seals, for God's sake. She walked over to the couch, where Marcus had reinstated himself. They certainly looked cozy enough. "Jac? Can I borrow you for a second?"

Jacqui blinked, looking a bit dazed and a little drunk. "Sure. What's up?"

Eliza helped her friend to her feet and walked her over to a shadowy alcove by the cash registers, out of earshot. Eliza noticed Jeremy trying to signal her from across the room, but she ignored him for now. This was more important.

"Those guys want to shoot my line, but only if you'll model it!" Eliza whispered fiercely.

"I know. They asked me." Jacqui smiled, wondering what the fuss was all about. "I told them no."

Eliza looked pained. "You don't understand. If you don't do it, they won't shoot my clothes."

"Really?" Jacqui asked, shocked momentarily into sobriety. "But that's so silly."

"I know, but that's what they said. C'mon, will you do it? For me?" Eliza pleaded. "I promise I'll be there every step of the way."

"Model?" Jacqui asked, making a face. Her brief brush with modeling had totally turned her off from the profession. Everyone she'd met in the industry—designers, makeup artists, stylists, editors—treated models like cattle: dumb, barely sentient beings who needed everything done for them. They even had a name for them: "clothes hangers." No thanks. "You know I can't stand it." She shook her head.

"I know." Eliza bit her lip. "I wouldn't ask if it didn't mean a lot. If it didn't mean everything to me."

Jacqui exhaled. She looked at Eliza's nervous, hopeful face. Maybe she could do just one shoot, as a favor to Eliza. Like the beach fashion show, or even tonight's task to walk the room. Come to think of it, she'd done a lot of modeling assignments as favors for Eliza in the past, so just one more couldn't really hurt. And the way Marcus was grinning at her from across the room . . . this would mean she would get to see more of him, a prospect that was starting to look very appealing.

"Oh, all right," she relented.

"Hooray!" Eliza cheered, pulling Jacqui in for a close hug. She dragged her back to where the boys were waiting for their answer. "She'll do it!"

"Brilliant!" Marcus cried, grabbing four flutes of champagne from the nearest waiter while Midas got his camera out again to capture the moment.

*I'm just being a good friend,* Jacqui thought as she glanced at Eliza's beaming face. She couldn't very well have said no. And besides, a little modeling here and there shouldn't interfere with her au pair duties at all. How hard could it be to mix kids and couture?

## www.blogspot/hamptonsaupair1

### it's 10PM—do you know where your children are?

This week flew by crazy fast. Time flies when the kids have jam-packed schedules. Thought it would be hard to get back in care-giver groove, but the job's turning out to be nothing but a glorified chauffeur gig. Kids are either in class, a seminar, or a tutorial every second of every minute of the day. Their mother, S., says it's good for them. But is it good for them never to see their mom? S. is up at 4 a.m., when the London stock market opens, and works till 10 p.m.each night. Every time she sees me and J., she grills us on the children, but I'm not so sure her hands-off managerial style is the best way to raise your kids. Then again, she's the one with millions of dollars and an enormous empire, so what do I know about man-agement?

On the plus side, the kids are v. independent. Logan and Jackson are self-contained and have amazing imaginations. The other day they asked if they could have a referendum on a later bedtime. They explained that they wanted the nursery run as a democracy. Unfortunately, they lost their bid in appeals court. J. and I voted 2-0 on the eight o'clock statute. Took Violet to a birthday party for a friend

at her mom's insistence yesterday. Twenty-four twelve-year-olds sipping mocktails and having makeovers at the Burberry store in
Bridgehampton. There were mani-pedi stations, massages, blowouts,
and a DJ blasting hip-hop. Those twelve-year-olds know how to
party! But Violet spent the afternoon standing in one corner talking to
no one. Sad.

**love is in the air. . . .**

J. has a massive crush on a cute Aussie photog named M. Poor Pete
from Indiana is of course long forgotten. Every time J.'s phone rings, she
runs to get it and is disappointed when it's just our boss, S., reminding
us to make sure the kids are doing their Mensa quizzes. As far as I can
tell, J. and M., who she'll be working with a lot this summer, have a
strictly business relationship—so far. Which, I'm sure, means lots of
subtle eyelash-batting and coquetry on the part of my Brazilian friend.
Will be sure to update on the status of this "business partnership."

In other news, E. is engaged!!!! Engaged!!!!! Insane. So excited for
the first wedding! Wonder if she's having bridesmaids? Must remember to ask her next time I see her—she hasn't said a word about the
wedding, and I haven't seen her much since the store opening. These
days, the papers seem to have more info on the blushing bride than
I do. The media's been in a frenzy with E.'s engagement, which is
great for her career, if not for her love life, since the publicity's done
wonders for her super-busy store. Will have to grill her during our next
weekly catch-up meal.

### except i'm out of oxygen

I tried. I really did. Every time D. sent a sweet text or e-mail—mind you, never a call—I told myself that was the most he could do. But frankly, a girl's got needs. And this girl needed to spill the beans. The day before yesterday, I sent him a sort of nasty e-mail telling him the total truth: that part of me wishes he was here, but the other part wishes he'd drown in a Venetian canal for ditching me at the airport. Okay, so maybe the overly harsh wording was fueled by a glass of red wine. And maybe honesty is not the best policy, as I haven't heard from him since. Should I grovel for forgiveness, or be smugly satisfied that his silence proves my point exactly?

**Till next time,**
**HamptonsAuPair1**

# mara feels roasted
# over the coals

THE FOURTH OF JULY WAS BLAZING HOT, THE SUN SHINING
and the skies a cloudless blue. Perfect weather for an afternoon
barbecue. Outside, the pool was sparkling and hummingbirds
were chirping in the imported dwarf cherry trees.

Mara turned from the window and took one last look in the
mirror, fluffing her hair and putting on one more layer of lip
gloss. She was wearing the white string bikini with a gauzy
embroidered peasant top and a pair of simple tan leather flip-
flops. Jacqui had loaned her a pair of vintage Ray-Ban aviators,
and she was all set.

"How do I look?" she asked, walking out of the bathroom and
striking a pose for Jacqui, who had wandered into their room.

Jacqui grinned. "Like you're armed for battle."

"What does that mean?" Mara asked, puzzled.

But Jacqui just shook her head and continued overturning the
pillows and rugs as she looked for Cassidy's pacifier.

"Seriously, what are you getting at?" Mara prodded.

"Nothing. Just have fun, okay?" Jacqui said gently. Mara would never admit to it, but Jacqui understood what Mara was doing. She wanted to let Ryan know what he was missing. And her bikini-clad body would certainly remind him.

Jacqui decided to hold her tongue—she'd been around long enough to know that the saga of Mara and Ryan never ended. Those two were either always on the verge of making up or breaking up. Mara couldn't live with Ryan, but apparently she couldn't live without him either. But you could never tell that to someone. They had to find out on their own, especially concerning matters of the heart.

Besides, she was in a good mood. She was going to see Marcus again tonight. The two of them had been flirting ever since the store opening, meeting with Midas and Eliza to brainstorm the shots for the "reality fashion" spread. It turned out that "reality fashion" was just as scripted as reality television. Although the photographs were meant to look like they were documenting a "day in the life" of a normal person, everything was carefully thought out and planned beforehand. Midas had suggested they start by shooting her at a fabulous party to create a glamorous, jet-setting image, and what better venue than the annual *Hamptons* magazine Independence Day bash? The party at the publisher's waterfront estate was the hottest ticket in town—the biggest, most exclusive, and most extravagant party of the season.

"I'll be back by five," Mara promised, deciding to drop it. They had agreed to switch off on the kids for the day so that she could attend Ryan's beach party early and Jacqui would be free to fulfill her modeling duties at the magazine party later.

She hugged Jacqui goodbye and walked out the back door toward the beach path that led to the Perry estate. She began the trek with a light step, but by the time she arrived at the right hedges ten minutes later, the heat had caused her hair to frizz and her floaty top, which had been so airy and breezy in her air-conditioned bedroom, was wet with perspiration and stuck to her body in a most unflattering manner, bunching up in her underarms and against her butt. She huffed from exertion and cursed a little bit at the sand that had stuck to the soles of her feet.

The smell of grilled meat and the soft sound of reggae greeted her as she approached the Perry house. She felt a wave of nostalgia as she opened the terrace's low gate. There was the patio where she'd played poker with Ryan and his buddies that first summer, and that was the pool where her then-boyfriend Jim Mizekowski had caught her and Ryan skinny-dipping that same night. Too many memories. Mara sucked in her breath, wiped the sweat from her brow, and walked toward the crowd gathered by the Weber grill.

Ryan's surfer friends were scattered about the pool area, some bobbing in the water on floaties and a few seated by the edge, their tanned legs dangling in the water. Like he'd said, it was a casual event—although this being the Hamptons, the girls were decked out in their Eres bikinis and matching Gaultier sarongs.

Mara was glad she'd dressed up, even if the peasant top had left her drenched in sweat.

She said hello to a few familiar faces as she made her way to the cooler, placing the six-pack of Corona she'd brought inside. She straightened, looking around for Ryan. She took off her cover-up—dear God, it was hot!—and stretched, making sure she wasn't popping out of the bikini. She'd never worn a two-piece that small before, although Jacqui had assured her tangas were more comfortable since they were cut close to the body and better for swimming. A few of the assembled guys did double takes when they saw her, although she was too busy retying the strings on her left hip to notice.

Now where was Ryan?

She was determined to prove to him that they could be friends—real friends—just like he and Eliza were friends. She could live with being called "dude" so long as he remembered how totally hot she was. Really, though, there was no reason they had to be estranged from each other just because they'd once been so close they could finish each other's sentences and knew each other's deepest secrets. (Mara's was that she'd once cheated on a math test, Ryan's that he'd actually attended an American Idol tour concert—with his little sister, of course). The two of them should be able to hang out, do everything they used to do—well, not *everything*, but she wanted him back in her life in some capacity at least. She could really use a guy friend, especially now that David, still silent after her vindictive e-mail, seemed to be out of the picture.

She was on her tiptoes looking around the party, the tiny strings on her bikini dangling sexily down her back and from her hips, when she saw him.

Sitting in the middle of the circle by the grill, holding hands with a head-turning blonde. A girl who looked all too familiar, and who was wearing an all-too-familiar teensy turquoise bikini.

Tinker!

The chick from Ryan's frat at Dartmouth who had lived in the yacht next to theirs last summer.

Mara felt a stab of—what? Shock? Jealousy? She couldn't be sure. But she was determined—there was that word again—to ignore it. So what if Ryan and Tinker were now an item? Wasn't that just natural? After all, they shared so many things in common—they were both great surfers, they lived for the outdoors, they both looked great in pastel polo tops, and their families both had truckloads of money.

It was almost sickening how absolutely perfect they were for each other. Mara had always suspected that Ryan would be a lot happier with a girlfriend who shared his interests. Now it looked like he'd found her.

She should just go. She felt awkward and out of place. But before her flip-flops could take her back to the safety of the shadowy hedges, Ryan spotted her and waved her over with a smile. She walked toward him slowly, as if approaching the lion's den.

"Hey, you made it," he said easily, seemingly unaffected by her presence.

"Yeah." Mara hoped her smile looked natural. She felt even more naked in the tiny tanga than she had the other night when she really *was* naked.

"Hey, Mara," Tinker greeted her with a smile, leaning over to massage Ryan's shoulders. If she was surprised to see Mara there, she was certainly doing a good job of hiding it. "Nice to see you."

"You too," Mara said. "Hot out," she added awkwardly, fanning herself with her bunched-up top. Had she really just reverted to talking about the weather?

"It's insane." Tinker nodded politely, her hands still on Ryan's bare shoulders. "Hottest summer in the Hamptons ever, I think."

"Have a beer, take a seat," Ryan offered. "Hey, Chuckles, move over," he said, ordering his friend Charlie to make room for Mara.

"Nah . . . I've got to go, actually. Another party. You know how it is." Mara shrugged and sighed, as if her schedule were just way too busy for her to even contemplate staying one more minute. "I just wanted to come by over and say hi."

"Oh—of course." He nodded. "'Tis the Fourth, after all. The Hamptons Christmas." Mara gave him a small smile, feeling the slightest bit more comfortable. They'd always compared the busy social schedule on the Fourth of July weekend to the jam-packed winter holidays. It was part of their secret language—which she'd been worried Ryan no longer spoke.

"Right," Mara agreed. "Well . . ."

"I guess we'll see you around then," Ryan finished with an upbeat, friendly smile. He was being so polite and maddeningly *nice.* Sure, Mara wanted the two of them to be friends, but he was treating her as if she were just another guest at the party—not the girl he'd lived with on a freaking boat just last summer!

"Yeah." Mara nodded lamely as Tinker got up to greet some new arrivals. She noticed Ryan squeeze Tinker's leg gently as she stood.

"Hey, man, can you pass a beer?" Charlie asked from his perch on the hammock. As Ryan reached into the cooler to get him one, Mara seized the opportunity to duck away as quickly as possible.

As she approached the gate, Mara took one last glance back at the two of them. Tinker had jumped on Ryan's back, and he was giving her a piggyback ride all the way to the edge of the pool. They fell into the water, laughing and screaming as their toned, athletic bodies splashed about.

Why did she even want to be friends with him? She couldn't remember the reasons. She was too angry and confused, her mind racing as she remembered all those times she'd come home from work and found Ryan hanging out with Tinker. She wondered if Ryan had ever really been such a great guy to her after all—or if their relationship had been just a sham. Was it possible there had been something between him and Tinker even then? Mara felt her cheeks burn from the heat, inside and out.

# jacqui enjoys the view from the top

"ARE YOU READY?" MARCUS ASKED, GIVING JACQUI A hand as she stepped out of his Jeep onto the red carpet that lined the driveway up to the Swan estate, where the *Hamptons* magazine bash was being held.

She nodded and inhaled deeply. It was her first official modeling shoot—or at least as official you could get, since it was taking place at a party—and she was nervous and excited. Especially since the shoot meant a night out on the town with Marcus. A few hours earlier, a two-man hair-and-makeup team had arrived at the Finnemore mega-mansion to prepare her for the evening. It had taken them three hours to transform Jacqui from merely devastating to billboard-worthy.

She swiveled her legs forward, locked together at the knee so that she wouldn't show her underpants to the world, and exited the car gracefully. With her bronzed skin, dewy lips, and hair worn in loose, mermaid-like waves, she was radiant in a short white jersey minidress—an Eliza Thompson design, of course—

with a back that dipped dangerously low to show "back cleavage." Hordes of paparazzi stationed at the party's entrance immediately descended on her like honeybees around a queen. It was pandemonium bordering on hysteria.

"Jacarei!"

"Over here!"

"No, over here!"

"To your right!"

"To your left!"

"Jaaaaacareiiii!"

Jacqui glanced questioningly back at Marcus. She noticed Midas standing a little removed from the paparazzi horde with his bulky professional camera and tripod, intently taking photographs. "What's going on?" she asked.

"It's all part of the shoot," Marcus explained with a smile. "It's a day in the life of a glamorous jet-setter, so we tipped the paparazzi to treat you like one."

They had advised her there would be some staged scenes at the party, but Jacqui was unprepared for the level of commotion the Easton boys had instilled in the photographers. The buzz surrounding "Jacarei" (one name only, at Marcus's insistence) had officially begun.

The Easton boys had envisioned their photo spread as a showcase of Jacqui as a busy Hamptons glamour girl, and tonight would be the first of many shoots. Midas seemed to have the more formal shoots all planned out: they'd get shots of Jacqui attending the biggest parties, hopping off fifty-foot yachts, sunning on Main Beach, riding a horse at the Hamptons Classic. They intended to divide the work between them, and Marcus had readily volunteered to take care of the "behind the scenes" cinema verité moments—Jacqui brushing her teeth over the sink (wearing items from Eliza's new lingerie line), chatting on the phone, or texting on a BlackBerry, having a cup of coffee. Jacqui was excited at the idea that Marcus would be trying to capture such intimate moments and hoped that it would mean having him around a lot.

"What am I supposed to do?" she whispered, unsure of how to proceed. Her hesitation was causing a backlog on the red carpet. An assistant to an actress who was idling in her limousine waiting for her moment in the limelight came up to Marcus to complain about the holdup.

"Very simple, my dear. Model," Marcus said, whispering huskily in her ear and stepping aside to let her commandeer the spotlight solo. He removed a tiny Canon Elph from his jacket pocket and began taking shots of her as well.

Jacqui flushed. She turned on her heel and began to pose, causing the paparazzi to shower her with attention. The popping of flashbulbs was intense, but she focused on Midas's voice, which she heard distinctly above the fray.

"Over to your left, look over your shoulder. That's it. Beautiful. Now chin up, like you've spotted someone you know. Give them a wave. Yes, yes, beautiful."

She noticed Eliza standing next to Midas, pointing and giving suggestions. She gave Jacqui the thumbs-up sign when she caught her eye.

"This is crazy," Jacqui muttered to herself when two photographers began shoving each other for a better vantage point. How much of it was real? How much of it fake? Like most things in the Hamptons, she couldn't tell.

Midas's steady voice helped her focus. "Keep your feet facing forward, but swivel your hips to me; that's it. Gorgeous. Now laugh. As if someone has just told you the funniest joke in the world. That's it. Good girl."

Jacqui felt herself begin to relax. Modeling was all about acting, which required more brain cells than she'd previously assumed. But with Midas's coaching, she began to let herself loose and enjoy herself. She caught Marcus's eye and naughtily hooked a thumb underneath the opening of her dress and pulled it to the side, showing even more skin—a taunting, tempting sight that drove the paparazzi wild for more.

Marcus gave a loud wolf whistle, quickly echoed by the fifty other male photographers who were now shooting in earnest. Several partygoers stopped and stared at Jacqui, and the crowd around her began to grow.

Jacqui laughed. This was *way* more fun than it should be. Did she say she hated modeling? Maybe she hadn't given it enough of a chance before. Besides, it was just a bit of harmless fun since it was only for the summer anyway. Jacqui blew several kisses and the photographers cheered.

"That's enough, boys," Marcus said, holding up his hands to signal that the photo shoot was over, but the press pack wouldn't let her leave. Even when the famous actress finally left her limo, they still trained their cameras on Jacqui.

"One more!"

"This one is for the *New York Post*!"

"Over here for *People*!"

Lucky Yap came up to Jacqui and asked her to spell her name, carefully writing it down on his notepad.

Jacqui looked over at Midas for guidance. Should she continue to pose? But he was already packing up his camera. He gave her a wordless, amused shrug. Apparently their "staged" paparazzi scene had evolved into a real one. It was all up to her. Jacqui sucked in her stomach and stood with her hand on her hip and a confident smile on her face, looking every inch the nascent supermodel.

Finally, the photographers put down their cameras. To Jacqui's complete surprise, they began applauding her performance. She gave them a courtly curtsy.

"You were perfect," Marcus said, gliding up to her and gently steering her into the party. "But work is over, and you're all mine tonight," he added in a low voice as they made their way from the red carpet to the house's magnificent entryway.

"That's it?" she asked. This modeling gig was all play and no work.

"That's it, love." He nodded.

A voluptuous girl in a revealing belly dancer's outfit greeted them at the door, and they discovered that the house and the two-hundred-foot tent in the backyard had been transformed into a sultan's palace. It was the Fourth of July, Moroccan style. The bombastic magazine publisher was known for his love of theme parties, but even for him, this was over the top.

"What the bloody . . . ," Marcus said as they took in the billowing silk draperies, the lavish Oriental rugs, the ceiling-tall hookah pipes, and the dizzying array of grilled meats, fruit, yogurt, twenty different kinds of hummus, stuffed grape leaves, and whole roasted lamb and goat, all sitting in authentic tagines on the buffet table. Low tables were set up with fat, overstuffed silk pillows, and *Casablanca* was projected on a fifty-foot screen.

"Welcome!" Christopher Swan, the genial host and owner of *Hamptons* magazine, greeted them personally. Jacqui had only met him once before, when Mara was writing for the publication. Mara had told her he was a bit of an eccentric. "Happy Fourth of July!" he boomed. He was dressed for the occasion in a fez, a short vest, and balloon trousers.

"What's the big idea?" Marcus asked, obviously amused by the decidedly unpatriotic flair of the event.

"Ssshh, don't tell a soul, but I got a great deal from this new Moroccan restaurant. They charged me a quarter of the cost to cater the party in exchange for publicity in the magazine." Christopher shrugged. Like a good mogul, he knew a good deal when he saw one. "Besides, who wants hot dogs and beer when you could have veiled dancing girls and camel rides?"

Jacqui nodded as she looked around, agape at the fantastic spectacle. There were ornately costumed drummers, acrobats, and dancers everywhere. Fire-breathers were stationed every couple of feet on the beachfront, and an African drum circle was set up around a bonfire.

"Just don't leave early," Christopher cautioned. "At midnight, there's going to be a re-creation of a cavalry charge, the men firing muskets into the air. Just like the real Fourth of July. Much better than fireworks, don't you think?"

Jacqui and Marcus hastened to agree, both of them straining not to look too shocked. A Moroccan theme and a cavalry charge at the same event? Only in the Hamptons.

"C'mon, I've got you guys up at the main table." Christopher pointed to a couple of gem-encrusted chairs on a dais in the center of the party.

He led them to their assigned seats, and Jacqui noticed the crowd parting deferentially as they walked by. She overheard a few of the guests' whispered commentary. "That's Jacarei—she's going to be bigger than Gisele. And that's Marcus Easton with her. Aren't they just the luckiest people in the world?"

As Jacqui surveyed the action from the vantage point of her golden throne, she wondered if life could get any more fabulous than this.

Marcus seemed to read her mind. "Pretty lovely at the top, isn't it?" He grinned, plucking a grape from the ornate tray on the table and plopping it into his mouth. He leaned back in his gilt chair and surveyed her admiringly. "It's where you're meant to be, I think."

Jacqui blushed. "That was more fun than I was expecting," she admitted. When she'd realized that the staged shoot had ended and the *real* paparazzi had been making a fuss over her, the attention had made her head fizzle, like bubbles in a glass of expensive champagne.

"*You're* just as much fun as I'd been expecting." Marcus grinned wickedly, leaning forward in his chair. Jacqui held her breath as she saw him lean in toward her, wanting to freeze this moment in time. She was on top of the world, and the most handsome guy she'd met in ages was right there with her.

She giggled and closed her eyes and felt his soft lips press on hers. He caressed her hair as he kissed her gently, his hand finding its way down her back. She felt butterflies in her stomach at his touch.

When they pulled apart, he kept his hand firmly on the small curve of her hip, and she decided that she was going to stay within reach of him for the rest of that night.

Who cared if she had to get up at 6 a.m. the next morning to make the kids their organic breakfast?

# is midas interested in eliza's designs, or does he have designs on eliza?

**WHEN THE SHOOT WAS OVER AND JACQUI HAD** finished preening for the real paparazzi, Eliza tried not to feel too piqued that none of the photographers had bothered to take *her* picture. After all, wasn't she someone too? Not too long ago, Eliza Thompson had ruled the glam-girl private school crowd, her photograph appearing everywhere from the *Times* social diary to *Town & Country* and *Vanity Fair*. But her high school days were over, and already a new crop of hot young heiresses ruled the society pages. The new girls even had websites and rankings and online fan clubs.

Midas saw the slightly distressed look on her face as he stowed away his gear. "You know the press—they're rabid for a new face. It's much better to stay in the background without all the fuss, don't you think? Funny how so much is made of the models when they'd be nothing without the designers."

"You're right." Eliza nodded, jollied out of her temporary irritation and silly jealousy. After all, Jacqui was promoting *her* line.

She'd just been sort of touchy recently because all anyone seemed to be interested in when it came to Eliza Thompson was her "engagement" to the "Greyson heir." The papers had been having a field day with the story. Not that she could complain—she'd started it. And at least the publicity had been paying off, since sales in her boutique were through the roof in just its first week. She smiled shyly at Midas, glad to have such a gentleman at her side.

"Let's leave them to it, shall we?" He handed his camera and tripod to an assistant and escorted her into the party. The two of them giggled at the outlandish extravagance. "I didn't realize Morocco was one of the fifty states," Midas quipped. "But perhaps I need to catch up on my American history."

Eliza laughed. "Nope, you're just in the Hamptons—aka an alternate universe." She was used to the quirks of the Hamptons high life. She'd once attended a black-tie square dance: the richest people in America line dancing among bales of hay, for the bargain price of five thousand dollars a plate.

While Marcus and Jacqui had been seated at a grand table at the center of the action, she and Midas opted for a booth in a quiet corner, sinking back into the plump cushions. Midas ordered a bottle of champagne from a passing waitress and they watched as a gyrating belly dancer approached their table, her finger cymbals clanking.

Eliza felt slightly awkward at the sight of the woman's undulating stomach, but Midas looked completely at ease, clapping to the beat and smiling. At the end of the performance, he discreetly tucked a ten-dollar bill into the top of her skirt as the dancer indicated.

"Thank you, sir," the dancer said, before bowing and leaving them to dance for another table.

"Very welcome," he replied. He noticed Eliza staring and explained. "Audience participation is a big part of belly dancing. I learned that in Lebanon."

"You've been to Lebanon?" Eliza asked, impressed.

Midas nodded. "We did a shoot for French *Vogue* in the city ruins. It's a shame what's happened to that country. They've rebuilt a lot since the war, but it's a slow process, and the recent skirmishes obviously haven't helped." Midas shook his head, saddened. "Beirut was the Riviera of the Middle East. The most fantastic nightclubs, and the food was amazing. Try this, it's delicious," he added, passing Eliza a plate of merguez sausages.

Eliza took a little bite. He was right—they were yummy. Tonight was purely business, but she couldn't help feeling that the circumstances were rather enjoyable. As an intern with Sydney Minx, she'd helped out on fashion shoots before, but those had been drawn-out affairs, with teams of stylists arguing with the photographer and Sydney about how the clothes should look. The Easton boys worked "light," with just a handful of assistants, and Midas had been so confident in her vision that he'd let her style the shoot without any help from outside professionals.

She felt a tiny bit guilty about enjoying the party when she'd left Jeremy alone for the night, but they had made plans to catch the fireworks from his dock later. Besides, as she'd told herself a dozen times, he wouldn't have fun at a party like this, especially not with her and Midas wrapped up in fashion talk.

In the short time they'd been working together, Eliza had quickly divined that Midas made all the decisions for team Easton, while Marcus seemed to be content to go with the flow. As far as she could see, Marcus's main task consisted of talking up the project to anyone who would listen—he was the mouth of the operation, Midas the brain. But when she'd hinted as much, Midas explained that while he usually took the bulk of the photographs with his professional Canon, Marcus tended to capture great candid moments with his little Canon Elph that added texture to the shoot as a whole.

"So, where else have you been?" Eliza asked, reaching for the crock of couscous on the table and spooning some onto her plate.

"Oh my, everywhere," Midas said. "Let's see, last month we were in Hanoi for *Visionnaire*," he said, naming a very avant-garde fashion magazine. "We had snake for dinner."

"Snake?" Eliza shuddered.

"It's supposed to be an aphrodisiac. You eat the heart and the blood," Marcus explained, smiling as Eliza looked askance. "We couldn't offend our hosts, so we did it."

"What did it taste like?" she asked, happy to be chewing on a baked fig and not some uncooked reptile's guts.

"Chicken." Midas laughed. "Ever had fugu?" he asked, naming the rare Japanese blowfish.

"Isn't that poisonous?" Eliza asked, dipping a falafel ball into the cup of yogurt. She usually skipped the food offerings at a party, but the spread was too tantalizing to resist.

"Not if it's cooked correctly. Besides, I like to live danger-ously," he said, raising an eyebrow James Bond style. "Easton. Midas Easton," he added for effect.

She laughed and took a bite of the falafel ball, careful not to let the yogurt drip onto her dress. "So what's the scariest thing you've ever seen?"

"When we went scuba diving in Palau with Quentin Taran-tino, we came face-to-face with a great white. Thought that was it, that was the end. But he just bumped us, scared the shit out of me—and went on his merry way."

Eliza raised an eyebrow, impressed. "I went running with the bulls in Pamplona one year when I was little. With my parents. We didn't know they didn't let kids do it. I got separated from them and cried my eyes out."

Midas whistled in sympathy. "Bet you gave the bulls a good run, though," he teased.

She smiled at Midas. For all his celebrity-studded stories and global travels, he was so down-to-earth and easy to talk to. He leaned back in his chair and studied Eliza thoughtfully, his shaggy bangs falling into his eyes. "By the way, I looked at the fall port-folio you sent over. It's really quite fantastic."

"Thanks." Eliza smiled, coloring with pleasure.

"I worked for a season with Phoebe Philo, of Chloé. Your

work reminds me of hers. It's incredibly modern and fresh," he continued.

Eliza gaped. Phoebe Philo was pretty much her hero. "Go on," Eliza said demurely.

Marcus chuckled. "You're going to get a lot of attention because you're so young and beautiful, you know. But you've also got the chops to back it up. I won't be surprised if you start get-ting backers. Or if the Vuitton group snatches you up, launches you like they did Stella McCartney. Of course, you can look like a troll and still be successful in this business—I won't name names." He grinned wickedly. "But if you have the looks as well as the brains and the savvy, nothing can stop you."

Eliza lowered her lashes and blushed. It was so flattering to have someone—especially someone who knew the fashion industry—understand and appreciate her work. Plus, he'd said she was beauti-ful, hadn't he?

"So who's the lucky guy?" Midas asked, nodding toward the rock on her finger.

"My boyfriend, Jeremy," Eliza replied. "We've been dating for three years," she added, almost apologetically.

"What's he like? What does he do? Describe Mr. Right to me." Midas settled back into the plush cushions behind him, as if waiting for Eliza to unveil all the secrets of womankind.

Eliza tucked a lock of hair behind her ear before answering. "He's really nice. Sweet. He's from here. The Hamptons. But not 'The Hamptons,'" she added quickly, making air quotes with her fingers. She explained about Jeremy's modest background and how he'd overcome it.

"So why him?" Midas asked, reaching over and lighting the gold hookah pipe that sat in the middle of the table. He took a puff and the sweet smell of fruit-scented smoke filled the air.

"That's a personal question, don't you think?" she asked tartly, lightly slapping him on the knee. "Why are you so interested?"

Midas didn't answer her and instead blew out a smoke ring, passing her the pipe.

"I don't know—because he's the nicest guy I ever met," Eliza said before inhaling the sweet tobacco.

"And that's enough for you?"

Of course it was enough . . . wasn't it? Eliza felt her brow furrow. What were Jeremy's goals? What did he want to *do* with his life? For the life of her, she couldn't remember anything he wanted to do except renovate a big old house and have a soccer team of kids. But surely that wasn't all. . . . Jeremy had big plans, didn't he? Eliza racked her brain. Something to do with building his landscaping business? Maybe?

"Nice guys finish first, huh?" Midas smiled, a slight sadness in his deep blue eyes.

"I guess." Eliza shrugged. She'd never really questioned the reasons why she and Jeremy were together before. He was cute and loving and he made her laugh, so why was she feeling so defensive suddenly?

"And where's Mr. Right tonight? He doesn't like parties?"

"No, he does . . . ," Eliza protested. He came with her to events like this when she asked him to, but she knew all the air-kissing and talk of fabulousness just wasn't his thing. Jeremy was completely supportive, but she knew all the fashion stuff bored him—bored most guys, really—to tears.

"Not his thing, got it." Midas nodded, seemingly glad to have figured out "Mr. Right."

Eliza shrugged uncomfortably. She didn't want to say anything to Midas about Jeremy that was disloyal. Especially since it suddenly occurred to her that Midas was the type of guy she'd always thought she would end up with—sophisticated, well traveled, culturally savvy. Until she'd ended up with Jeremy, who thought a trip to Connecticut was exotic.

Just then her cell phone rang. The display read J STONE, and oops, 10 p.m. She'd promised she'd meet him at the dock for fireworks a half hour ago. "I'm almost there!" she sang into the phone, even though she knew she couldn't make it there for another half hour at least. She started to get up from the table just as the waitress finally returned with their champagne.

"Sure you can't stay for one drink?" Midas asked, taking the bottle from the bucket with a flourish and preparing to pop the cork.

Eliza glanced at the label. Cristal. And this was about business, after all. . . . She eased back down onto the cushions.

"To Eliza Thompson, this generation's Coco Chanel!" Midas proposed as the champagne bubbled over their glasses. "To the best spread ever," he added as he handed her a flute of bubbly, his blue eyes shining.

Eliza accepted the glass. How could she leave when she was being toasted as the next big thing? She'd go meet Jeremy after this one drink. After all, it was the Hamptons. Nobody was ever on time.

### galloping gourmands

The other day we had to prepare five different lunches for the kids, who are encouraged to "explore their personal palates" and "discover new tastes and new experiences" according to their gifted programs and therefore demand individually crafted meals with stringent specifications. Violet wanted a soy burger cooked extra-crunchy, Jackson wanted quinoa-and-tofu teriyaki, Logan a Provencal pot-au-feu, and Cassidy spit out the mashed organic zucchini I prepared for him until I got the texture just right (not too lumpy!). Thank God for Wyatt, who was happy with PB and J. My kind of guy.

### miss crankypants in the hamptons

J. is a supermodel! Her photos from the Fourth of July party appeared *everywhere*. E. can't stock enough of that dress. . . . J. is also now dating that handsome photog, who's a bit too slick for my taste but is definitely a cutie. J. is over the moon, singing while she changes diapers; she's in such a good mood she didn't even blink when S. called us in for an emergency meeting after Wyatt failed his KRTs. Poor kid's gotta go in for remedial kinder-tutoring.

As far as I know, E. and J. are on the road to the altar, although E. is so busy with the store she hasn't begun to plan the wedding or even picked a date. Gotta get that girl on the ball. Doesn't she know it takes a year to get everything together? Oh, well. From the way she waves the subject off every time I ask about it, she isn't in any sort of rush.

Meanwhile, D. is officially out of the picture. Haven't heard from him since the day before I sent my nasty e-mail, when he was in Rome. (Apparently, D.'s last words as my boyfriend will have been to convey that the pasta in Italy is beyond scrumptious. I'll never know.) I really should have waited just a *little* while to get drunk and mean, since I'd asked him to pick me up a fake Hermès bag from this guy E. knows who has a table by the Trevi Fountain a while back. I can't really hope he'll still bring me one now that we no longer appear to be together, right? Is there such a thing as a breakup parting gift?

And not to keep whining, but I really, really don't want to run into my ex R. and his new gal pal T. Thank God, I haven't seen them anywhere, not even at the tea shop where R. gets all his super-antioxidant green tea that he's addicted to. Phew. I don't want to be a bitch (but I will be), but T. isn't all that great. I know she's gorgeous and athletic and good-spirited and all (at least that's what R. always said about her—sans the gorgeous part, although that was obvious enough to everyone). But can I just point out that she has a slightly horse face and a hyena-like laugh. A veritable zoo in one package. Okay. That was so *Mean Girls*. But whatever. I'm allowed. No one reads this blog anyway, right?

**Till next time,**
**HamptonsAuPair1**

# dalai lama says: enlightenment means making friends out of enemies

**MARA WOKE UP TO THE SOUND OF THE BABY CRYING** from the monitor. As she eased her feet into her slippers, she shot a grumpy look in the direction of Jacqui's empty bed. It was Jacqui's turn to give Cassidy a bath and a bottle, but the Brazilian au pair was nowhere to be found. Since hooking up with Marcus on the Fourth of July, she'd spent almost all of her free time with him, even after the shoots. She was usually good about getting back to the mansion before the kids woke up, but this time, she was late.

Mara dialed her cell number. It rang and rang and then went to voice mail. Not willing to give up that easily, she tried again. Jacqui picked up on the last ring.

"Jac? Where are you?" Mara asked, trying to sound more concerned than irritated.

"Mmmpph?"

"It's seven; we need to get the kids ready. It's Dalai Lama day, remember?"

"*Merda!*" Mara heard the phone clatter as it fell to the floor and then Jacqui's voice again. "I'm so sorry, I overslept. But I can get there and be ready to go in an hour."

Mara sighed. The kids had to be in Southampton's largest auditorium before then. Their father, before he'd gone on his walkabout and never returned, had raised his kids as Buddhists, the religion he was practicing at the time. Suzy, who wasn't religious, made sure the kids kept to the noble eightfold path so that they'd feel close to him when he came back—whenever that was. The Dalai Lama was in town for a whole week of events, but the morning's special lecture, "Making Peace," was to be the highlight of his trip.

"Don't worry about it," Mara told Jacqui. "I'll take care of it."

"Are you sure?" Jacqui asked, although the relief in her voice was all too evident.

"I'm sure," Mara said with a huff, keeping an eye on the clock. She had to get the kids dressed, fed, and out the door as soon as possible if they were going to make it.

"We were out last night with some friends of theirs from Auckland, and *Deus*, can those Kiwis drink! We didn't get in until five in the morning. Marcus promised me he'd set the alarm, but—Marcus . . . what are you doing? Don't, I'm not ready. . . . Oof! He just took my picture!" Mara heard the sound of Jacqui pummeling her boyfriend with a pillow. When Jacqui came back on the line, she was still giggling. "Seriously, though, if you need me, I can meet you there," Jacqui offered.

"I told you, it's okay. Do you know where the kids' togas are?"

"Togas?"

"You know, the Tibetan prayer robes they have to wear. I asked you to send them out with the dry cleaning on Friday."

"Oh." There was a pause. "I forgot," Jacqui admitted in a small voice.

Mara sighed. She didn't want to complain—after all, Jacqui was now the "face" of the Eliza Thompson line, and being seen at all the right events was part of that job—but it was the third time that week that Jacqui had messed up on the job. Last Thursday she'd been out all night with Marcus and had been so out of it the next day that she'd brought Violet to chess camp and the twins to ballet. Mara didn't want to say anything, but it was getting ridiculous.

Plus, life was getting a little lonely. Eliza and Jacqui were always out, doing fun things together, while Mara was left at home with the kids. Jacqui and Eliza invited her to everything, but after one party where a guest asked if she was Eliza's assistant and another one where she bumped into Ryan and Tinker together—if you could call catching them making out in one of the cabanas at the Star Room "bumping into them"—Mara had decided it was better to stay at home with the kids or to work on her blog. When she'd first launched it, she was elated to receive a handful of hits, but as she began posting more and more of her adventures, she found her audience growing steadily.

The more time Mara spent alone, though, the more time she spent wishing she hadn't been so cold to David. If he were still in her life, she'd at least be getting texts and e-mails that let her know *someone* was thinking about her. But she was too proud to rescind what she'd written. Everything she'd said was still true—she *was* hurt that he'd left her at the airport and then never even bothered to call. She blamed it on the stupid modern world. If there wasn't such a thing as texting and e-mailing, he'd have had to call her the old-fashioned way from the start, and maybe then she'd still have a boyfriend.

"Listen, I owe you," Jacqui said gratefully. "Thanks, *chica*."

"Don't worry about it." Mara sighed. "We'll catch you later." She turned off her phone and hurried to pick up the baby, who was squalling loudly on the monitor, seemingly aware that Mara was now behind schedule.

When they arrived at the auditorium, the line to the entrance stretched around the block, all the way to the village green. The sidewalk was littered with tents, pillows, plastic chairs, sleeping bags, illegal charcoal grills, and assorted garbage, since some people had camped out the previous evening. Apart from stopping by the UN, this was the only public stop the Dalai Lama was making in the country, and people had traveled from all over the eastern seaboard to see him.

"What's that smell?" Jackson asked, crinkling his nose as they hurried past the Porta Potties the town had hastily set up to accommodate all the pilgrims.

"Don't ask," Mara said grimly as she hustled them to the front of the line.

Only a handful of tickets had been made available to the

public, and all had sold out in a matter of minutes, but the mood was oddly cheerful and politely cooperative for the Hamptons, where scowls were regularly exchanged at Citarella over the last slice of Scottish lox. Since the holy man was a guest of the Southampton Cultural Board, where Suzy was a trustee, the kids had received VIP tickets. Mara scissored her way expertly through the crowd, waving their laminated passes over their heads, the kids clutching their prayer beads.

Many of the town's wealthy denizens were dressed in orange prayer robes accessorized with Blahnik slides and Verdura earrings, mingling with the friendly Tibetan monks. The festive air was similar to that of a fashion show, with a lot of air-kissing and jostling over seats. Mara noticed that a good number of sleek scenesters were carrying elaborate floral bouquets, overstuffed picnic baskets from the Barefoot Contessa filled with imported truffles and handmade brownies, or beautifully wrapped boxes from Tiffany and Christofle.

"What's up with all the gift baskets?" Mara asked Lucky Yap, whom she spotted snapping photos of socialites demurely bending over their prayer wheels.

"Ritual offerings," Lucky explained over the click of his camera. "The uninitiated can make sacrifices to move up in rank. Food, flowers, or water—symbolized by bowls. Hence the run on crystal bowls at Tiffany. They're all gone."

"Gotcha." Mara smiled, bemused. The Dalai Lama probably didn't care if the offerings were from the supermarket or the gourmet store, but the Hamptons crowd certainly wouldn't dream of making a donation that was less than what could be found in their own, utterly gourmet kitchens.

After a quick goodbye, Mara found their seats up front, and the kids quietly settled in. She marveled again at how well behaved the children were being. Violet was already chanting her fifth mantra, while Jackson and Logan were intently studying the geometric mandalas they'd found on their seats. Cassidy was lulled to sleep by the low hum of the crowd. Only Wyatt was wriggling in his seat, already bored to death.

The lights dimmed, and the head of the organizing committee welcomed the Dalai Lama to the Hamptons amid an explosion of applause. Mara clapped heartily along with everyone else. The holy man walked slowly to the middle of the stage and climbed on a generously proportioned armchair that had been provided for him, which allowed him to sit with his legs crossed underneath his body.

During the hour-long lecture, the crowd was rapturously silent. Not even an errant cell phone ring or BlackBerry buzz or the sound of gratuitous sniffling broke the spell of the Dalai Lama as he spoke of compassion, kindness, and gentleness.

Mara listened intently, surprisingly moved by his wisdom. The kids were even quieter than usual when the speech was over until Wyatt tugged on her sleeve.

"What's individual reponsi . . . responti—" Wyatt scrunched up his face in frustration at being unable to pronounce the word.

"Individual responsibility?" Logan interrupted. "It means we can choose to be happy by helping others and the world. You know how you always hog the remote? You shouldn't do that anymore."

"Er . . . right." Mara nodded, although she didn't know if that truly counted as "helping others." Still, if Logan could get Wyatt to stop hogging the remote, it would mean a lot less individual responsibility for *her*. But maybe that wasn't a very charitable thought.

The kids wanted to get their prayer books signed, so they joined the group congregating around the Dalai Lama for an autograph.

"That was just so . . . inspiring!" the blonde ahead of them was gushing. "I'm so glad I gave everyone donations to Tibet instead of Christmas gifts this year!"

Mara craned her neck to see who had been the Christmas Goody-Goody Grinch. That was the title her family had quickly given her older sister Megan one year, when she decided to "give" everyone notes saying that she had "donated to their favorite charity"—in the amount of five measly bucks each—instead of adding to the gaily wrapped presents under the tree. She wasn't surprised to discover she knew this particular Goody-Goody Grinch: it was Tinker, in all her blond and perky glory. She was chatting with a bunch of bald monks, her prayer beads jauntily wrapped around one arm, her orange robes styled into a sexy one-shoulder dress.

"Oh, hiii," she said, her voice practically tinkling as she spotted Mara. "Wasn't that amazing? I can't believe we were actually in the presence of the Dalai Lama!" She beamed at Mara with positive, radiant energy, her bright blue eyes looking like they might just jump out of her face.

"It *was* really great," Mara agreed reluctantly. She wasn't a fan of trendy religions, but given that Buddhism had been around for thousands of years, she supposed it wasn't *exactly* trendy.

"It just makes me want to go out there and change the world . . . starting with myself," Tinker said quietly. "You know what I mean?"

"I guess." Mara nodded, not quite sure if she felt that heroic but unwillingly charmed by Tinker's exuberance. It seemed Tinker had joined their group as they moved up the line, and as they made their way toward the exit, the silence between them became slightly awkward. "So, um . . . what would you change?" Mara asked, not sure if the question was too personal but curious to find out what the beyond-perfect Tinker might say.

"Well . . . ," Tinker began, "I know this is so ridiculously shallow, but I've gained, like, five pounds because Ryan insists on grilling everything with butter, and I totally don't fit in any of my clothes anymore." Tinker blushed furiously as she fiddled with her prayer beads, clearly feeling as self-conscious as Mara had the other day in her tiny tanga. "And it's not just about appearance, it's that I've always been such an athletic person, and I sort of hate not recognizing myself, if that makes sense."

Huh. Mara cast a sideways glance at Tinker's moving form. She certainly looked as slim as always. But then again, Mara didn't notice those things too much. Maybe Tinker wasn't completely perfect after all.

"Oh! Is that one of your kids? He's climbed up on the stage," Tinker cried worriedly, interrupting Mara's thoughts.

Mara whipped her head around and spotted Wyatt climbing up onto the stage, attempting to get to the chair the Dalai Lama had sat in. "Wyatt! Get down from there!" Mara ordered, nervous about accident-prone Wyatt falling off the stage and getting seriously hurt. She'd been so distracted by Tinker she hadn't been giving the kids her full attention.

"Don't worry, I've got him," Tinker said, making her way to the stage in a few sprightly steps. She wrapped Wyatt in a big hug as she plucked him off the stage, and he seemed to be quite pleased with his rescuer. "They're a lot of work, aren't they?" She sighed sympathetically, ushering the five-year-old toward his nanny. "I used to babysit my cousins, but there were only two of them—I don't know how you do it!"

Mara thanked her for her help and did a quick head count to make sure all the Finnemores were indeed alive and with all their limbs intact. Wyatt was squirming in her arms, Violet was asking a monk if women could join the monastery, the twins were debating Tibetan versus Japanese Buddhism behind her, and the baby was gurgling happily in his stroller.

"So when did you become Buddhist?" Tinker asked, once they finally reached the front of the auditorium.

"I'm not," Mara explained. "But the kids are."

"Well, it's nice that you're so open to it."

"Yeah, I guess." Mara shrugged.

Tinker played with her beads as they shuffled forward. "Actually, Mara, I'm glad I bumped into you." Her smile faltered a bit and she looked slightly nervous. "I've been wanting to tell you something, but it's sort of a weird thing to say and I wasn't sure how to bring it up. . . ."

"Oh?" Mara pretended to fiddle with the baby's stroller, hoping her burning curiosity wasn't completely obvious.

"I just want you to know that nothing ever happened between Ryan and me when you guys were together," Tinker said earnestly, still playing anxiously with her prayer beads. "It's an awkward thing to talk about, but I just . . . wanted you to know that. We were always just friends. We didn't even get together till the spring semester."

"You don't have to tell me anything—it's none of my business," Mara said bluntly.

"Oh, I know, but I know what I would think if I was in your place, and I just wanted to make sure there wasn't that kind of tension between us," Tinker explained, looking worried. She placed a light hand on Mara's arm.

"Okay. Thanks." Mara nodded. That really *was* nice of Tinker.

"We should all hang out sometime," Tinker suggested. "I'll call you."

"Sure." Mara had never really liked Tinker, but all her stubborn animosity was starting to fade. It was just too hard to hate someone who was so darn *nice*. Especially after the Dalai Lama's speech. Could it be that the road to inner peace began with making peace with your ex's new girlfriend?

# a picture's worth a thousand words

**ELIZA RUSHED ACROSS THE PATIO OUTSIDE JLX BISTRO,** tottering on her heels as she balanced two large garment bags and a rolling suitcase. "There's my girl," Jeremy said to the maitre d' as he spotted her. He smiled tightly. "Better late than never."

"I'm sooo sorry." Eliza was slightly out of breath as she made her way into the restaurant. "The shoot ran longer than we thought. Did they give away our table?" she asked worriedly, craning her neck and peering into the restaurant's depths as if she might be able to spot the evil table stealers themselves. She handed over her baggage to the hostess.

"No, madame, right this way," the Frenchman said curtly, collecting two leather-bound menus and leading the couple briskly through the restaurant.

"Did you get my text?" Eliza whispered, grabbing Jeremy's hand and giving it an apologetic squeeze as they tried to keep up with the fast-walking server. She'd let him know she'd be five minutes late, but in reality it'd been more like a half hour, once again counting on "Hamptons" time.

The server stopped so quickly that Eliza almost plowed into him. They had been led to a private table with a view of the ocean. Eliza paused for a moment, waiting for Jeremy to pull out her chair for her the way he usually did, and then seated herself.

"Yeah, I got it," Jeremy said tersely as he plopped down into his chair.

"I'm so sorry," Eliza repeated, knowing that Jeremy had all the reason in the world to be upset, since this wasn't an unusual occurrence—her lateness had become a bad, and predictable, habit of late. She couldn't help it; the store and the various shoots took up so much of her time. The other night she'd almost stood him up at the movies, arriving just in time before the previews ended, and last week she had completely forgotten they had made plans for brunch and had left him stranded at Babette's alone.

"Don't worry about it," Jeremy said softly, finally relenting and giving her a small smile. He reached for her hand across the table and stroked it, then stopped. "Hey, where's your ring?"

Eliza looked at her ringless finger and panicked for a second, then remembered she'd taken it off herself. "I took it off because I didn't want it to fall off while we did that shoot on the boat," she explained. Jacqui had taken the kids water-skiing while she and the Easton brothers had rented a boat and followed her out on the water.

"Oh, right." Jeremy nodded, but it was obvious its absence bothered him. Neither of them wanted to say what they were thinking—that the shoot had been three days ago.

The server returned and took their orders. Eliza was momentarily relieved by the interruption, but as soon as they were alone again, she knew it was her turn to speak.

"Jer . . . about the ring," she began. She had been meaning to have this conversation since he'd given it to her, but it never seemed to be the right time. They'd hardly seen each other in the past month, what with her busy schedule and his workaholic tendencies. Eliza slept over at his apartment a few nights a week, but he was busy renovating the Greyson house and often worked well into the evening, and she was out the door early to open the store while he was still sleeping. When they did see each other, it was in bed, and they were both too tired to do anything but cuddle.

"Is it too big? Is that why you were worried it might fall off? Because we can get it fitted," he said helpfully, reaching for a roll from the bread basket and slathering it with butter.

"No . . . it's . . ." She looked out over the ocean, where the sun was setting. The colors bled orange, red, and crimson all over the dark water. She would never get tired of looking at the sunset. It was postcard-ready romance, but Eliza had never been one for cheesy Hallmark moments. She just loved anything that was beautiful.

"Then what is it? Did I get something wrong? I thought it was what you wanted. Princess cut. Neil Lane. Colorless." He looked up from his roll, his face awash with concern.

Eliza's heart melted. God, he really was such a sweetheart. "No, it's perfect." She sighed. Maybe she could just postpone the conversation for another time. Besides, she still didn't know exactly what she wanted to say. What was the difference between a promise and an engagement ring, anyway? He was perfect, they were perfect together, and the ring was . . . well, it *was* the ring she'd always wanted. She took a sip of her wine and relaxed into her chair.

Jeremy grinned and gave the saltshaker a little push across the table. Whenever they were at a restaurant, they liked to play air hockey with the salt- and pepper shakers, pushing them across the table and seeing who could get theirs to slide closest to the edge. It was a silly gesture, but it meant Jeremy was in a better mood.

She smiled back at him and playfully pushed the salt back in his direction. She opened her mouth to speak, but they were momentarily blinded by the flash of a camera. She blinked to find a young reporter with a tape recorder standing in front of them.

"Hi, I'm from the *Hampton Daily*; sorry to interrupt. Can we get one with the two of you leaning closer together?"

Eliza looked apologetically at Jeremy, who nodded, clearing his throat to hide his annoyance with the interruption. "Sure," she told the reporter, and arranged her face into a serene smile. She was glad she'd had her hair blown out that day so it hung perfectly straight down her back, setting off her new black silk ruffled Phillip Lim shirt and Prada cigarette pants (she couldn't wear her brand *all* the time) and that Jeremy looked handsome in the pale blue Thomas Pink oxford she'd bought him.

Jeremy excused himself to the restroom, though Eliza was sure he just wanted to avoid having his picture taken anymore. She knew Jeremy didn't like how the press was so obsessed with their engagement—mashing their names together to create some kind of Frankenstein romance monster, with numerous breathless articles about the upcoming nuptials—which they had yet to really talk about.

But it was a slow news summer in the Hamptons. Chauncey Raven had finally put on underwear and had settled down to raise her two children rather than raise hell at a nightclub. Everyone was already used to the gaudy monstrosity of the Reynolds Castle, and Garrett Reynolds himself had been keeping something of a low profile while his new house was being built. There was no one to write about except for the Greyson heir and his pretty designer fiancée, whose clothes had become the de facto Hamptons uniform.

"So, can you tell us about the proposal?" the reporter asked Eliza once they were alone, his thumb resting gamely on the red record button as if it were a trigger.

The proposal? Was there even one? Too deep into her little charade with the press to go back, Eliza thought quickly. "It was magical," she said breathlessly. "We were standing in a gazebo at sunset, with a view of the ocean, when Jeremy went down on his knees and read a poem he'd written for me." Okay, so neither detail was technically true, but the reporters demanded a story and Eliza knew the more Harlequin it sounded, the better it was for publicity. "I was wearing my spaghetti-strap column dress, which you can find at the boutique!" she added. Why not milk it? In Eliza's mind, she was wearing a Holly-rock—a Hollywood-style ring whose only purpose was to show the world one was loved enough to be gifted with major bling.

Their food arrived just as Jeremy returned to the table. Eliza beamed at him, trying not to feel too guilty about embellishing a few details. She had a flair for the dramatic, and she knew the public would be so disappointed when they heard he'd just put the ring on her finger without even saying or asking anything. What kind of proposal was that, anyway? Eliza vacillated between being thankful it was a non-proposal proposal—the kind she secretly thought was the most understatedly romantic—and worrying that it wasn't shout-at-the-top-of-your-lungs romantic enough to share with the world. Or, more specifically, to share with the press and her adoring public.

"Can you tell us about the poem you wrote?" the reporter asked, turning to Jeremy and shoving the tape recorder toward his face.

"What poem?" Jeremy asked, looking puzzled and waving the recorder away with a hand.

Eliza interrupted before the reporter could say anything more. "Can we finish this later?" she said sweetly, plastering on her best put-off smile. "As you can see, my boyfriend and I are in the middle of dinner." She gestured to the steaming plates before them as if to emphasize her point. The newsman nodded gruffly and left.

Jeremy grabbed his knife and tore into his steak. When he finished chewing, he looked up at her intently. "Why do you keep calling me your boyfriend?"

"Last time I checked, you seemed to be pretty fond of me," she said playfully, grabbing the saltshaker from its post dangerously near the edge and sprinkling its contents lightly over her grilled sole.

"Ah, but I was reading, uh, Page Six." Jeremy spread a little Grey Poupon over his steak before taking another bite. "And in their interview you called me your, and I quote, 'handsome fiancé.'" He made air quotes as he said it and smirked to show that he was joking, but there was a hint of annoyance in his eyes.

"Is something bothering you?" she asked worriedly, putting the salt back down on the table.

"No, it's nothing." He shrugged, leaning back in his chair and wiping his hands on the napkin in his lap. "It's just funny how you make a big deal out of our engagement to the press whenever they ask you about your store."

"You read Page Six?" she teased, trying to make light of it, even though she *was* guilty of making a big deal about it for the press—playing up the blushing bride angle was keeping her store in the news.

Jeremy took a swig of his beer. "Sure." His lips twitched. "Don't worry. It doesn't bother me either way. It's just funny," he said again, though it was obvious he didn't find it all that amusing. He grabbed another roll and tore it apart with his teeth.

Jeremy was about to say something else when another photographer walked by. "Smile for the *Hampton Star*!"

He rolled his eyes and she shrugged, but they both leaned in and flashed what Eliza thought of as their "eyebrows-at-the-same-level *New York Times* wedding-announcement" pose.

The newspaper would have its shot: the perfect picture of a couple in love. But as Eliza pulled away, her brow furrowed, and Jeremy brooded behind his beer; it was obvious to anyone who'd care to look after the camera flash had passed that there was something less than perfect going on there.

# what good is a thirty-minute meal if your friends are more than thirty minutes late?

ONE DASH OF OREGANO. TORN BASIL LEAVES. A TEASPOON of salt . . . or was it two teaspoons of salt? Mara checked the recipe again. *One* teaspoon. Oops. So dinner would be slightly salty. She picked up a pepper grinder and ground it for a few seconds above the steaming dish. There. Maybe the spiciness would combat the saltiness.

"Mmmm . . . what's cooking?"

Mara looked up and smiled when she saw Eliza's father. "Hey, Mr. T." They never saw him around much since he was always on the golf course, having a sail, or out at dinner at the Maidstone. But Mara felt comfortable around Mr. Thompson, since she had spent a fair amount of time with Eliza's family in New York over the years. He was a lot older than her father—almost a grand-father, really—and she liked him a lot.

"I'm making spaghetti Bolognese," Mara explained as she grabbed some cloves of garlic from the enormous Sub-Zero.

"Fantastic." Ryder Thompson settled onto one of the bar

stools and fixed himself a drink. He looked at his watch. "Suzy better get down here soon, or we'll miss the dinner and have to join you! Though the way things are smelling, that wouldn't be the worst thing in the world." He smiled and Mara began to understand where Eliza got her charm.

Suzy blew through the kitchen wearing a wrinkled black evening dress, her hair its usual frizz bomb, magenta lipstick on her teeth. Mara knew Suzy worked so much she hardly had time for her kids, let alone for grooming herself before going out on a date with her boyfriend (though it was weird to think of Eliza's dad as somebody's boyfriend). "Mara!" Suzy cried when she saw her. "Does Cook know you're in here?"

"She does, and it's cool." Mara wiped her hands on her apron and tried to look as responsible as she could. Earlier today she'd had to practically beg the Finnemores' formidable cook to let her use the kitchen. Florentia was very strict about keeping order in her domain and had tried to convince Mara to just get takeout. Mara had to swear on her life that she wouldn't touch the complicated oven controls, since Florentia seemed equally worried that Mara would soil her pristine kitchen as that she'd burn the mansion down.

"Okay." Suzy nodded dubiously. She turned to Ryder. "Darling, are you ready? Do you have the tickets?"

"I thought you had them," he said, his forehead wrinkling in concern.

"Oh!" Suzy exclaimed, opening her clutch and dumping the

contents on the kitchen counter. Out tumbled a BlackBerry, a cell phone, a mess of gum wads, and a broken makeup compact as well as a dirty white envelope.

"Yes, here they are. Okay." Suzy nodded and began to haphazardly stuff everything back into her purse.

Ryder Thompson raised his eyebrows at Mara and then downed the rest of his drink. "Well, we're off. If you see my daughter, tell her that she does still have a curfew and that while she thinks I don't notice when she doesn't sleep here, I certainly do."

"'Kay." Mara giggled. Parents. "Bye, Mr. T., Ms. F. I promise I won't burn the house down!" she called after them as they made their way out the door in a frenzy of smiles and a frizz of red hair.

Mara hummed cheerfully as she chopped up the garlic and tossed it into the sauce. It had been weeks since she and her friends had sat down together, as they'd all been remiss in making their weekly catchup meals. Earlier in the summer they'd been better about hanging out, but lately it felt like they were three different trains running on separate tracks. Of course, Jacqui and Eliza spent a lot of time together, but from what Mara could gather, hanging out gave them little time to chat—those Saucy Aussie boys, or whatever the hell they were called, were always around.

She put some chopped vegetables in another pot to steam and glanced up at the clock. Eight thirty already. Jacqui and Eliza were running late. Typical.

* * *

An hour later, Mara sat at the counter, quietly simmering as much as the pasta sauce. She was about to clear the pots and pans when she heard the front door slam.

"Ouch!" There was a yelp from Jacqui. "*Deus,* who moved the umbrella stand there?"

"Shhh . . . ," Eliza whispered, laughing.

Hearing her friends joking together while Mara sat alone, waiting, stung. It reminded her too much of their first summer in the Hamptons, when Jacqui and Eliza tore up the party scene while she was left to take care of the Perry kids on her own. Bored and lonely, she'd spent her nights pining for Ryan, who didn't even know she existed back then. It was three years later, but had anything really changed?

Mara tried to tell herself things were different now as she got up and turned the heat on under the sauce to warm it up. First off, Jacqui and Eliza were now her friends—not two strangers who gave her the cold shoulder. And second, her days of pining for Ryan were well over. Sure, she'd felt the odd flash of jealousy on seeing him with Tinker, especially at first, but her weird fixation with making Ryan see what he was missing earlier in the summer had just been about missing her *own* boyfriend and needing some male attention.

Finally, the kitchen door swung open and Jacqui and Eliza tumbled in, giggling and holding on to each other. They smelled of champagne and cigarettes, and their faces were red and flushed. Both girls wore floor-length, exquisitely draped goddess gowns, samples from Eliza's upcoming fall collection, Jacqui's with a cutout in the middle to show off her sleek, tanned stomach. They looked red-carpet glamorous, if a little worse for wear.

"About time," Mara said irritably. Not only were they late, they were drunk? "What's so funny?"

They told her about some prank the boys had pulled on an insufferable bore at the party. The twins had pretended they were one and the same person and kept popping up at opposite ends of the party, making the poor guy think he was losing it.

Eliza leaned on the counter, still laughing, while Jacqui investigated the pots and pans simmering on the stovetop. "Mmm, *chica*, this smells great," she said, sticking a ladle into the thick sauce and licking it. "I'm starving."

Mara handed the two of them plates. "I thought you guys would have eaten by now," she said curtly. Neither of them had thought to apologize for their lateness, and she wasn't about to let it slide.

"Nah, you know what those parties are like. Lots of standing around. Cocktails, but no one eating anything," Eliza said, scooping up pasta from the pot onto her plate, not caring that it was getting cold.

"I wouldn't really know." Mara tried to sound wounded as she grabbed silverware from the drawers.

"Aw, Mar, don't be like that," Eliza said soothingly, noticing the resentment in Mara's voice. "We're sorry we're late, but you know how it is. Anyway, we asked you to come with," she pointed out, settling down into a bar stool at the counter.

"Well, I can't really get off at, like, six to go to a cocktail party, can I? Not with five kids to watch," Mara added, setting the silverware down in front of them with a clang and looking meaningfully at Jacqui. She felt a bit like the nagging, irritated housewife, complete with dirty apron.

"I'm sorry, Mar, I know I promised I'd be back," Jacqui said guiltily, looking down at her empty plate. She felt bad about leaving Mara with the kids so often, but she couldn't help it that she had a busy shooting schedule to attend to, could she? Fashion waited for no man (or woman), and it certainly wasn't going to wait for her to clean up baby spittle. "How about you sleep in tomorrow and I'll take the kids to gifted camp?" she offered, making her way to the stove to get some pasta now that Eliza had cleared the area.

"All right," Mara relented. She stood up and grabbed a bottle of white wine from the fridge. She could never stay mad at her friends for very long anyway. "So how's the shoot going?"

"The photos are insane," Eliza said proudly, grating cheese on her spaghetti. "Wanna see?" She dug out a black binder from her bag and placed it on the counter. The three of them crowded around to look.

"Wow, Jac. Is that you?" Mara gushed, taking in the glossy, gorgeous shots. "You're a superstar!"

Jacqui blushed. She hadn't expected to enjoy modeling so

much. It was almost too easy to be believed. But the boys had told her it was difficult to find models as photogenic as she was and who responded to direction so naturally. And it certainly didn't hurt having Marcus at every shoot—it made her practically glow with happiness.

"Did you see this one?" Eliza asked, pointing to a risqué photo of Jacqui lying facedown in bed, wearing only a languid smile and a black Gucci thong. She was barely covering herself with a pillow.

"Whoa," Mara cried. "Racy!"

"It's going to run in 'Socialite Centerfold' in *Hamptons* mag," Eliza said proudly.

"Marcus took it one morning," Jacqui explained, blushing slightly. She smiled as she remembered the morning Marcus had taken the photo, the admiring look in his eyes. He was everything she could possibly ask for: a funny, fabulous, and sexy guy who was crazy about her. She'd been single for so long, she'd forgotten how incredible it was to have a boyfriend. With NYU in the bag and Marcus in her arms, Jacqui was on top of the world. The whole supermodel-for-a-summer thing was just icing on the very sweet cake.

"Don't forget, tomorrow we have to be in Bridgehampton early for the equestrian shoot," Eliza reminded Jacqui, getting up to refill her plate. "I'm famished," she said apologetically as she took another heaping portion.

"Oh yeah . . . I guess I can't cover tomorrow," Jacqui said, looking anxiously at Mara.

Mara blew out her bangs.

"Anyway, you know how it goes, *chica*. I covered your ass two summers ago," Jacqui added playfully, still engrossed by the book of photos. She turned the page. "When it comes to the whole au pair thing, we've always traded off doing the actual work, right?"

Mara was about to protest when there was a buzz from the intercom. Eliza flipped the screen on the television to the security channel.

"Who ordered pizza?" Mara joked, picking up an errant piece of pasta off the countertop.

"Oh, whoever he is, he's cuuuute," Eliza cooed, leaning in for a closer look. "Tall, dark, handsome. Kind of looks like Ewan McGregor in that movie. . . ." Eliza snapped her fingers, trying to recall. "He's wearing horn-rimmed glasses and a varsity fencing jacket. And he's carrying one of those backpacks that sit on those metal thingys."

"A fencing jacket?" Mara asked, standing stock-still over the garbage disposal. That sounded awfully familiar. . . .

She raced over to the screen. "Oh my God!" she exclaimed. "It's David!"

She felt her heart beat faster. What on earth was David doing in the Hamptons? How had he tracked her down? Had he come back just for her? What did this *mean*? She was thankful she looked presentable, wearing one of Eliza's tissue-thin James Perse T-shirts she'd borrowed from her closet and low-riding Nuala yoga pants. She'd learned from her friends the secret to looking sexy but casual.

"Really?" Eliza raised an eyebrow. She had never had a chance to meet David in New York. Since it was so impossible to find time to get together, she always wanted to spend time with just Mara, and then every time they made actual plans to double date, one of them would cancel.

"Why do you sound so surprised?" Mara turned to Eliza, a slight edge in her voice.

"It's just—Mar, he sounded a little nerdy every time you described him. But if it's any consolation, I was so wrong. He's a regulation hottie."

Mara knew Eliza could be blunt, so she wasn't insulted. Much. "What's he doing here?" she wondered aloud, wiping her hands on her apron. "He's supposed to be in the Ukraine by now." Mara playfully shoved Eliza over and looked at the little black-and-white image of David on the screen. She had almost forgotten how cute he was. She was still angry at him, but seeing him standing there under the porch light, her heart melted a little.

The intercom buzzed again.

"Well, what are you guys waiting for? Let the poor boy in already." Jacqui laughed. And with that, Eliza buzzed the door open.

# love means knowing how to say you're sorry

**THE KITCHEN DOOR SWUNG OPEN AND DAVID ENTERED.**
He carried a traveler's pack on his back, and his suitcase was still in his hand. It looked like he had stepped off the plane and come straight from the airport.

"Hey, David," Mara said, as if she wasn't at all surprised to find him in her kitchen instead of in Kiev. She kept her voice cool, but the sight of him looking so humbled and modest—David always looked confident and assured—moved her. "Aren't you supposed to be in the Ukraine by now?" *And what made you think I'd even want to see you after that e-mail I sent?* she added silently.

"I can explain," he said, casting nervous glances at her two friends. Jacqui and Eliza were studying him with hooded eyes from behind their glasses of wine. Mara knew they could be an intimidating pair.

"David, you've met Jacqui before, and this is Eliza," she said, remembering that it was her place to make the introductions. Both girls gave David a guarded smile.

"Nice meeting you. Mara talks about you constantly. It's nice to put faces to names." David looked tan and weather-beaten, his eyes tired and red from lack of sleep, but he smiled politely.

"Nice meeting you too," Eliza drawled, eyeing him up and down as if she were taking inventory.

There was a short silence, and then David cleared his throat. He put his backpack down on the floor. "Mara, do you think we could, uh, go for a walk?"

They excused themselves and walked out the back toward the beach trail. It was another cool night, and Mara shivered in her thin shirt. David offered her his jacket and she accepted it thankfully. They walked for a few minutes in silence. Finally David stopped, took a deep breath, and looked at Mara. "Listen, I know you're angry at me. I would be angry too. I feel terrible about what happened at the airport."

"So do I," Mara deadpanned. She dug a toe into the gravelly sand, not making eye contact. "And I haven't really been thrilled with the whole lack of response to my e-mail for two weeks. I didn't even think we were together anymore."

"I know." He looked out to the dark water and sighed, as if the endless ocean would grant him the forgiveness he was seeking. "I felt so guilty about leaving you the whole time I was there. It's just, I couldn't walk away from the job. Ever since I was little, I've always wanted to be a writer." He sat down on the cold sand, and Mara sat down beside him.

"I know," she said quietly. She did know. She had always wanted the same thing.

"I should have just quit on the spot. But my family expected me to go. What would I tell my mom?" He picked a pebble up off the beach and tossed it into the water.

David's mother was Pinky Preston, the most famous—and most feared—literary agent in New York. Pinky had discovered all the biggest names in publishing: the literary brat pack of the eighties, the Gen-X memoirists of the nineties, the too-clever-for-their-own-good postmodernists of the twenty-first century. David hardly ever talked about his parents, and Mara had gotten the impression they were very cold.

He dug a heel into the damp sand. "I mean, I told you what she's like."

Mara nodded. She'd never met Pinky before, despite the fact that she'd once accompanied David to his parents' apartment in the famous Dakota apartment building to pick up some laundry. She'd stayed outside, too afraid to come in, figuring she'd meet his parents when he was ready to set up a formal introduction. "My dad's a writer, and she dumped him as a client when his books didn't become bestsellers." David sighed. "If I don't become a famous writer, she'll probably disown me."

Mara inched slightly closer to him on the clammy sand. Having such a demanding and overachieving mother explained a lot about David—the high standards he set for himself and for others.

"Anyway, I just couldn't handle the idea of telling her I gave up the Lonesome Planet gig. If I'd told her I was just going to spend the summer bumming around Europe with my girlfriend, she'd freak." He shrugged helplessly.

"Well, why didn't you say so?" Mara asked pointedly. This information would have been helpful a month ago.

"I don't know. I didn't want you to think I was some kind of mama's boy, you know?" He turned to Mara and grabbed her hand, his blue eyes earnest. "But Mara, the minute I got on the plane, I knew I'd made a mistake. I got to Europe, and I missed you so much. But I knew if I called you and spoke to you, I'd just come back, so I e-mailed and texted instead. It was a total cop-out."

Mara listened quietly without interrupting. The waves crashed softly on the shore.

"But then when I got your e-mail, it hit me how much I'd really hurt you. I was so miserable. I cut myself off from everything. I couldn't concentrate. I couldn't write—at all. I quit the guide and just wandered the streets of Europe by myself. After two weeks, I knew the only thing I could do was come back here and try to get you to forgive me. I called Alicia to ask if she knew where you were, and she told me, so here I am." Alicia was Mara's roommate, the Southern debutante.

"Here you are," Mara repeated quietly, still unable to believe that he really *was* here.

"You can hate me if you want," he offered, biting his lower lip. The air was chilly, but her hand was warm in his.

"I don't hate you. I'm not even sure I can be angry at you anymore." As soon as she said it, she knew it was true. She wished she could be stronger and hold on to her anger, but seeing him made her realize how much she'd missed him. She'd missed him so much she'd even convinced herself she still had feelings for Ryan Perry.

"Oh, Mara." David's shoulders sagged in relief and he pulled her in for a close hug. She nestled her head against his neck, remembering how strong and solid he felt. "I missed you so much," he whispered gently in her ear.

When they finally pulled apart, David smiled mischievously. "And I almost forgot, I got you something."

She knew instantly what'd he'd brought her—a copycat Birkin, from the famous stall near the Trevi Fountain. He'd gotten her text after all. He really had been listening.

She pulled him close, and as their lips met by the crashing sea, Mara's heart filled with contentment. A boyfriend and a Birkin—what more could any girl want?

## www.blogspot/hamptonsaupair1

### it's not just a job, it's a relationship

There's something that they don't tell you and that you totally don't expect until you start taking care of other people's children. It's that you start thinking of them—and loving them—as your own. S. needn't have worried. Those kids are my life. Wyatt finally scored a decent grade on his KRTs (PHEW!) and to celebrate, I let him have a video game. (SHHHH!) The twins surprise and delight me every day with their inquisitive and unique view of the world. Yesterday after they found me scribbling notes for my book, they told me they too were going to pen their memoirs. (*Tales of a First-Grade Nothing? Heartbreaking Works of Staggering Precociousness?*) Cassidy is the happiest baby ever—not just on the block. If only Violet would come out of her shell a little. I wish I could find a way to let her know it's okay to have a little fun sometimes.

On a harsher note, it's easier to spot Christie Brinkley at the yacht club than J. at work these days. Her modeling shoot has taken over most of her time, and I know she's in the busy process of becoming an international sensation—this week she did a five-minute spot for a Japanese car commercial and had to learn how to say, "Take the wheel," in Japanese—but really, couldn't she pay a *little* attention to

178

the home front? While I don't mind (much), I just wish she'd tell me when to expect her (or not expect her) so I'm not waiting around for her to burp the baby or take the kids to squash lessons all the time. I don't want to get in the way of her transformation into "The Body" (as everyone is calling her since that saucy photo of her ran in *Hamptons* mag). I just wish she'd bring her body over to help with doing the baby laundry sometime.

But the good news is that D. is back!!! I have a boyfriend again!!! He's staying at his parents' rarely used summer home in North Fork (they're not exactly beach types, or vacation types for that matter, if you know what I mean) and has claimed that his only job for the rest of the summer is to make his prior absence up to me. So far, he's been true to his word. He's been really great with the kids—we took them sailing in his boat the other day, and tomorrow we're all going to the Nautical Museum out in Riverhead. It's been wonderful to have him here. I take back all my bitching and whining. Yesterday he took me to the annual Writers & Artists softball game (his mom sponsors the Writers team) and we met all these famous authors. It was v. cool. They all seemed to know him—he's like everyone's favorite godson or something. He was nice enough to mention that I was a writer too, although I don't think a few clips in *Hamptons* and *Metropolitan Circus* really counts. Still, it was nice to pretend.

**Till next time,**
**HamptonsAuPair1**

# is midas the guy
## not taken?

AFTER A LONG DAY AT THE STORE, ELIZA SENT THE
salesgirl home, preferring to close up shop herself. This was her
favorite part of the day—tallying the day's receipts, putting back
all the clothing on the racks, tidying up and making sure everything was in order. It was her own tiny little retail kingdom, and
she loved the peace and quiet.

She was folding the last of the linen sweaters when there was a
knock on the door. Eliza glanced up to see Midas in the store
window, waving to her. She buzzed him inside.

"Are you busy?" he asked, glancing at the pile of sweaters in
her hand. "I've got something to tell you, and it deserves a bit of
champagne."

"What is it?" she asked warily, setting the sweaters gently on a
lower shelf. "I have to warn you, I hate surprises. . . ." Her voice
trailed off as she remembered the last time a guy had a surprise
for her—it had ended with a very heavy rock on her finger.

He shook his head with a grin. "Mum's the word until we've

got drinks in our hands." He ushered her out of the store. Main Street was emptying as the shops closed, but the streets glowed with late-summer light. "Let's just pop in here." Midas motioned to a tiny hotel bar along the avenue.

They walked into the dark recess, feeling the cold blast of the air-conditioning hit their skin. The bar was cozy, with plush red velvet cushions on cane-backed chairs, and bamboo lining the walls.

"I like this place," Midas proclaimed as his sharp blue eyes took in the decor. "It's like a pub in Rangoon, you know—men in white linen suits and fedoras, the sun setting on the British Empire, all that jazz."

"Mmm. The British raj. Khakis against pink saris." Eliza nodded. She too viewed every unique setting as a possible stage for a fashion shoot. It was also the way she dressed—every outfit told a story. Today she had put on a pretty, floral-print forties-style Rodarte dress with a nipped-in waist and bell sleeves, matched with her black-and-white Brian Atwood spectator pumps, because she was feeling very Scarlett Johansson in *The Black Dahlia.* Not that she'd even liked that movie, but the clothes were to die for. Pun intended.

The waitress approached, and they ordered—a martini for her, a Manhattan with bitters for him.

"So, khaki with pink . . . I can see your mind working." Midas leaned back in his chair, scrutinizing her from across the table.

"I need ideas for my resort collection," she admitted, running a finger over the bamboo coaster. She shivered slightly in her thin silk dress and wondered if she could ask the bartender to turn down the air-conditioning.

When the waitress returned with their order, Midas hoisted his lowball glass. "Now, then. Let me be the first to congratulate you"—he paused dramatically—"on being the youngest designer ever to grace a twenty-page spread in *Vogue*. I think Zac did it before he was twenty-five, but I don't know anyone who's done it before they were legal to drink," he added with a smirk, clinking his glass against hers.

"Oh my God! You're *joking*!" Eliza cried. Did he just say *twenty pages* in *Vogue*? She knew the Eastons were in the Hamptons on *Vogue*'s dime, but that they were working on spec for the shoot—which meant that the magazine hadn't approved it yet, and there were no guarantees. Eliza had hoped for two or three pages at the most . . . but *twenty*? That was every designer's dream.

"I'm serious as a priest." He put a hand over his heart, his eyes twinkling mischievously, looking quite a bit like his twin brother. Midas looked very much the cool auteur that day, with his five o'clock shadow, chain belt, and distressed Paper Denim jeans. "It was originally scheduled for August, but when Anna saw some of the shots, she flipped. They're running the whole thing in the September issue."

"Midas!" She leapt from her chair and threw her arms around

his neck. Twenty pages in September *Vogue*, the biggest issue of the year!

He kissed the top of her head, and she felt a frisson of electricity spark between them.

"I'm sorry." She blushed, extricating herself from his lap.

"Oh, go right ahead." He laughed, pulling out her chair for her so she could sit back down. "Though in case you feel like jumping again, let me tell you the rest of the news—they want to throw you a big party at the end of the summer at Calvin Klein's beach house."

Eliza grabbed Midas's hand across the table and squeezed it tightly. "You have no idea what this means for me."

He squeezed her hand back. "You deserve it, kiddo."

"Please. You're not that much older than I am."

"I graduated from university two years ago," Midas protested. "I'm practically a dirty old man," he said cheekily. Noticing Eliza's empty glass, he waved the waitress over for another round, handing her his platinum card.

"You went to college?" Eliza asked, remembering that in England they called college "university," so in Australia it was probably the same. "I figured you went to art school."

"Nah, I'm an Oxford man." Midas took his glass from the waitress as their drinks arrived.

"Oxford, really? Not design school?" Eliza asked, totally floored. She spiked an errant onion in her martini with the little plastic sword that came with it.

"Design's school's all well and good, but if you want to work in fashion or media, everyone went to Cambridge or Oxford. And while I'm loath to admit it, who you know is always part of making it in this business."

Huh. Eliza brought the martini glass to her lips and took a slow sip. She *had* heard from friends who worked in the industry that the staff at all the top magazines were Ivy bred. But she couldn't imagine going to school just to make connections. "So that's why you chose Oxford?" She had to decide pretty soon if she was going to Princeton or back to Parsons in the fall. Princeton had only allowed her to defer a year, so if she didn't enroll this fall, she'd have to reapply for admission, and who knew if she'd even get in the second time? After such a successful year at Parsons, she hadn't really been considering it. "I can't imagine committing to a school for four years just to rub shoulders with the 'right sort of people,'" she said, making little air quotes. "I think . . . ," Eliza started, realizing she really meant it as the words tumbled out of her mouth, "I'd go to college to explore what's out there, to get a well-rounded education."

"Of course." Midas nodded. "It was a twenty-four-hour schmooze fest, yes, but I loved learning the Great Books. I majored in philosophy, if you can believe that." He chuckled, taking a sip of his drink. "But my dear, you just have to do whatever's best for you."

Eliza set her glass down on the table. As she mused on Parsons, which would teach her everything she needed to know about design, her first and current love, versus Princeton, which meant exploring everything she might ever want to learn, Eliza couldn't stop herself from looking down at the ring on her finger. If she married Jeremy, she'd be committing to her *other* first love—the only person she'd ever really been with. What if she was closing the door on other experiences too? She played with the diamond ring, turning it around and around so that it caught the light, reflecting a thousand rainbow colors on the dark bamboo walls. Between Parsons and Jeremy, it was starting to feel like her whole life had been decided for her.

# it's miniature golf,
# not the pga grand slam. . . .

**"GREAT SHOT!" MARA CHEERED AS DAVID SHOT THE**
ball through the windmill, past the wooden cow, and into the
tiny cup at the end of the felt fairway.

David took a little bow and walked over to the hole. "Your
turn, man," he called to Ryan as he bent to pick up the robin's-
egg blue ball, a smug grin on his face. He came to stand beside
Mara and gave her a little peck on the cheek. "We've got 'em
where we want 'em," he whispered in her ear. She giggled.

"Show him, baby!" Tinker cried from her post behind Ryan,
swinging her golf club in the air. "Give 'em hell!"

David had only been back for a week when Mara had run into
Tinker and Ryan and they'd invited her to a late-night bonfire.
When Mara demurred, saying her boyfriend was in town, Tinker
suggested they all double-date sometime. Mara had accepted the
invitation, not sure if it would actually happen, but here the four
of them were. She was pretty sure she owed the evening to
Tinker's enthusiasm rather than Ryan's—he'd seemed a little

stunned to find out she even *had* a boyfriend, which she had to say was strangely gratifying—but since they'd been having a good time tonight, she was genuinely glad it had all worked out. They had met at Lunch for dinner, ordering mouthwatering lobster rolls and platters of assorted fried fish, the guys swigging back longnecks and talking sports while the girls gossiped about people they knew.

They were going to call it a night when David suggested a round of mini-golf in Riverhead, on the North Fork. It was a nice respite from the high-flying Hamptons scene, as mini-golf was way too corny and suburban for the Hamptons elite. True to form, the course was populated by suburban types in wash-and-dry cotton rather than dry-clean-only denim.

"Isn't this fun?" Mara giggled, a little tipsy as they moved on to the next hole. She and David were beating Ryan and Tinker—a miracle, considering the other two were athletes. She'd been teasing them about it mercilessly.

Ryan bent down and set his ball, which was fiery red, on the slotted black rubber pad that served as a tee. As he set up his shot, practice-swinging his club back and forth in the air, he accidentally nudged the ball with his club and it rolled off the tee and onto the forest green fake grass.

"That counts as one stroke," David called.

"Oh, man." Ryan laughed at his own clumsiness. "I think I had one too many back there." They had left more than a half-dozen empty beer bottles on the rickety wooden tables back at the restaurant and had decided to cab it to Riverhead. "Can I get a do-over?" he asked.

"No way, dude, those are the rules." David was the one keeping score, and he'd already reached into his pocket for the stubby golf course pencil to add a stroke to Ryan's score.

"Rules are made to be fixed," Ryan grumbled good-naturedly as he set the ball back down on the tee for take number two.

"What's that?" Tinker asked, looking up from her beer. She was wearing a pristine white knee-length Lacoste dress, a wide grosgrain headband in her thick blond hair, and a string of real pearls around her tanned neck, the epitome of polished patrician chic. Mara had been briefly intimidated when they first met up. Tinker looked like one of those country club queen bees for a moment—but as soon as she'd greeted Mara, rather sweetly asking about the kids and their "enlightenment," the feeling had quickly passed. Besides, Mara felt confident about her own, Eliza Thompson–approved outfit: a cotton voile bib-front Chloé top and tailored pinstripe Bermudas that Eliza had pronounced the "look" of the season.

"Oh, nothing," Ryan mumbled as he set up his shot again.

"You know, rules are made to be fixed. The early bird releases the worm. Idle hands are the devil's workplace." Mara grinned at Ryan from across the course. Back when they were dating, the two of them would try to come up with as many subverted clichés as possible.

Ryan looked up from his club and grinned back. "The heart despises what it despises."

"Ah, but I don't think 'despises' is the opposite of 'wants,' really," Mara pointed out, leaning jauntily on her club. "Good try, though. Half a point for effort!"

"I don't get it." Tinker frowned, taking a long slug from her plastic cup of Bud Light, the only drink the golf course offered. The red Solo cup looked hilariously mismatched with her chic outfit.

David looked back and forth between Ryan and Mara, shaking his head with a sigh. He yawned.

"We keeping you up, man?" Ryan teased. He tapped the golf ball lightly but didn't hit it.

"No, but if you don't take the shot anytime soon, I may just fall asleep standing up," David ribbed him back, holding his club over his head as he stretched his arms.

Mara looked back and forth between them. Boys could be so competitive. Though she couldn't help but feel that David's jabs were less good-natured than Ryan's had been. "David, I forgot to tell you—Ryan hates to lose," Mara sang out teasingly, trying to infuse some estrogen into their testosterone standoff. "And he hates even more to be distracted," she added, jutting her hip out the slightest bit as she leaned against her club, a gesture she knew he used to always find seductive. She couldn't help herself.

Ryan, as if on cue, flubbed the shot and then cursed impressively. He jogged after the ball and hit it vigorously once it had come to a stop, finally whacking it through the big bad wolf's head. "Three strokes," he said definitively to David.

Tinker came to stand beside David, looking over his shoulder at the scorecard. "Don't worry, babe," she called to Ryan. "We're only losing by, um—eleven. I suck! I'm so sorry."

"You guys do suck," Mara taunted, sticking out her tongue at Ryan. It was so refreshing to be actually good at a sport—all those years spent at Chuck E. Cheese were finally paying off. Ryan and Tinker, who'd grown up with parents who didn't believe in cheap amusement parks, were completely hopeless at mini-golf.

They moved onto the next hole, which featured a series of blue ramps painted to look like rivers. David set up his shot and then hit the ball briskly. It hit the side of the ramp with a clang and then went spiraling off the course, where it bounced out onto the concrete and started rolling away.

"Out of bounds, automatic forfeit of the course," Ryan cried gleefully, waving his cup of beer in the air.

"What? No way," David argued, pushing his glasses up on his nose and grabbing his ball from outside the course.

"Those are the rules, dude." Ryan shrugged, looking smug.

David just set his ball on the tee again and took another shot. The ball careened up the ramp, rolling swiftly down the other side and making a beeline for the hole, where it settled with a satisfying plop. "Hole in one!" he cheered, pumping his fist triumphantly into the air.

"It doesn't count. You forfeited, remember?" Ryan reminded him. His face was a bit red, probably from all the beer.

Mara was laughing at something Tinker was saying when she noticed the boys were facing each other, neither of them smiling. Seriously, why couldn't they just relax?

"Dudes, it's just a game," Tinker said cheerfully. "Mara, it's your turn."

Mara looked from her current boyfriend to her ex, confused at how the pleasant evening had suddenly turned frosty. She could swear it looked like they wanted to punch each other but were being too polite to let it show.

"C'mon, guys," she said, trying to defuse the situation. "It doesn't really matter who wins, does it?"

"Winner takes nothing," Ryan replied smoothly, easing back into his and Mara's own private in-joke. Tinker looked uncomfortable and giggled nervously.

"Whatever." David shrugged. "I'm going to go get another beer."

"All's fair in hate and war," Mara couldn't resist replying to Ryan, setting up her shot and slicing expertly, sending the ball flying through the air and landing perfectly in the clown's mouth.

# jacqui models fall's latest accessory: baby puke

**"LOGAN—I MEAN JACKSON—I MEAN WYATT—DON'T TOUCH** that!" Jacqui begged as Wyatt reached curiously for a steaming brown lump on the ground that could only be horse poo. She had taken the kids to a nearby farm with a petting zoo, which featured pony rides, tractor pulls, and a varied menagerie. She grabbed the little boy's hand and brought him over to the shady spot where she'd been tending to baby Cassidy, who seemed none too happy to be experiencing the great outdoors.

Jacqui had offered to take the kids for the day so Mara could get in some alone time with David. She'd felt guilty about fobbing the kids off on Mara all summer so she could play supermodel, and she wanted to make it up to her. Although at this particular moment, she wished she hadn't been so generous.

She'd forgotten Cassidy was allergic to cats, so the baby's nose was running and dripping all over everything. She didn't know that Violet was scared of horses. The twins thought a "farm zoo" was beneath their intelligence and had boycotted the event by taking seats under a shady tree and refusing to budge. Only Wyatt threw himself into the activity with gusto and had already fallen into a bale of hay, been chased by a pig, and been bitten by an angry duck.

She wiped Cassidy's nose with a baby wipe and tried to manage her frustration just as the now-familiar flash of a camera momentarily blinded her.

"Hold it, just like that. . . . Marvelous," Marcus directed.

On top of everything, the afternoon was also supposed to be a fashion shoot for *Vogue*. The editors had flipped when they heard Jacqui was also an au pair—they declared that children were the hottest accessory of the season, what with all the big stars making child care a fashionable event, and Marcus was quickly dispatched to take some quick shots of Jacqui tending to her young charges.

He had promised that it would be fun and that he would help with the "rug rats," as he playfully called them, but so far all he'd done was jump in her face with his camera and get in her way.

"Don't mind me, just go on with what you're doing . . . ," he said cheerfully.

Easy for him to say. She jiggled Cassidy on her shoulder, trying to soothe him. The baby suddenly vomited all over her new cross-back sundress. It was the only sample in existence. How exactly was she going to make this look glamorous?

"Ick," Marcus said, making a face. "You're going to have to change. Puke is not fall's new color," he joked.

Jacqui put the baby back in his car seat and scrubbed at the stain with a baby wipe, hoping Cassidy would be good. She hadn't expected Marcus to be hands-on with the kids, but she wasn't prepared for utter revulsion either. She briefly remembered how attentive and sweet Marcus had been with the kids on the day they'd met. Was that all an act, part of the courtship process? And if that was an act, what else was? Jacqui shook off the thought as she wiped baby Cassidy's pink cheeks, hoping he wouldn't throw up again—she was almost out of wipes.

Marcus studied the photos in the small viewing screen of his camera. "I don't know why you're wasting your time cleaning up spittle," he said. "You should be on the runway in Milan, not running a day-care center."

"I like working with kids," Jacqui said defensively as she hunted down juice boxes in her backpack for the kids' midafternoon snack.

"That's not the point, love," Marcus said, coming over to squeeze her waist and give her a kiss on the cheek. "You're better than this," he added in a whisper as Jackson, Logan, and Violet approached from their perch under the shady tree to partake of the snack.

Jacqui smiled to hide her annoyance. Who was he to tell her what to do with her life? She'd done a damn good job taking care of those Perry kids for three years, although no one ever gave her any credit for it. Madison was now a well-balanced teen at a normal weight, William was far from the hyperactive little boy he used to be, Zoë had finally learned to read, and Cody was toilet-trained. And that was a serious feat.

"C'mon, everyone, how about we go on a hayride?" she proposed as she passed out the juice boxes, trying to muster up enthusiasm. She was met by five blank faces.

"A hayride?" Logan wrinkled his nose. "You mean an hour spent sitting on itchy bales of hay while driving around a brown, muddy field?"

Looking around at the children's unhappy faces, Jacqui was unsure what to do. The more trouble she had with the Finnemores, the more she began to doubt herself and her abilities. Maybe her work with the Perrys had just been a fluke?

"If it's all right with you, babe, I'm taking off. I'll meet you later," Marcus said, stowing away his camera and giving her a quick kiss on the cheek, leaving her to deal with five grumpy children on her own.

*Maybe Marcus is right,* Jacqui thought as she proceeded to practically drag the children over to the area where eager kids were boarding large red trucks filled with hay. Covered in baby drool, with a sulky pre-teen, two bored seven-year-olds, and a five-year-old who wouldn't sit still, she wasn't exactly super-nanny.

"Where's Mara?" Jackson asked plaintively, not for the first time that day.

"She'll be back tomorrow," Jacqui promised, feeling a little hurt.

"I want her noooowwww!!!" he suddenly screamed.

Maybe it was indeed time to throw in the burp cloth and put on the stilettos.

# david plays dunne
# to mara's didion

**THE AUGUST SUN FELT WARM AND PRICKLY ON HER** skin and Mara turned onto her stomach lazily, feeling genuinely relaxed for the first time in ages. "You're slacking on lotion duties," she teasingly told David, pushing the St. Barth's tanning oil she'd found in the bathroom toward him.

She put her head in her hands and glanced out toward the water. From their vantage point, she could keep an eye on the kids playing by the shore. Violet was completely engrossed in the latest issue of the *New Yorker*. Logan and Jackson were fascinatedly using a metal detector. Wyatt was building sand castles. Cassidy was dozing in his stroller underneath the Bugaboo sunshade. The children were all as they should be—occupied.

When Mara woke up for work that day, Jacqui was nowhere to be found—as usual. It was a whole week since she'd taken the kids to the farm, and she had been missing from the mansion since then. Apparently, now that she was officially a model for *Vogue*, Jacqui wasn't going to bother to show up for work anymore.

Taking care of five children entirely on her own was becoming exhausting, so Mara was thankful when David called and proposed a day at the beach. There were only two weeks of summer left, and she wanted to squeeze at least a little fun out of them.

David inched toward her and began rubbing the buttery lotion into her shoulders, giving her a little massage as he did. Mara sighed. It was heavenly having him back in town. He was amazing with the kids. He was the one who'd brought the metal detector for Jackson and Logan, he'd shown Wyatt how to build a sand castle, and he'd gotten the baby to say his first word, "Dah." He'd even had a heart-to-heart with Violet, whom he'd confided in that he'd been a gangly smart kid in high school. Violet seemed really happy to know that introverted kids could turn out cool, and she'd even whispered to Mara that David was "really cute."

Mara sighed in pleasure as his strong hands worked their way down her back, tugging playfully at her bikini strings.

"So . . . I had a chance to look up your blog the other day," David said, removing one hand from her back to dab a little sunblock on his nose.

"And?" Mara asked, holding her breath. She'd told him about the blog and how she was thinking of maybe turning it into some kind of novel one day. But that was a week ago and he hadn't mentioned it, so Mara had assumed he hated it or thought it was trivial.

"It's hilarious. I particularly enjoyed all the death wishes for your slacker boyfriend 'D.,'" he added with a grin.

"Oops. I forgot. I had to vent, you know," she said, pulling herself up on her elbows and looking at him underneath the brim of her straw hat. "But what'd you think?"

"I told you, I thought it was really funny. You have a great voice—very appealing to women, I think. Very chatty," he added, capping the suntan oil. He regarded her thoughtfully. "I think you have something there. I would concentrate a little more on the social aspect—do it as a comedy of manners. An upstairs/downstairs kind of thing. You know, like *Remains of the Day* but for teens."

"Huh." Mara nodded, gratified that he took her work so seriously. Although wasn't *Remains of the Day* a bit highbrow for what she was doing? But then, David always was a literary snob. He once gagged when he found Stephen King in her book collection.

"Anyway, I want to show it to my mom," he said, putting on the clip-on shades for his eyeglasses and leaning back on the blanket.

"Your mom?" Mara breathed.

"I can't guarantee anything—but I think she should meet you. Mom's always looking for new clients. And I get points too if it all works out," he added with a smile.

"You really think your mom would rep me?" Mara asked in disbelief.

"Sure, why not?" David's tone was casual, as if the opportunity to talk to New York's most fearsome literary agent happened every day in a writer's career. He lay all the way down on the blanket, grabbing his copy of *Crime and Punishment*—which he was reading for the fourth time—and putting it on top of his face to block the sun. "She's giving a dinner party at the end of the month at Daniel, in a private room, and I want you to come. If you ever wanted to meet Salman Rushdie and Jay McInerney, now's the time."

She felt her heart thump in her chest. David was very protective of his mom. Other kids at Columbia were always slipping him their manuscripts, asking if he would show it to his mother, and he always just tossed them into the trash.

"What day was that again?"

"August 28."

Mara grabbed her BlackBerry from her purse—which Suzy had provided so that she could keep track of all the kids' schedules—and checked her calendar. That was the same night as Eliza's *Vogue* bash. Shit. Eliza had been so excited when she told her about it, and she'd be heartbroken if Mara didn't go. But she couldn't say no to dinner with the Prestons and their literary circle—this could be her big break. Writers would rather die than miss meeting Pinky Preston, let alone be invited to dinner. Mara knew David was going out on a limb for her, so the night meant a lot for them both.

"Thank you," Mara said, removing the book from his face so she could kiss him on the cheek.

David nuzzled Mara's forehead, and soon they were kissing, rolling from their blanket onto the damp sand.

"Oops," Mara said, pulling away, a smile on her face. "The kids."

They looked up to see all the Finnemore kids watching them, horrified looks on their faces. Mara had a feeling this wasn't *exactly* what Suzy meant when she'd told Mara the kids needed exposure to "ample stimulation" this summer. . . .

# jacqui meets some model citizens

**"THIS WAY, LOVE—THE POOL IS OUT BACK."** **MARCUS TOOK** Jacqui's hand and led her through the spacious two-story Georgian house to the Olympic-size infinity pool in the back, where a party was in full swing. Tall, beautiful girls were tossing a beach ball lazily over a volleyball net, sunning on the custom-made rocks, and drinking mojitos out of frosted glasses. There was a sprinkling of moneyed moguls, A-list actors, and hip-hop stars mixing with the girls. It was a good-looking and very European crowd, and Jacqui felt right at home overhearing the babble of many different languages.

When Marcus had suggested they stop by the Chrysler Model house in Southampton for the weekly Sunday afternoon pool party, Jacqui had jumped at the chance to check out the outfit that was so hot to sign her up. Chrysler Models was one of the biggest and most prestigious modeling agencies in New York, and they'd been actively courting Jacqui all summer long. Chrysler girls had a solid reputation in New York as professionals instead of party girls, so Jacqui was curious to see what all the fuss was about.

"Come meet some friends of mine," Marcus said, bringing Jacqui to where a group of models were splayed out on beach chairs facing the pool, their bodies tanned and lean. "This is Jacarei," he said to the group at large, presenting her to them as if it were her first day in kindergarten. "Be nice to her, ladies, or by next year she'll have all your jobs," he added naughtily.

Jacqui shrugged apologetically but was pleasantly surprised to find that the models, instead of glaring at her, were smiling indulgently at Marcus.

"Don't worry, honey, we're used to old Marcus here," a stunning redhead with a pixie haircut and an Eastern European accent consoled, inviting Jacqui to sit by her on an empty lounge chair. "I'm Katrinka. That's Fiona, and next to her is Sam."

Marcus laughed, perching on the arm of a lounge chair and grinning wickedly at all the girls. "Jacarei's the star of our new *Vogue* spread. We're doing twenty pages," he added, throwing down the gauntlet. He looked around the party and jumped up from his seat. "I'll be right back; I just want to say hello to someone," he told Jacqui, squeezing her arm before loping off to greet a friend.

Jacqui settled down in the lounge chair, a little nervous to be left alone with all the models.

"Twenty pages. You must be so excited!" Fiona, a petite British girl who was a dead ringer for Kate Moss, smiled, putting aside the issue of French *Vogue* she'd been reading. She poured Jacqui a margarita from the pitcher beside her and Jacqui took it gratefully.

"Is it your first?" Sam, a tan, raven-haired, green-eyed girl asked. She had a slight midwestern accent. "I remember my first *Vogue* with the boys," she added, looking off into the distance as if she were reminiscing about years past. "We went to Paris. I was so excited—I'd never been out of the country before that."

Jacqui took a sip of the ice-cold drink. Other than São Paulo, she'd never been anywhere but New York and one trip to Florida with the Perrys, and she felt the slightest bit jealous. But then, she would be starting NYU in the fall, her dream, so who was she to complain?

"How'd you like working with the Eastons? They are very sweet, no? Midas can be a bit of a stickler, but the pictures come out beautiful," Katrinka jumped in, pushing her sunglasses back on her spiky red hair.

Jacqui nodded. "I like it. To be honest, I didn't expect to, but it's a lot of fun," she admitted. She was surprised at how friendly these girls were. The models she'd met in the past had been distinctly bubble-headed, catty, and hostile. And it was sort of nice to be able to talk to people who understood what she'd been up to all summer.

"When my issue came out, I got signed by Versace to do their ads," Sam said, piling her luxurious dark hair on top of her head. "Just wait—your life is totally about to change," she added excitedly, her green eyes sparkling as she smiled eagerly at Jacqui.

"How do you mean?"

"It happened so quickly," Sam said, folding herself in her arms and tucking her legs underneath her chin. "I mean, one minute, I was just nannying on the Upper East Side, kind of bumming around, not really doing much, and suddenly I was on a private jet to Morocco with Marc Jacobs and André Leon Talley."

"You were a nanny?" Jacqui asked, surprised. She removed her Tory Burch cover-up and began to lather the body oil Sam handed her on her skin. She was feeling more at ease by the minute.

"Yeah. No one can work a juice box like me." Sam winked. "Is that an Eliza Thompson?" she asked, critically studying Jacqui's swimsuit.

Jacqui nodded. "She's a friend of mine, actually. And I'm an au pair."

"Not for long," Sam said wisely.

"I'm not sure I want to make modeling my life, though," Jacqui told them.

"Oh, it doesn't have to be. Do you think I'll be doing this when I'm twenty-five? Be serious." Sam shook her head. "I'm totally doing the Christy Turlington thing. Retire, start up a company, marry a cute guy, have a great family."

"In the meantime, the traveling is awesome," Fiona gushed. "Last week I was in Shanghai, Milan, and the Canary Islands. The lifestyle is great—it's so flexible. You can work if you want, but if you don't want to, you don't have to get out of bed."

"And of course, there are the parties." Katrinka nodded. "Not to mention getting to stay in this little cottage here." She waved a hand at the enormous stately house behind her.

"Your agency put you up here?" Jacqui asked. A little shack on the beach this was not.

"Yup, it's their little gift to us to let us relax and get away from the city. We're all roommates in New York too. In a little loft in the Bowery. You should come by sometime."

"I will," Jacqui agreed, thinking that a loft in the Bowery sounded a whole lot cooler than a tiny little dorm room. Looking around at the three confident, beautiful girls—each with a distinctive look and a lucrative contract—she began to think that if she ever were to model full-time, she could do worse than become a Chrysler girl.

"Can I steal you for a moment?" Marcus interrupted, coming over with a fresh drink and holding out a hand. Jacqui bid the girls goodbye, and he brought her over to a more private area of the pool patio.

"Big news," he continued once they were alone. "That was Gilles Bensimon I was just chatting with. Midas and I sent him some outtakes from the *Vogue* shoot last week and he loved them. We're going to Paris!" he said gleefully, picking her up and spinning her on the grass.

"*Meu Deus!* Paris?"

"The City of Lights! *Singin' in the Rain*! *Funny Face*!" Marcus laughed. "Picture it: you and I walking along the Seine together. Dancing at Les Bains. It's going to be absolutely brilliant."

"But why?" Jacqui asked, still shocked.

"Midas and I just scored the *Elle* cover. Gilles doesn't want his magazine left out of trumpeting the new girl. They've booked Versailles for the location, and we have to get there the day after the *Vogue* party. But no worries, they're sending a private jet to take us straight there."

"In ten days? That soon?"

Marcus nodded. "August 29."

"But that's the first day of orientation at NYU," Jacqui said, her face falling. "Couldn't we shoot it the weekend after?" she asked hopefully, even though she knew it was a stupid question.

Marcus scoffed. "You don't tell Gilles Bensimon when to schedule a shoot. He tells you and you go, no questions asked. Darling, it's all very simple." He grabbed both her hands and squeezed them, looking deep into her eyes. "You need to forget about NYU. Come to Paris and we'll stay at my flat; I've got plenty of space. Midas and I have big plans for our muse."

Give up NYU? She'd worked so hard to get in for so long. But the opportunity to be an international supermodel certainly didn't come along every day. She'd just met a bunch of pretty normal girls back there who led amazing, extraordinary lives. Traveling to the most beautiful places on the globe. Free designer clothes. Invitations to the best parties. Here was a chance to join the jet set. The beautiful people.

Marcus smiled at her, and the sun hit the blond highlights in his hair. She could picture it—photographer and muse, living in a charming flat on the Left Bank. It would be so romantic, like her favorite movie, *Moulin Rouge*, except she wasn't going to die of consumption anytime soon. All she had to do was turn her back on NYU.

She had never been a great student—she'd had to work so hard just to maintain a B average—whereas modeling came so easily to her, it was like breathing. Could this be the one thing she was good at? She thought of Eliza and her designs and Mara and her writing. Maybe this was her talent. Maybe this was what she was meant to do.

"Give it a think. You've got a week and a half. But listen to me. You won't want to miss spending autumn in gay Paree with me." Marcus took her in his arms and dipped her low.

Jacqui laughed as she felt the blood rush to her head. *Paris.* She'd come to the Hamptons from São Paulo three years ago to track down the boy she thought was the love of her life. She was older now and wiser. But what should stop her from following another guy—one who had *invited* her to go with him—to the most romantic city in the world?

## www.blogspot.com/hamptonsaupair1

### it's 10 PM—do you know where your friends are?

Seriously, do you? Because I don't. J., E., and I are like three ships passing in the night. Make that a foggy night, without foghorns. Not that I think we're in any danger of crashing anytime soon, but it would be nice to know they're still out there. On the rare occasion that J. and I cross paths, she seems really out of it, like she's so busy thinking about something she's got no brain cells left for everyday cognition (did I mention she's a model? Jk!). E., on the other hand, is simply an invisible wonder. She's so busy at her store, working on her fall line, and generally being so on top of the world that she's got twenty pages in *Vogue* that she seems to have literally exited this earth. I guess I should just be happy that they're both happy. . . . That's what friends are for. . . .

Speaking of E.'s party, I'm totally torn up about missing it to go meet D.'s mom. I've always been the type to put hos before bros (tee-hee,), but this time I must confess I'm leaning toward the dinner. So without further ado, a list of pros and cons re ditching my friends to solve the matter:

### pros

Dinner with Manhattan's top agent could make me a literary superstar.

**cons**

Might no longer be alive to launch my literary career once E. finds out I'm missing her bash.

I think I'm willing to take my chances. . . .

**Till next time,**
**HamptonsAuPair1**

# you know what they say about people who live in glass houses. . . .

"WHAT'S GOING ON?" MARA ASKED WHEN SHE ARRIVED at their table in a cozy little restaurant not too far from the house. The three girls had been remiss in meeting up for their weekly catch-up meals, and all of them had made an effort to get together that evening. Summer was almost over, and it was criminal how little time the three of them had spent together. Mara had come straight from putting all five kids to bed and had found Jacqui and Eliza looking tense.

"Jacqui is moving to Paris," Eliza announced in grave tones before soaking a piece of bread in a pool of olive oil on her plate and taking a delicate bite.

Mara took her seat and unfolded her napkin on her lap. "What? Why?"

"Marcus wants me to go to Paris," Jacqui explained a bit defensively as she perused the menu. "It's the next step for me, he said. There's a chance I could be on the cover of *Elle*."

"But what about NYU?" Mara asked. She reached into her

oversize Alexander McQueen tote bag and removed a large white envelope with the purple NYU logo on the right-hand corner. "This came for you today. You're never at the house anymore, so I thought I'd bring it tonight."

"Oh." Jacqui accepted the envelope. She opened it and its contents spilled out—registration forms, cheerful color-coded information memos on housing and meal plans. "It's the orientation packet," Jacqui said flatly, brusquely stuffing all the papers back into the envelope.

"So wait—back up—you're moving to Paris and not going to NYU?" Mara asked, completely floored. All Jacqui ever talked about for two years was how NYU was her dream. She remembered how ecstatic Jacqui had been when she called Mara to tell her she'd just been accepted. "Just so you can model?"

Jacqui shrugged. "NYU will still be there when I'm done with modeling." She was miffed that her friends weren't more excited for her, but if they weren't going to be supportive, she preferred they not talk about it at all. "Have you guys had the salmon here? Is it good?"

Eliza snatched the menu out of Jacqui's hands. "You can't be serious," she said. "Jac, I hate to break it to you, but modeling is not that easy. The world is full of models who never made it living in, like, ghetto apartments. You're better off going to school."

"I have twenty pages in *Vogue*," Jacqui said defensively, reaching back for the menu and scanning the pages with an annoyed look on her face.

"Granted—but think about it. Most girls don't get paid for anything until they score a cosmetics or designer contract. Editorial pays for shit. You might never hit it big, and then what?" Eliza raised her eyebrow haughtily. She didn't meant to rain on Jacqui's parade, but she'd seen too many of her friends in New York fall into the same trap. They left for Paris, Milan, or Tokyo with their portfolios and dreams of magazine covers dancing in their heads, wasting years appearing in beer ads in Ginza rather than the Galliano runway before giving up completely.

Jacqui grimaced. Eliza could be so bossy sometimes. She knew Eliza was right—Marcus had explained to her that she had to work for the lowest pay scale until she joined a proper agency, her rates went up, and a huge brand signed her. She knew her friends had good intentions, but she hated the way they always thought they knew what was good for her. Well, Jacqui could think for herself, and she thought Paris sounded pretty grand, thank you very much.

"And anyway, I think there's something off about Marcus," Eliza added, thinking about what Jeremy had said after he met him briefly earlier in the summer—that he seemed like a player. How could Jacqui just run off to another country with a guy she'd only known for a matter of weeks? She and Jeremy had been dating for three years, and *they* weren't even living together.

She motioned to the waitress to refill their bread basket. All this talk of modeling was making her hungry, almost as if she were unconsciously rebelling against the strict diet Jacqui would have to adhere to once she officially signed on. Eliza remembered being accosted by a modeling scout herself and being told she had to lose another ten pounds to be considered runway ready. Hello, she was already a size zero—she wasn't about to get into the negative figures. No thanks, she'd rather dine on pasta than on promises.

"How can you say that?" Jacqui asked, now completely irritated. "That's ridiculous. He and Midas are making your career."

"What?" Eliza cried, turning pink. Now it was her turn to feel the sting. "Jac, I can't believe you don't think I wouldn't be able to make it on my own."

"That's not what I meant." Jacqui backed off quickly. "But you guys have to understand—it's not every day that regular people get handed opportunities like this. Some people spend their whole lives waiting for their big break." Jacqui looked down at her hands and bit off an errant hangnail.

Mara looked at Jacqui curiously. Regular people? Since when did Jacqui consider herself ordinary? Her otherworldly good looks always saved the day for her. The girl had never had to pay for a meal, a cab, or a drink in her life. She quietly took a sip of her water, not wanting to get involved.

"If you flake out on NYU, you'll hate yourself," Eliza pronounced, her voice carrying to the other tables so that the well-heeled patrons turned around to glare at her for breaking through the restaurant's cozy murmur. She closed her menu definitively, as if closing the book on Jacqui's character.

"How can I expect you to understand—you've always had it too good," Jacqui said sourly. "Where is that waitress? I really need a drink."

"Hey!" Mara said, unable to watch from the sidelines anymore. "Stop it, you guys. Let's not spend the evening bitching at each other. C'mon, are we ready to order?"

"No, I'd really like to hear what Jacqui meant by that," Eliza said, her color high. She took a furious gulp from her water glass. Always had it good? Hadn't she suffered humiliation when her father lost their fortune and her family had to hightail it to Buffalo? It wasn't such ancient history that Eliza had forgotten what being poor was like.

"Nothing," Jacqui said sullenly, refusing to meet Eliza's eye. She usually didn't seek out confrontation, but if Eliza pushed, she would give it to her.

"No, go ahead. Please. Tell me," Eliza challenged.

Jacqui put down her napkin. "I don't know. It's just sometimes you take everything for granted. Didn't you pay for your store with your trust fund? I'm sorry, Eliza, but some of us don't have parents who can buy them careers."

"Anything more you have to say?" Eliza asked, her face now as red as her Chloé Gladys bag.

"Actually, yes," Jacqui said fiercely. If Eliza was going to tell her all the mistakes she was making in her life, well, then she deserved a little wake-up call herself. "You don't even take Jeremy seriously. You don't want a commitment; you're just wearing that rock on your finger for show." There. She'd said it. Well, somebody had to.

"You're one to talk about commitment!" Mara jumped in before Eliza, who'd turned completely ashen beside her, could respond. "Jac, you're the one who bailed on me all summer! I've had to do *everything* for those kids!" Mara wiped her hands on her napkin in dismay.

"See what I mean? You've flaked out on Mara," Eliza said in a triumphant tone, the color coming back to her face, although Jacqui's words had hit home. She knew Jacqui wasn't entirely wrong, but she didn't want to give her the satisfaction of acknowledging it.

"Don't take her side—she's not even going to be here for your big *Vogue* party." Jacqui folded her arms over her chest. It was going to be a completely sober evening, apparently. The waitress was nowhere to be seen.

"You're missing the *Vogue* party?" Eliza asked, turning to Mara. She looked more hurt than angry.

Mara flushed. "I was going to tell you," she said, wringing her napkin. "I'm having dinner with David and his mother, Pinky Preston. She's a huge literary agent—you both probably have never heard of her, but she's really famous in publishing. I can't miss it." Mara shrugged. She hadn't wanted the information to come out this way, but Eliza couldn't really blame her, could she? Give up the biggest opportunity of her young career to go to a party?

"So let me get this straight—you're missing my big night, and possibly Jacqui's last night in the country, for some lame snobby literary thing?" Eliza said icily.

"It's not lame," Mara snapped, now on the defensive.

"Whatever, Mara. All summer long, you don't want to come to any parties and you act like you're so above it all, with your pseudo-intellectual better-than-thou boyfriend," Eliza huffed. She was glad to have an excuse to change the subject, and for the opportunity to pass the feeling of guilt on to someone else. "And now you're missing out on the biggest night of our lives!"

"Of *your* life—you've already established that Jacqui's modeling career is going nowhere," Mara said coolly.

The waitress arrived, smiling as she pulled a pencil from behind her ear and a pad out of her belt. "What can I get you girls? Can I start you off with some drinks?"

"I'll have a mojito," Jacqui decided.

"A margarita for me," Mara added.

"Martini." Eliza nodded. "Dirty, with extra olives."

"Sure." The waitress kept smiling. "I just need to see some IDs."

For a moment, the three girls looked askance at each other. They *never* got carded. They were so used to drinking whatever they wanted at fashion parties, at the house, and at VIP rooms that they had taken the lax policy in the Hamptons for granted.

"You know what, forget it," Eliza said curtly, standing up. "I'm not hungry."

"Neither am I," Jacqui agreed, tossing her dark locks.

"Fine," Mara said through gritted teeth. "I'll see you guys later."

The three of them left the stunned waitress behind and exited the restaurant without so much as a word. Eliza jumped in her convertible without offering the other two a ride, Jacqui hailed a cab, and Mara decided to walk. Was this what friends were for?

# romance on the rocks, warning: major iceberg ahead

ELIZA PULLED UP TO THE OLD GREYSON ESTATE THE next afternoon, surprised to see how much work had been done on it since she'd last been there. Those late nights Jeremy had spent working on it had really paid off. The portico was refurbished, the house shone with a new coat of paint, and the crumbling columns had been replaced with new ones. A crew of construction workers milled around the grounds, and there was sawdust all over from the new fence being built.

"Jer?" she called. She hadn't told him she was coming, but she had hoped she'd find him here. After Jacqui's comment at last night's disastrous dinner, she knew she needed to really talk to Jeremy. She wasn't sure exactly what she was going to say, but she'd find the right words when the moment came.

He walked out of the front door in paint-splattered jeans, his dark brown curls plastered to his forehead and his face covered in a light sheen of sweat. "Hey, beautiful. What a nice surprise." He gave her a kiss and brought her inside. "Come take a look."

He took her first to the kitchen, which had been demolished, creating a huge open space. "It's going to have an island right here and then stainless steel counters and appliances," he said proudly. "But don't worry, I'll do all the cooking," he added with a sly grin. Eliza couldn't help but think of that day earlier in the summer, when she'd laughed off the thought of Jeremy ever thinking of her as a housewife. That seemed so long ago now.

She followed Jeremy around the house as he pointed out the work that had already been done—two bathrooms restored with marble tiles and Japanese toilets, as well as the refinished floors, sanded down and stained to a clean, light gray color. It was all incredibly beautiful and exactly to her taste.

He brought her to the master bedroom, which was still a mess of plaster and dust. "Looks like there's a lot of work still to be done," she observed.

"Yeah, but I think we should be finished by Christmas. I want to be moved in by December."

"Kind of big for a bachelor pad, isn't it?" she asked playfully.

"I think the two of us should keep it warm," he said, coming up behind her and folding her into his arms.

"About that . . ."

"I know, I know, you need to be in New York. I understand. But we can stay out here on the weekends. The Hamptons are really beautiful in the winter. So quiet. And then once the spring rolls around and you're done with classes, I was thinking we should come out here full-time and have the wedding in June. You know, the month we met."

"June?" Eliza said. "That soon?" Jacqui's words from last night's disastrous dinner were still ringing in her ears. *You don't want a commitment; you're just wearing that rock on your finger for show.*

Jeremy turned her around to face him, holding on to her arms and looking deep into her eyes. "Liza, I don't want to wait, and I've got no reason to. I've been working hard my whole life, and now I've gotten this big break. Best of all, I've got the girl of my dreams to finish the package. I see the future, and I want it now. I know we're young, but we're not stupid. I love you."

"Jer—I can't," Eliza said, pulling away. She looked at the five-carat rock on her finger. Wearing it meant she was engaged to be *married.* Jeremy was dead serious about them, about the ring. "I can't move into this house with you."

"But . . . don't you want to be with me?" His eyes searched hers, his brow furrowed in concern.

"I do, I do, I do," Eliza said, shaking her head. She could feel the hot tears welling in her eyes. She'd just uttered the very words she would have to say at the altar, but she wasn't ready to say them in a church.

"Then why are you crying?" Jeremy asked, mystified.

"It's just—it's too soon." She looked into his eyes, begging him to understand. "I'm only nineteen. It's all too soon. I want more. . . . I want to experience more of *life* before I settle down. . . ." The words spilled out from her lips before she could even think about them. But they were all true.

She took off the ring. It felt heavy in the palm of her hand, but not as heavy as her heart. "Jer, I have to give this back to you."

She closed his hand over it, and, choking back a sob, she ran away from him, from her Barbie dream house, and from their future.

# the heart wants
# what it wants

MARA WAS THROWING IN ANOTHER LOAD OF THE KIDS'
laundry when her cell phone rang. She grabbed for it eagerly,
hoping it was Eliza or Jacqui. The girls hadn't spoken to each other
since their fateful dinner, almost a week ago. Jacqui was now at
Marcus's 24/7 and had ceased even pretending to be an au pair. Eliza
was busy gearing up for the big *Vogue* party, meeting with the magazine's party planners to prepare for the event, and Mara hadn't so
much as run into her at the house. And since the shoot with the
Aussie boys was wrapped and done, she knew Eliza and Jacqui's paths
weren't crossing either. She missed her friends, but she didn't want to
be the one to apologize, since she hadn't really done anything wrong.

"Hello?"

"Hey, what's up." The voice on the phone didn't belong to
either Jacqui or Eliza—it was Ryan's. "I'm out by the beach right
now. Can you hang out?"

That was kind of a shock. Other than their über-competitive
golf date, she'd only run into Ryan in passing. It made her kind

of sad, actually. This summer was so different from years past. "Um, sure. I have to throw something into the dryer first, but then I'll come meet you."

"Glad to see you've got your priorities straight, Mar."

"Shut up. See you soon." She grinned as she hung up the phone. At least he'd stopped calling her "Waters" or "dude," but really—what was this all about?

She walked the short distance to the Perry house and found Ryan waiting for her, sitting on a fallen log, not far from where he'd surprised her when she was skinny-dipping earlier that summer. Come to think of it, it was the very spot where they'd first slept side by side in sleeping bags. She wondered if all those old memories flooded him when he came here too but shook off the thought.

"So, how's it going?" Mara asked, feeling shy all of a sudden. They hadn't been alone together since the start of the summer, and she still wasn't quite sure how to act around him. She sat down on the log beside him, the bark scraping her ankles.

"Good." Ryan nodded. "You?"

"Things are okay," Mara said tentatively. She was about to launch into the positives in her life—how much the kids had been improving, how glad she was to have David back—when she realized she could tell him what had really been on her mind. "I had a big fight with the girls last week, actually," she admitted quietly. "I haven't spoken to either Jacqui or Eliza since. Which is pretty impressive considering we all live in the same house." It felt so good to get it off her chest. She hadn't even told David about it—she was afraid he'd never like her friends again if she told him everything they'd said.

"Oh, man. You all right?" Ryan asked.

"I will be." Mara sighed. She reached down and grabbed a handful of sand, opening her hand again and letting the grains fall softly down onto the ground. "The fight was sort of a long time coming, I guess."

"Some things are like that," Ryan said with a small smile. He looked out to the water, and his eyes were distant. Mara glanced at him curiously, wondering what he was thinking about.

"I broke up with Tinker the other day," he said quietly.

"What? *Why?*" Mara blurted. She was shocked. They'd seemed so happy together. What could two people who were so much alike possibly find to disagree about?

He shrugged. "I guess I was just starting to feel like I was with her because I felt like I should be, not because I wanted to be." He looked out to the water again. The waves were crashing angrily against the shore. "I'm sure you know what that feels like," he added softly.

"Um, no . . . ," Mara said slowly. Was he implying what she thought he was?

Ryan turned to face her on the log, his green-blue eyes filled with concern. "Oh come on, Mar. I know David's a writer too, but really . . . He's totally not right for you."

Mara felt herself stiffening. She knew Ryan was upset about his breakup with Tinker, but why did he have to bring David into this?

"You deserve better," he added, almost as an afterthought, but she was too incensed to notice.

"You don't even *know* David," Mara said hotly, the color coming to her face. Was this why Ryan had called her? To pick a fight? He was clearly upset about his own breakup, but that wasn't her problem. Well, she wasn't going to let him drag her into it.

"I know enough," Ryan mumbled, looking down at the ground and kicking up a little sand with his foot.

"What is that supposed to mean?"

"Mara, he's just . . . he seems like the kind of guy who's always looking out for himself." He paused. "And not after you," he finally finished, looking down and kicking the log with his heel.

She sat there, for a moment too shocked to speak. "You're one to talk," she said angrily, her eyes flashing. "You were *so* considerate of my feelings all summer—hardly acknowledging my existence, making out with your stupid happy-go-lucky Buddhist girlfriend all over the place, and being so freaking *smug* about it," she spat. She felt bad about dragging Tinker into this, since she really *had* been sweet to Mara. So much for inner peace. But all was fair in love and war, right?

"Whatever, Mara." Ryan shook his head disappointedly and stood up. "I was just trying to help," he added.

She sat there bristling, but before she could say anything more, he turned and walked back inside his house, not looking back at her once.

## www.blogspot/hamptonsaupair1

Sorry I haven't been blogging for a while. I heard that's a blogger's cliché—apologizing for not posting to your readers. :) So I doubly apologize. Things have been hectic over here. D. and I are going to New York this weekend, and I'm so looking forward to getting back to civilization. Don't get me wrong, the Hamptons are civilization too, but the Hamptons are like Gaul to New York's Rome. The weather is better, the food is great, but ultimately, you want to be back where the action is, and I miss the city.

How are the kids? Well, thanks. Violet has talked to a boy! Sure, it was just the hot dog vendor on Sag Harbor, but still. Logan and Jackson have received their GREs and are contemplating colleges. They'll probably get into a better one than mine. Cassidy is walking already! And Wyatt has learned how to tie his shoes.

As for J. and E. I wouldn't know . . . and I don't care. Much.

**Till next time,**
**hamptonsaupair1**

# eliza finds an aussie band-aid can't quite heal her all-american broken heart

**"IS IT TRUE?" MIDAS ASKED THE SECOND ELIZA WALKED** in the door of the temporary *Vogue* offices. He and Marcus had chosen the photographs that were going to be in the spread, and she was dying to see the final edited collection. "You and Mr. Right—it's off?"

As if her breakup with Jeremy wasn't difficult enough on its own, the papers had had a field day with the disintegration of Jereliza, and it seemed that every conversation she'd had for the last week had begun with that sentiment—*"It's really over?"* Eliza had drunkenly confessed about their breakup to a gossipy friend at a bar, and the next day it was everywhere. Luckily for her, two days after that, Chauncey Raven had gotten back together with her loser ex-husband, despite the fact that he'd once cheated on her with a nineteen-year-old, and everyone forgot about the Greyson heir and his designer girlfriend again.

Eliza nodded. "It is." It was bizarre to say it, much less to think about it. She and Jeremy were no longer a couple. She felt too shocked to be sad. She was merely numb.

When she left him that night in a fit of melodrama, she had assumed that he would immediately come after her and demand that she change her mind. But he hadn't. And now that a week had gone by without her hearing from him, she'd realized that he probably never would. How could they ever get back together after she'd shattered his dreams like that and strung him along so cruelly the whole summer? She couldn't blame him for giving up on her.

"I offer my condolences," Midas said softly. "To the poor bastard."

"Excuse me?" She wasn't sure if she'd heard him correctly.

"What I meant to say is, fancy having dinner with me tonight?" Midas said a bit more loudly, his blue eyes sparkling and a wide smile on his face.

"Sure." She nodded. Having not spoken to Mara and Jacqui in a week, she could certainly use a sympathetic ear. "Dinner sounds great."

"Splendid. I'll pick you up at eight." He closed the portfolio, handing it to her. "I've got another meeting, so I'm afraid I have to run, but I'll see you later."

Eliza stood up, taking her things. Wait. What just happened here? Had they planned a friendly dinner, or had she just agreed to go out with Midas on a date?

* * *

JLX Bistro was more crowded than it had been in a while, filled with the late-August flood of now-or-never vacationers. There were lawyers and bankers who put in hundred-hour weeks and didn't see their families all summer until the very end, as well as the Hollywood crowd who breezed into the Hamptons to catch the last round of parties and premieres of the season.

Eliza was surprised that they were still given a choice seat out on the patio with a view of the ocean, what with all the famous faces surrounding them. But she shouldn't have been. When it came to connections, fashion people always did well for themselves, and Midas was given a bear hug by the owner of the establishment as soon as they arrived. Hollywood actresses might come and go, but the style pack had been summering in the Hamptons forever.

Midas was in top form at dinner, regaling Eliza with stories about growing up in Sydney and hanging out in Bondi Beach. She had been to Sydney once, so they chatted about bars and restaurants and where to get the best beer. Midas was being his usual funny and charming self, but as was the way with her lately, Eliza found she could hardly concentrate on his words, and her mind kept drifting off.

"You should show at Sydney Fashion Week." Midas's voice broke into her thoughts. "The field is growing and Aussies are mad for fashion."

"I'll keep it in mind." Eliza nodded, hoping that he hadn't noticed her zoning out there for a bit. "Are you going?"

"Not this year," Midas said. "I'll be working on a documentary, actually."

"Something fashion related?" Eliza asked, idly playing with her cell phone and wondering what Jeremy was doing right then. Did he even *miss* her?

"Nope. The fashion world's just a stepping-stone. I want to be a real artist, maybe pull a David LaChapelle," he confessed, suddenly looking a bit shy.

"Really?" David LaChapelle had started out shooting fashion spreads for avant-garde magazines like *The Face* and *Black Book*, then pervy-cool portraits of Pamela Anderson and Paris Hilton for *Vanity Fair*, and had recently directed a well-received documentary on inner-city kids. "So what's your film about?"

"Carnies," he said with a grin. "After Paris, Marcus and I are traveling around the world documenting the carnival underground. It's wild."

"That does sound wild." Eliza smiled. It seemed strange to trade in the fun, fabulous world of fashion for a chance to hang out with circus freaks, but she understood Midas's desire to branch out into something different and acquire a bit of art-world credibility. Though she knew with Midas it wasn't about anything snobby—it was about trying something new and being his own boss rather than having to pander to the fashion world's finicky tastes.

But wait. Did he say he and *Marcus* were traveling together after Paris? Where did that leave Jacqui? "You and your brother are so close," Eliza observed, hoping to get more information out of him.

"He's a good mate," Midas said simply. "Although he can be a bit of a wolf with the girls." He grabbed one of his fries and dipped it in ketchup, wolfing down the bite as if to emphasize his point.

"Really," Eliza drawled. She hated to be right about things like this.

"Like a cat around the birds, that one." Midas took a sip of his drink. "I hope your friend can take care of herself."

"She's a big girl," Eliza said, though she wasn't so sure. Even though they were fighting, she wanted to look out for her friend. Especially if Jacqui was ready to throw everything away for the chance to live in Paris with a guy who would be out the door in a month.

"And you? Are you a big girl too?" Midas teased.

He was smiling at her over his steak frites, and Eliza couldn't help but smile back. Midas was so unbelievably charming. With his piercing blue eyes and messy, tousled, David Beckham–like hair (not to mention his toned David Beckham–like bod), he was by far the best-looking guy in the restaurant—everyone had turned to look at them when they'd entered. As they well should—they looked great together. And now she was free to date him. So why didn't she feel more excited?

Looking around her, Eliza realized with a hollow thud that she was sitting on the very same patio where she and Jeremy had had that awkward date earlier in the summer, that fateful night when neither of them had the chance to say what they were really thinking and feeling about their relationship.

If only they had really talked about what the ring meant when he put it on her finger. If only she had told him then what she had been truly feeling instead of being too scared to hurt him. Maybe if she'd just laughed and told him he was being silly, he would have put the ring away and they would have waited to talk about marriage again when they were ready, years down the line. Instead, she'd hurt him in the deepest way possible.

Lucky Yap chanced by and, seeing Eliza and Midas together, promptly snapped a photo. "It'll be in *Hamptons* next week," he told them gaily. *"Elidas,"* he added to himself with a grin.

Eliza flashed a smile at Midas but shuddered to think what Jeremy would feel when the picture was published, seeing her on a date with someone else so soon after they had broken up. It hurt just to think about it.

*Gotcha.*

# "chick lit" is not a
# four-letter word

LATE AUGUST IN NEW YORK CITY MEANT HEAT
compounded by sweltering humidity, but the day Mara and
David returned to Manhattan was one of the rare, extremely
pleasant late-summer days. A breeze blew across the Central Park
trees, the air was cool and refreshing, and everyone on the street
was in a good mood, from the Wall Street types with their
folded-up sleeves, to the girls in billowy white sundresses and
flip-flops who hurried between shops, to the hot dog vendors and
the falafel guys.

They spent a wonderful day together, stopping at the
Metropolitan Museum of Art to see the new Rembrandt exhibit,
watching Shakespeare in the Park in the afternoon, and grabbing
coffee at David's favorite bookstore on Madison Avenue. Mara's
head was dizzy from all the cultural activities and deep conversa-
tions. After a summer spent changing diapers and stopping by
the occasional Hamptons glitz fest, she'd forgotten what a day
with David in New York was like—stimulating and full.

His childhood bedroom at the Dakota was wall-to-wall bookshelves, and she was gratified to see that they owned a lot of the same books. She fixed her makeup in the tiny mirror on his desk, making sure not to get lipstick on her teeth. They had fifteen minutes before they had to meet his mother at Daniel.

"You look great—don't stress," David assured her from the bathroom, where he was fixing his tie.

Mara nodded and smoothed down the folds of her skirt. She'd chosen a pretty Diane von Furstenberg shirtwaist, a crisp black cotton dress that she hoped said "serious writer." "So, how many pages of the blog should I bring?" she asked, kneeling down and unzipping her suitcase to show him the printout of all the posts she'd done. It was a hefty stack of paper. "Do you think the first fifty are enough?"

"Don't worry about that; you can just leave it here." David waved his hand as if it were a silly suggestion as he pulled his tie into a knot with a definitive tug.

"I shouldn't bring it?" Mara asked, surprised. She put on her best heels—the silver Manolo Blahnik rhinestone sandals she'd gotten for free one summer. If the dress was meant to communicate her serious ambitions, the shoes were to remind everyone she had glamorous aspirations as well. "But what will your mom look at?"

"You're so cute." He came back into the room to kiss her on the head. He stroked her hair, petting her like a puppy. "She'll look at *you*." He shook his head as he moved over to the dresser, slipping into his navy blazer.

"What's that supposed to mean?"

"You know what I mean. . . . It's all about fitting a marketing profile." He buttoned his gold cuff links and shrugged. "Young, cute, perky blogger girl writes a chick-lit book; publishers will salivate at the sight of your author shot alone," he finished, putting on his horn-rimmed glasses and smiling at her. "I'd drool at your author shot," he added huskily, with a wink.

Her author shot? Mara's face fell. "But you said it was funny. . . ."

"You *are* funny," David assured her. "You're a very *entertaining* writer." She knew he meant it as a compliment, but "entertaining" sounded a lot like "dumb" to Mara's ears.

He grabbed a pair of argyle socks from his drawer and slipped them on his feet. "It's the reality of the market these days. It never matters what the writing is like anymore; it's the concept of the thing. My mom just sold some memoir from twin seven-year-olds. I'm sure it's awful, but who can resist precocious young kids writing a book?" He shrugged and grabbed his wallet from his desk, sticking it in his pants pocket.

Mara stopped putting on her shoes and sat down on the bed, suddenly feeling a bit dizzy. "So what exactly is *my* hook?"

"You know, cute au pair lit. Chick lit with the nanny angle. From the cutest au pair of all." He came and sat down beside her on the bed, smiling. "What's wrong? Are you feeling sick?"

Okay, so maybe she wasn't writing *Remembrance of Things Past* here, but she'd worked hard on that blog. She slaved over every sentence. It was very difficult to make writing look effortless.

"Seriously, are you okay?" David asked, leaning over and putting a hand on her face to check her temperature.

Mara couldn't look at him. All this time, she'd thought David was interested in her writing, but he was really just being condescending.

"So you don't think my writing's any good."

"Mara, I just told you," he said, looking exasperated. "It's not *about* that. Your writing isn't what's going to sell your book."

Something in Mara snapped. She didn't need him or his mother. There were other agents in the city. Besides, she had a lot of readers now—who were interested in what she had to say, not just what she looked like. She did *not* have a webcam, thank you very much, and she wasn't about to whore herself out to an agent who simply wanted a sexy author photo.

"You know what? I'm not okay." She stood up and began stuffing her clothes back into her suitcase haphazardly. She grabbed her cosmetics from the bathroom and threw them in, not caring if the shampoo spilled on her new Eliza Thompson tunics.

"What are you doing?" David asked, aghast. "My mother is waiting for us."

"I'm not going to dinner. I'm leaving," Mara said, looking him straight in the eye. "I'm not your little squirrel," she added icily.

"Squirrel?" he asked, confused.

"Ibsen. *A Doll's House*," she snapped, just to show that she too could make hoity-toity literary references if she wanted to.

"But why? I don't understand." He looked truly distressed, and for a moment she felt bad for him. He really didn't get it. "Just because I said you couldn't bring your blog? For God's sake, bring it if you'd like. It doesn't make a difference to me."

It didn't make a difference to him? She didn't feel so bad anymore. Mara stuffed her manuscript into her laptop bag and it bulged a little. "It's not just that, David. And if you can't figure it out, then I can't help you."

"Mara, don't be an idiot. You clearly have no clue what a huge opportunity this is," he warned. His voice suddenly had a frightening edge, one she'd never heard before.

"Oh, I don't, don't I?" She hoisted her suitcase upright and marched for the door, wobbling on her heels a little. It was a little difficult to make a graceful exit in a tight dress and spindly high heels.

"No. You're being ridiculous," David said angrily, throwing up his hands. "You're going to embarrass me in front of my mother and her friends. Now put that suitcase down and let's go to dinner. All right?"

"No." She turned as she reached the door, trembling slightly. She looked at David, in his expensive-looking blazer, his trendy horn-rimmed glasses, and his shiny monogrammed cuff links and couldn't remember what she had found so attractive about him anymore. Ryan was right. David was an impossible snob. Worse, he was kind of a jerk.

Suddenly she thought back to last summer, when she was

living with ˙Ryan on the yacht and writing her column for *Hamptons*. Ryan never understood the writing thing the way David had—it just wasn't one of his interests. But there was a huge difference between her two ex-boyfriends. Ryan would never, ever look down on her.

"What am I going to tell my mother?" David asked, his angry expression crumbling into doubt. Suddenly he looked like a whiny little mama's boy.

"I don't know, David. Why don't you make up a story? That's what writers do, isn't it?"

She slammed the door in his face and raced out of the Dakota and onto West Seventy-second Street, hailing a cab. She hoped she could still catch the last Jitney and make it to the big *Vogue* party. Maybe it wasn't too late to make everything right.

# jacqui doesn't seem to like surprises either

"IS IT EVERYTHING YOU EVER WISHED FOR?" MARCUS asked with a grand wave of the arm, gesturing at the scene before him.

"More," Jacqui said breathlessly.

She had expected the usual Hamptons blowout for the *Vogue* party celebrating Eliza's collection: a cadre of security at the front gates, bedlam at the door, valets hustling guests out of their shiny new Porsches. But the fete at the Calvin Klein mansion was a far cry from the extravagant, over-the-top, anything-goes bacchanalian parties that put the Hamptons on the map.

Instead, the spare, modern spaces of the large and airy home were as artfully decorated and well edited as any *Vogue* spread. The pristinely white walls were adorned with enormous, elegant black-and-white blowups from the shoot, and classical music was piped in from the invisible overhead speakers. The magazine had invited only an intimate handful of the most powerful, influential, and well-known style arbiters who had passed muster with the publication's exacting editor in chief. It was a chic and stylish crowd, comprised of old-money scions and blue-chip heiresses like the Lauders and the Hearsts. Needless to say, Chauncey Raven wasn't on the guest list.

Jacqui couldn't stop looking at the humongous life-size photographs of her. She was inescapable. She was no longer Jacqui Velasco, pretty girl from Brazil, but the one-named wonder "Jacarei." She couldn't cross the room without being accosted by several different people—editors, modeling agents, PR reps, reporters, designers, photographers, who all wanted a piece of her. The attention was almost overwhelming.

"I'm . . . everywhere," she said as she took it all in.

"My dear, that's how Jacarei was meant to be experienced," Marcus drawled, nodding in pleasure at the enormous wall-high photographs.

Whether or not that was true, the sight gave her a bit of a headache. She wished she hadn't left her purse in the coat check, since she always kept a few Tylenol pills stashed away. She excused herself and made her way to the grand staircase and the coat check beyond.

As she walked up the stairs, she adjusted the front of her dress, making sure her bra straps weren't peeking out of the neckline. Knowing that most would expect her to show off "the Body," Jacqui had decided to trump expectations by choosing a loose, poufy baby-doll dress from Eliza's fall line. She'd worn it with sky-scraping six-inch Pierre Hardy wedges that made her tanned legs look endless. The effect was stunning and subversively sexy and showed that Jacqui could command a room without having to show off her figure. See? She didn't need Eliza to style her after all.

From the top of the landing, she could see the main hall below, where Eliza was holding court in the great room, looking poised to take over the global fashion market. She wore a smashing red dress with flamenco ruffles—for her resort collection, she'd decided to channel 1950s Cuba. Not that Eliza had told Jacqui that. She'd had to hear about it from Marcus, since she and Eliza still weren't speaking, despite the fact that it had been an entire week since their argument.

Eliza had come up to her when she'd first arrived at the party and hissed in her ear that she needed to talk to her about Marcus. But Jacqui had angrily waved Eliza away. She didn't want to hear another warning about Marcus and the evils of modeling, and she was sick of Eliza thinking she needed to be taken care of. She'd made up her mind, and there was no going back: she'd signed up with the Chrysler agency and was leaving for Paris the next morning. She would have to let NYU know she wouldn't be enrolling in the fall at some point—after all, they'd probably notice when she wasn't at orientation tomorrow—and the thought brought a little sadness. But she was determined, and nothing was going to stop her.

She was feeling a little dizzy from all the cocktails she'd drunk. They'd created a special drink in her honor—the

Passionate Jac, made from Jack Daniels and Brazilian passion fruit juice. She looked for an empty bathroom where she could at least clear her head. As she stumbled around a corner, trying to find her way, she crashed into something. Make that someone.

"Oh, excuse me," she said. She looked up, feeling a bit disoriented. "Don't I know you . . . ?"

"Jacqui Velasco." The person in front of her was six-foot three, blond, and beaming, in a tailored shirt with nice wool pants.

"Pete? Pete Rockwood?" Jacqui asked in disbelief. "Am I dreaming?"

"Nope. Not at all." Pete broke into a wide grin. "It's me."

"What are you doing here?" she blurted, too shocked to have any manners. Was this really the guy she'd met at the duck pond? He almost looked like a sophisticated Hamptonite and not the sweet tourist she'd met back in June.

"It's a long story," he said, smiling at her so widely that she couldn't help but smile back. "Are you going downstairs?"

She nodded, unable to remember what she'd been doing before she bumped into him, and he led the way.

"I think there's an elevator around here somewhere—I took it on the way up." They walked down the length of the hallway to a small elevator next to the library that was almost hidden in the wall.

"So, would you like to tell me the long story?" she prodded, her curiosity getting the better of her.

"Well, it all started at the dentist's office," he said in a practical tone as he punched button to call the elevator.

"The dentist's office?" Jacqui burst out laughing. She couldn't help it; it was all too surreal. Where could this story be going?

"Yeah," he said with a grin, letting her step inside the car first. He pushed the elevator button and the doors closed behind them. "Anyway, there I was, waiting for Dr. Finklemore, when I pick up a magazine and there *you* are. Your picture, that is. The article said you were spending the summer in the Hamptons, modeling for some store. So I stole the magazine and called up the boutique—Eliza Thompson? Anyway, the girl there said she knew where you were. So here I am."

Jacqui stood there looking at him, totally stunned. All that effort just to track her down? But then, hadn't she spent the first weeks of the summer madly Googling him?

"So basically, I came here looking for you. Does that make me a stalker?" His blue eyes twinkled and perfect dimples formed in either cheek. For a moment, all Jacqui could think about was that any girl would be happy to have Pete Rockwood for a stalker.

She suddenly remembered herself and shook her head, as if shaking water out of her ears. "But how—how'd you even get into this party? I thought you were from Indiana," Jacqui said as they arrived at the first floor with a ding. How did a small-town boy end up at an exclusive fashion event?

"I am." He smiled as he ushered her out of the elevator. "I've got my methods," he said with a crafty grin.

She raised an eyebrow, more curious than ever.

"C'mon, a guy's gotta have a few secrets, right? All that matters is that I'm here now and you're here."

They stepped out of the elevator and into the main hall. "You're everywhere, in fact," he added with a laugh, gesturing to the enormous photographs of Jacqui plastered as far as the eye could see. "Anyway, I was thinking . . . maybe I could take you out? Tomorrow night?"

"Take me out—"

"On, like, a date?" he asked, his face hopeful. "Dinner. Movie. Awkward conversation. You know, that sort of thing."

"A date . . . tomorrow," Jacqui repeated. She shook her head, reality suddenly coming back to her in a rush. "I can't."

Pete exhaled, looking crestfallen. They stopped in an empty alcove where they could hear the murmur of the party in the adjacent room.

"It's not what you think," Jacqui said gently. "I like you. It's just I'm leaving for Paris tomorrow." *And I have a boyfriend now,* she thought but didn't say.

"So how about when you get back?" he asked. "Tell me if I'm trying too hard," he added, still managing a ghost of a smile.

She shook her head, more slowly this time. "No, it's not a vacation—I'm going to Paris to model. I'm staying there."

Now it was his turn to look shocked. "But what about

NYU? Didn't you need that down payment for tuition earlier this summer?"

"I'm not going to NYU," she said softly. She felt confident about the decision, but it still sounded foreign to say it out loud.

"I see." Pete frowned, biting his lip. He opened his mouth and then hesitated, shaking his head. "But at the duck pond, you said . . ." He trailed off.

"What?" Jacqui asked.

A white-jacketed server came out of the kitchen and looked curiously at the two of them. They waited until he was out of earshot to resume their conversation.

Pete sighed. "Look, I know I don't know you at all, but I think you're making a mistake. When you were talking about what you really want to do in life, you never mentioned anything about modeling. It was all about NYU, your future. Are you sure modeling is what you want to do?"

Jacqui felt her face burning with annoyance. This was just like the lecture Mara and Eliza had given her. "You *don't* know me at all. I mean, seriously. You met me once, for like five minutes, and that was months ago," she spat. She knew she was being totally unfair, but why couldn't anyone trust her to make her own decisions anymore? Why was everyone treating her like a child or, worse, like some airhead model, when that clearly wasn't what she was going to be?

"Jacqui—," he began, his voice soothing. But she wasn't going to be placated.

"It was great bumping into you again. Have a nice life." And with that, Jacqui returned to the party, certain for the second time that summer that she would never see Pete Rockwood again.

# kiss a prince,
# find a frog?

JACQUI WAS STILL ANNOYED WHEN SHE FOUND MARCUS,
who was saving a spot for her on one of the modern white
couches and keeping her champagne glass filled. She smiled when
she saw him. Everything was going to work out splendidly—she
was moving to the most romantic city in the world with her
boyfriend, and she was going to be an international supermodel. The more people told her otherwise, the more she was
sure of it.

Marcus smiled back as she sat down beside him on the couch.
"Great news, love—we can get a ride to Paris on my friend's private jet tonight. We'll get there early, and I can show you the city
before we have to get to work."

"That's fantastic," she purred, snuggling next to him on the
oversize white couch. The sooner the better. She couldn't wait to
get out of here.

"You'll love Paris," Marcus murmured, playing with her hair.
She rested her head on his shoulder and closed her eyes. *Paris,*

and they were leaving tonight. She was more than ready for her fantasy life to begin.

"The other girls are going to love you," Marcus continued, nuzzling her neck.

Jacqui opened her eyes with a start. "What other girls?"

"Your roommates," Marcus said casually, running a finger up her leg and tracing all the way up to her thigh.

She pulled away from his touch. Other girls? *Roommates?* Her Parisian dream was starting to look very crowded. "I thought we were going to be together in Paris, just you and me."

"You and me, and Natalie and Francesca and Zenobia," Marcus said casually, setting his glass down on the table. "Although I'll be gone for a little while after next month. Midas and I are doing a film."

"Excuse me?" Jacqui stared at him, her jaw agape. "Repeat that again. I know my English isn't very good sometimes."

"My flat's one of the Chrysler Model apartments. I rent it out because I'm not there a lot," he said matter-of-factly. "You'll like the other girls, I promise. You won't be lonely. I don't know how long I'll be gone, but you're welcome to stay as long as you want." His tone indicated that he thought he was being very generous.

"But I thought . . ." Her voice trailed off, and she began to feel the tears well up in her eyes.

"Oh, Jacqui, love." Marcus sighed, turning to her and taking both her hands in his. "You had to know that this was only for the summer?" He tried to look shocked, but somehow Jacqui got the feeling he'd had this conversation before, with a lot of other girls.

Jacqui's heart clenched in her chest. Another sucker punch. "But you said—to move with you to Paris," she said dumbly, drawing her hands out of his.

"I said for you to move to Paris and be a model and that you could stay with me," he corrected, carefully enunciating each word.

Jacqui shook her head, more disappointed in herself than in Marcus. She'd thought that he loved her and had let herself be swept right off her feet. But when she stopped to think about it, his words had always been so vaguely stated that there were no promises of the future, just empty remarks. Hungry for romance, *she* had filled in the rest.

"Darling. You know how much I adore you. And the two of us, it was great for business. Great for the shoot," he drawled, stroking her cheek. "And look at you, you're a star." He gestured to the enormous photographs on the walls.

She looked at all the photographs, the intimate shots he'd captured—of her in his bed, wiping the sleep from her eyes, sitting wistfully by the window and looking out at the stars. Her eyes closed, waiting for his kiss. Marcus had made it look personal, like he knew her. But in reality he had only presented to the world a perfectly packaged image, sold as the real thing.

"Reality fashion" indeed. It was all scripted, all staged, as fake as her relationship had been. *Women look more beautiful when they're in love,* he'd told her. But for him it was just the way the industry worked. A way to get a better picture. He had used her, and worst of all, she had let him.

"C'mon. If we leave now, we can wake up tomorrow on the Champs-Elysées." Marcus stood, holding out his hand. He didn't seem to notice anything was wrong.

"Marcus, are you ready?" Rupert Thorne appeared at his side. His eyes lit up immediately when he saw Jacqui. "Is this your friend?"

Jacqui felt like she might throw up. What an idiot she had been. She stood up from the couch, grabbed her drink, and threw it in Marcus's face. The surrounding partygoers gasped. Who was making a scene at such a civilized event?

Marcus shrugged as he wiped his face with a jet-black napkin. "I'm sorry you feel that way."

She turned on her heel and left the party, catching a glimpse of herself in the hall mirror. Her hair was put up in a complicated pouf, and she was wearing so much makeup it felt like her face was going to crack. Her dress was too short, and her heels hurt. She looked like a beautiful doll. Exactly what she'd never wanted to be.

This wasn't her. The real Jacqui lived in jeans and flats because it was easier to run around after the kids in those clothes. The real Jacqui was hardworking and determined and never took the easy way out. Mara and Eliza were right. Pete Rockwood was right. She shook her head, unable to believe that a stranger had known her better than she had known herself.

# best friends always know best

MARA TIPTOED THROUGH THE DARKENED FOYER OF THE
Finnemore mansion, making a beeline for the kitchen. She'd
arrived at the *Vogue* party just as it was winding down and, after a
disappointing lap of the party, realizing she'd missed Eliza and
Jacqui, she'd come straight home. She'd missed dinner and was
starving from the four-hour Jitney ride—which, she thought
sadly, had all been for nothing. The house was dark and silent, so
she was surprised to see a light on in the kitchen.

She found Eliza sitting by herself at the counter, wearing a
bright red gown with puffed sleeves, a chicken sandwich in hand.

"Hey. What are you doing here?" she asked. Only Eliza would
be casually eating a sandwich wearing a gown that looked like it
had come straight off the runway.

"I could ask you the same thing," Eliza said simply, wiping
mayonnaise from her lips with a napkin. Chunks of chicken salad
fell onto the floor around her, but she didn't seem to notice or
care. "How was your dinner party?" she asked dryly.

"I didn't go. I went to the *Vogue* party instead, tried to find you." Mara took a seat across from her friend.

"You did?" Eliza asked, her face lighting up.

"Why aren't you over there?" Mara asked. She reached for the bag of potato chips next to Eliza's plate, and Eliza moved it closer. Without even having to say anything, they both knew the fight between them was over.

"I have so much to tell you." Eliza sighed.

"Me too." Mara nodded. She raised an eyebrow. "Got any more of that chicken salad?"

"Left drawer." Eliza smiled.

"Where's Jacqui?" Mara got up and moved over to the Sub-Zero.

"Right here." Jacqui appeared in the doorway. She'd changed into a pair of sweats and an old NYU T-shirt. Of course, she looked as gorgeous as ever.

"What happened to you?" Eliza asked as Jacqui sat down at the counter and helped herself to Eliza's potato chips. "You left the party early. Everyone was looking for you for the photo op. They had to settle for pictures of me and Midas." Eliza had been a little upset when no one could find Jacqui but had shaken it off and enjoyed being the center of attention for a change. All the editors at *Vogue* were falling over themselves to compliment her on the clothes. She mentally reminded herself to send a flood of bouquets to their office tomorrow to thank them for the party.

"I broke up with Marcus." Jacqui told them about what he'd

said and her painful revelation. She sighed, pulling back her freshly washed black hair into a ponytail. "I should have listened to you guys."

"Me too," Mara admitted. She recounted the argument she'd had with David and how she'd left him high and dry. "We're done. It's over."

"You were right about him," both Mara and Jacqui said at the same time. They looked at each other and laughed.

"I'm such an idiot," Jacqui said. For the whole cab ride home, she'd felt like her world was falling apart. But after a long, hot shower, she realized she was being overly dramatic. After all, what had she lost? As far as NYU knew, she would still be at orientation. And she'd had a really fun summer. She'd wanted a boyfriend, and she'd imagined one for herself. But as a summer fling, Marcus really had shown her a good time. As for her heart—it was bruised, but it wasn't broken. She was okay with being single if that was what was in the cards for her right now. She knew now, though, that she didn't want to settle for anything less than the perfect guy next time.

"Don't be so hard on yourself, Jac," Mara consoled. "I should have known too—I can't believe what an awful snob David turned out to be," she confessed. She told them what he'd said about her writing and her chances for publication, and both girls immediately became incensed.

"He's an idiot," Eliza declared, polishing off her sandwich and eating the chunks that had fallen on her plate. "You'll publish that book without his dragon-lady mom. I know a great agent who can help you. Don't worry. We'll show him yet."

"I think he's intimidated by you," Jacqui said, opening another large bag of chips. "You're the one with all the clips from real magazines. He's just the editor of a student paper."

"Ryan was right. . . ." Mara sighed. "He told me David was a jerk, but I didn't listen . . . to any of you." She took a huge bite out of her sandwich. Love trauma always made her hungry.

Jacqui and Eliza just sat there, looking at her.

"Ryan?" Eliza said simply, raising an eyebrow.

"Oh. Yeah." Mara blushed a little. "I didn't tell you guys. We sort of got into an argument the other day. He said he didn't think David was right for me."

"*Chica.*" Jacqui shook her head. "Do you really think Ryan's impartial?"

Mara couldn't help but smile at Jacqui's sagelike pronouncement. But could it be true? Could it be that Ryan had said those things about David because he was *jealous*?

"He was your first love." Eliza sighed. "You just don't get over those," she added softly, staring off into the distance.

Mara looked at her critically. "You miss Jeremy," she said. Of course Eliza did.

Before Eliza could say anything, the kitchen door swung open and Suzy entered. She was wearing a red silk bathrobe that was the same color as her hair, and her usual frizz was even wilder than usual, sticking up all over the place.

"Don't mind me," she said cheerfully. "Just getting a glass of water." She pulled a Fiji bottle out of the fridge and turned to the girls. "Mara, Jacqui, I just want to say thank you so much for all your work this summer. The kids just adore you guys. I really can't thank you enough."

"You're welcome," Mara said. "They're great kids."

"I know." Suzy sighed. "They really are." She sat down at the counter next to the girls, and Eliza shuffled over a little to make room for her. It was starting to get a bit crowded. Suzy absent-mindedly reached for one of the potato chips and started munching on it noisily. "I realized how much of their childhoods I'm missing, so I'm going to cut back on my work hours a bit. The market needs me, but the kids need their mother more."

"That's wonderful, Suzy." Jacqui smiled. She'd known it was only a matter of time before Suzy realized her mother-as-manager theory was not the way to raise children.

"It's about time. I really shouldn't outsource everything." Suzy shrugged, putting the chips down and getting up from the counter, her moment of soul-searching apparently over.

"What else have you been outsourcing?" Eliza asked, suspicious.

"God, the house." Suzy rubbed her eyes. "I mean, I just wanted a nice little beach house. We hired this really pushy decorating team. And I turn around and I get this . . . this . . ."

"Mega-mansion."

"Castle."

"Fortress."

"Right." Suzy nodded. She raised an eyebrow. "Do you guys really think I would commission a copy of the *Pietà* for my front lawn?" The girls laughed. Suzy smiled. "Good night, girls," she called as she headed back upstairs, her red robe billowing out behind her.

"She's really not so bad," Jacqui declared.

"I guess not," Eliza said grudgingly. She had still hoped that her parents would get back together, but as a stepmother, Suzy really wasn't too bad.

"I love you guys," Mara said suddenly. "I'm sorry about how I was acting this summer. I wish I'd gone to some of those parties. They sounded fun."

"Me too," Jacqui added, tears springing to her eyes. "I mean, I love you guys too. And the parties *were* fun," she added, a playful gleam in her eyes.

"Well, I never think friends need to apologize," Eliza said slyly. "It's just understood."

They hugged each other tightly, not wanting to let go for a long time. With good friends and potato chips, who needed boys?

# jeremy is mr. right,
# just not right now

IT WAS ALMOST THREE IN THE MORNING WHEN ELIZA drove up to the Greyson estate after her late-night snack with the girls, but there was a light shining in the kitchen. Apparently someone else couldn't sleep.

She knocked on the door and after a minute Jeremy appeared, wearing old jeans with holes in the knees and a worn-out white Hanes tee. His eyes were rimmed with red, and he looked exhausted. He leaned his head against the door frame so that their faces were only five inches apart but separated by the screen. "What are you doing here?" he asked quietly, as if not wanting to disturb the silence of the night.

"Can I come in?" Eliza asked in a low whisper.

Jeremy stepped wordlessly aside, and she followed him into the living room. There were several couches in the room, still covered in plastic. He'd picked out the Mies van der Rohe collection—black leather modern couches that she had once admired in a catalog. He took a seat in an Eames lounge chair and she sat on the plastic of the couch across from him, almost sliding off the slippery covering.

"Why haven't you unpacked?" she asked, unable to think of anything to say but the obvious. "How do you live like this?"

"I'm renting it out," he said. "You're right—it's too big for a bachelor pad."

"Jer—"

"Eliza, I don't want to hear it," he said abruptly. "I don't even know what you're doing here."

Eliza nodded, understanding why he was still upset. She ran her fingers through her hair, and took a deep breath. "It was wrong of me to accept that ring," she said. "I just didn't let the implications sink in at the time. Because I was afraid of what it meant. And I was afraid that if I didn't, I would lose you."

He sat there, stony-faced, for a long time. The crickets sang outside, and moonlight poured in through the window. He sighed. "Part of it is my fault too. I guess I got caught up in it. That ring was the first thing I bought with the money from the Greyson estate. I just thought—here it is. Here's my chance to make Eliza happy." He pulled at the plastic covering the arm of his chair. "And I knew it was too soon—which is why I didn't say anything, I just put it on your finger. Because if you went along with it, I thought maybe . . ."

"Oh, Jer . . ."

"I know." He smiled ruefully.

"And here I thought I was the one with all the doubts."

"Nah. It's not like I've got it all figured out."

"Thank *God*." She sighed heavily, smiling as she got up to sit on his lap. He cradled her in his arms and she tucked her head underneath his chin. He smelled warm and woodsy. She relaxed in his arms. Who needed to meet or date any other boys when you'd found your one true love already? So what if they met so young? It only meant they could grow up together. Everyone should be so lucky.

He buried his nose in her hair and inhaled deeply, as if trying to catch up on everything he'd been missing.

She pulled her head out of the crook of his neck so she could look at him. "I wanted you to know, I'm going to Princeton in the fall. There's so much I want to learn and do. . . ." His warm brown eyes were locked on hers. He looked surprised but not unhappy. "And I hope we can do it together. But the question is, can you wait?" she asked quietly. She suddenly felt like a little girl, curled up on his lap, waiting helplessly for his answer. "Will you wait for me?"

"I'll wait forever if I have to," Jeremy promised, grabbing her hand and kissing it right where her ring would have sat. His answer was everything she'd wanted all along—a promise of forever, not a diamond ring. Jeremy cupped her face in his hands and they leaned in for a long, intense kiss. Eliza felt every part of her relax. This was right. This was home.

When they finally pulled apart, she smiled up at him wickedly. "So, um, whatever happened to that ring?"

# the more things change, the more they stay the same

**THERE WAS A MOVING TRUCK PARKED IN FRONT OF THE** Perry manor when Mara drove up to it the next morning. Movers were loading cardboard boxes and crates into the truck. Several oversize objects stuck out on the driveway—Ryan's surfboards, Anna's Marie Antoinette vanity.

Mara parked the Lexus and walked up to the front door, where she found Ryan directing the men on how to move the art installations.

She came up behind him. "You're leaving?" she asked bluntly.

He looked up, surprised to find her standing there. "My dad sold the house. They want to buy a summer place in Europe. Anna loves London, and she says she's tired of the Hamptons." He stuck his hands in his pockets. "I was lucky to even have the summer here, I guess."

"What a shame," Mara couldn't help saying. She looked up at Creek Head Manor, feeling as if she'd just lost a loved one. "We had a lot of good times in that house."

He shrugged, as if it didn't matter to him either way. "So what brings you here, Mara?" he asked, a little sharply.

She held her breath. She hadn't realized until she saw him how nervous she was. "I broke up with David," she said simply, and looked at him expectantly.

Ryan looked her square in the eyes and nodded. Then he turned and started to pack up the open cardboard box in the yard beside him.

Her heart dropped. Was that all? "Oh. Well. I just thought you should know," she said, swallowing the hurt that was building up in her throat. She turned her back and started walking toward the car. She got inside and shut the door, tears starting to well up in her eyes.

The hot sun poured through the windshield and Mara blinked, trying to see straight. She fumbled in her purse for the keys. Why had she even come over here? What did she think was going to happen?

There was a rap on the window. She looked up to see Ryan leaning on the car. She pressed the lever and the glass rolled down.

He exhaled loudly. "Mara. I don't know what you're thinking, showing up here and telling me that. What do you want from me?"

"I think—I want *you*," Mara said softly.

He wrinkled his forehead and shook his head sadly. "That day on the beach—I wanted you to say just that, but you didn't. And honestly . . . every summer we get back together and then you break up with me at the end of it. I mean, what's the point anymore?" His face looked pained, and she couldn't tell if he was more angry or upset.

She wiped the tears with the back of her hand and nodded vigorously. "Okay." She got it. He wasn't going to wait around for her anymore. Every year it was the same story. Ryan, standing there with his heart wide open, only to have her slam it shut.

He sighed deeply. "Listen, I need a change. I've been doing a lot of thinking lately, and I'm going to take a semester, maybe a year, off from Dartmouth and go to London with my family. I want to travel around Europe for a while. I'm not going to be around."

She blew her nose with a tissue she found in the glove compartment. "I'll see you, Ryan. Take care, okay?" She stuck the keys in the ignition.

But before she could start the engine, he opened the car door and got into the passenger seat. He turned to look at her, studying her face intently. He let out a long breath. "I'm leaving, but I had this stupid fantasy that maybe you'd want to join me," he said, the corners of his mouth turning up slightly.

Mara blinked. Bum around Europe? All of her unrealized dreams for the summer came back to her in a rush: Gondola rides in Venice. Eating chocolate croissants at sunrise on a bench on the Seine. Touring the winding streets of London in a red double-decker bus. But take a year off from Columbia? She'd always followed the straight and narrow path, had never been the type of girl to derail her long-term plans just because a guy had asked her to.

She suddenly remembered that poem, the one they made you read at graduation, about the road not taken. This wasn't just any guy, and this wasn't just any offer. Ryan Perry was standing there, giving her another chance. Giving *them* another chance.

"I'll do it," she told him.

"You will?" His face broke into a huge, innocent grin. He looked just as handsome as the day they had met, when he had stepped out of his Aston Martin onto the sidewalk, barefoot. Ryan would always be a free spirit. She would have to learn how to let go a little bit, take his example.

He leaned across the gearshift and pulled her close. "I love you," she whispered softly.

"I love you too."

And then Mara laughed. After a summer's worth of drama, she was finally going to get to see Europe. This time, with the right guy.

# another summer is gone, but autumn opens new doors. . . .

**"EVERYONE READY?" ELIZA CALLED FROM HER CONVERTIBLE** that afternoon as she beeped the horn loudly.

Mara ran out of the front doors, dragging her luggage, Jacqui right behind. The kids gathered around them. Mara gave them all kisses and hugs.

"Who are you?" Wyatt asked Jacqui.

Jacqui laughed and ruffled his hair. She'd heard that line before.

They piled into Eliza's convertible. They were all driving back to the city together. Eliza was spending a weekend at home with her mom before heading off to Princeton. Mara had to wrap up a few things at Columbia for her year off before she jetted off to Europe with Ryan, and they were dropping Jacqui off at NYU orientation.

Eliza took them slowly on the two-lane highway, and they drove through the sleepy hamlets. The sun was shining brightly on the calm ocean, and the surrounding countryside was green and vibrant.

"Here," Jacqui said, leaning forward from the backseat and plopping a fat envelope on Mara's lap.

"What's this?" Mara asked, opening the flap and finding a neat stack of hundred-dollar bills.

"My share of the au pair salary. It's yours. I didn't earn it—you did."

"I can't take this!" Mara protested, trying to give it back.

"Yes, you can." Jacqui nodded fiercely.

"But what about . . . Don't you need the money?"

"I did that Japanese commercial, remember? With the payment and residuals, I made enough for tuition," Jacqui said proudly.

"Are you sure?"

"*Chica*, I'm sure. Believe me, the check I got, it's got a lot more zeros than what's in that envelope."

Mara turned around and gave Jacqui a close hug. "Thank you."

Jacqui nodded. "I'm not giving up on modeling completely. Christy Turlington graduated from NYU, you know."

Mara shook her head and smiled.

The drive back into the city was quick, Eliza speeding around all the other cars with a dainty honk and a giggle. They made it to Washington Square Park by midafternoon, and Eliza parked the car by the curb in front of a building with a big purple NYU flag on the front steps. Jacqui looked out the window and took in the scene, near bursting with happiness. There were so many eager eighteen-year-olds, most with their parents in tow, carrying their purple NYU orientation packets and wearing their NYU Class of '11 T-shirts. Sure, they looked a bit like wide-eyed tourists, but she was one of them. And even if her parents couldn't come from Brazil to help her get settled in, she had two people who loved her to see her off, right here in this very car.

As her eyes scanned the crowd of bobbing heads, she suddenly recognized a very familiar head of blond hair. "Pete!" she yelled excitedly, not stopping to think for a second.

Mara and Eliza exchanged smirks in the rearview mirror.

"Is this the famous Pete Rockwood from Indiana?" Mara asked.

"Pete Rockwood? That sounds familiar. . . . Wait a minute—is this the guy who called the store from his dentist's office?" Eliza pushed her sunglasses up on her head to get a better look at him. "Talk about regulation hottie—this one is off the charts!"

But Jacqui was getting out of the car so fast she couldn't hear them. She didn't even bother to open the door, instead leaping over the side of the convertible. She ran up to Pete, who was standing under the grand arch in Washington Square Park, surrounded by cardboard boxes and suitcases.

"What are you doing here?" she said breathlessly as she approached him, not pausing for the usual civilities.

He put down one of the suitcases he was carrying, looking the slightest bit embarrassed. "I'm a freshman here, actually," he said sheepishly. "Remember when we met? I was in New York because I was wait-listed and had a follow-up interview. I was too embarrassed to admit I hadn't gotten in."

Jacqui nodded. That sounded familiar. When she was deferred for a year, she'd done the exact same thing.

"And besides, I didn't want you to think I was just telling you to go to NYU because *I* would be here." He shrugged. "Although that might have been part of it," he added with a small smile.

"So it's just fate." Jacqui nodded, smiling.

"Just fate," Pete agreed. "But what about you? Shouldn't you be in Paris?"

She shrugged. "Paris will always be there. I'll see it some other time. Isn't that what spring break is for?" She raised an eyebrow and flipped her dark locks over her shoulder.

Pete grinned at her, his dimples forming irresistibly in either cheek. "So, uh . . . need some help moving into your dorm? If it's not too forward of me to see your room on our first date," he added quickly. His shy but eager smile said everything, and Jacqui felt that familiar tingle up her spine.

"You bet." She grinned right back. "But just a second—I've got to say goodbye to my girls."

Jacqui ran back to the car, her glossy black hair flowing behind her, grinning widely, her face aglow. The three girls hugged one last time.

"So you're not going to be in New York this year," Eliza said sadly to Mara.

"Neither are you," Jacqui reminded Eliza.

"Princeton isn't too far away," Eliza assured her. "I'll come visit."

"And I'll write long e-mails, I promise," Mara said. "And you can always read my blog," she added with a grin.

After one last hug Eliza pulled the car away from the curb. She and Mara waved to Jacqui and Pete until they were mere specks in the distance, two figures standing hopefully beside each other underneath the looming arch of Washington Square Park.

Eliza steered the car uptown, the late-afternoon light streaming through the windshield. Another summer was over, and they would all be separated once again. But good friends were never too far away in spirit.

Mara turned on the car radio. They sang along to the Natasha Bedingfield song, the one they knew all the words to, and felt a little better.

*"The rest is still unwritten. . . ."*

## www.blogspot/eurogirl1

Europe is amazing! We got to Italy yesterday, first stop Venice, and everything is even more beautiful than I had imagined. R. and I are having too much fun. This afternoon we went on a gondola ride, where the gondolier was actually wearing a red-and-white-striped shirt and a silly black hat. R. joined in the singing, of course, which was hilarious, if not melodic. I'm currently typing from a Venetian Internet café. Did you know they have Internet here now? I had wondered how they'd get the wires through those canals, but apparently my notions are silly and outdated. Italy is just like home, except the pizza is better.

E. is having a blast at Princeton. She's already in the best eating club and is hard at work on her next collection—preppie basics! Of course. Guess she's taking inspiration from her surroundings. She and J. are going strong and have already booked the church for 2012. Here's hoping she designs the bridesmaids' gowns.

J. is dating P. at NYU and modeling on the side. They're planning to meet us in Paris for spring break so J. can go to some look-sees (and eat some escargot, obv.). She's been doing a lot of commercial work since the September *Vogue* came out—but, she assures me, only as much as doesn't interfere with her classes.

And in really exciting news, my blog is going to become a book! It sold to a big publishing house that wants to publish next summer. I'm so excited I don't know what to do with myself. My first novel! I even decided on a title yesterday: *The Au Pairs.* I want the cover to have three girls in bikinis. I know, I know. No sign of the children anywhere. But really—the book is more about the friendships I found there than about the kids or the partying. And, of course, the great guy who made every summer special.

**Till next time,**
**Eurogirl1**

PS—And no, I still don't have a webcam!

# acknowledgments

The Au Pairs was a great ride, and I'd like to thank everyone who made it a possibility. Writing this book series changed my life, and I am deeply grateful to everyone who made it happen. Emily Meehan and Josh Bank for being the books' godparents. All my fabulous current (and former) editors at Alloy who had a hand in making it wonderful: Sara Shandler, Ben Schrank, Siobhan Vivian, and Joelle Hobeika (thanks especially to Joelle for being so patient with the *Crazy Hot* drafts!). Thank you to Les Morgenstein for everything. Deep gratitude to Richard Abate and Josie Friedman at ICM who have my back. And Niki Castle, Karen Kenyon, and Colin Graham who help Richard and Josie have my back. Thanks especially to everyone at S&S who were such big cheerleaders for the series: Rick Richter, Elizabeth Law, Jen Bergstrom, Bethany Buck, Carolyn Pohmer and Courtney Bongiolatti. It means so much to me to be part of the S&S family.

Thank you to my dear friend Tom Dolby for his steadfast friendship and support. Thanks, Tom, for being so patient with me while I finished this book. We can work on our project now. Thank you to all my friends in New York and Los Angeles. I love you all.

Thank you to all my dear readers from all over the U.S. and the world (all the way from Sweden, Germany, Poland, and the U.K.) who e-mail, blog and MySpace-friend me. You guys are the best! I love hearing from you, so please keep in touch by writing me at melissa@melissa-delacruz.com.

Thank you to my amazing family—the DLCs: Mommy, Papa, and Chito. The Greens: Aina, Steve, Nicholas, and Joseph. The Johnstons: Mom J., Dad J., John, Anji, Alex, Tim, Rob, Jenn, Val, and Lily. The Gaisanos: Tita Odette, Isabelle, and Tina. The Torres family: Tita Sony, Tito Badong, Mandy, Stevie, and Miggy. And all the Ongs and de la Cruzes who are too numerous to mention, but especially my nieces Mica Calangi and Bianca Ong, who are big fans of the books!

Thank you to Nubia Alvarez, who helps me be a working mom.

And most importantly, thank you to the loves of my life, Mike Johnston and Mattie Johnston. I thought of you every minute I was writing this book.

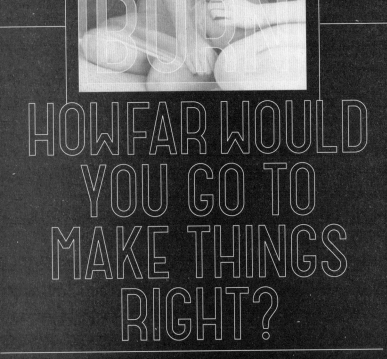

NEW YORK TIMES BESTSELLING AUTHOR

**JENNY HAN &
SIOBHAN VIVIAN**

BURN FOR BURN

HOW FAR WOULD YOU GO TO MAKE THINGS RIGHT?

FROM BESTSELLING AUTHORS JENNY HAN AND SIOBHAN VIVIAN
THE FIRST IN AN INCENDIARY NEW TRILOGY!

# Because *summer* should last forever.